The Other Elizabeth

Royal Sagas 2:

Tudors II

Betty Younis

D1470520

Copyright © 2016 Betty Younis

All rights reserved.

ISBN: 1533394245
ISBN-13: 978-1533394248

For MTC

Betty Younis

Chapter One

Winter 1536

She heard her mother's footsteps running frantically towards the house even as her horse reared, snorted and broke free of the shallow light provided by the stable's rag lamps. Like a beast possessed by all the demons of hell, the proud animal raced into the shroud of dank and silken darkness which cloaked the moonless night. Uncertainty and fear rendered the familiar terrain bleak and terrifying in its shifting monotones of gray and ebony, but even as her way became less known and her mount slowed to cope with the deepening void, her heart raced with the thrill of what would be her own adventure. Her own life. Yes, finally it could begin, removed from the shackles placed upon it by those who came before her. No more would she be bound by codes of silence, imprisoned by Coudenoure and all its hidden layers and meanings. She was free.

Her mount felt its way forward and even in the dark sensed the upcoming low stone break in the perimeter wall which kept the world apart from Coudenoure and Coudenoure separate from all else. It gathered sudden speed and leapt to clear the hurdle in a single bound. On and on it galloped into the night, taking her deeper and deeper into an unknown world until at last a faint light shown through the darkness ahead. She slowed and finally stopped, patting her ride gently on its side, hearing its heaving ragged breaths and feelings its muscles twitch beneath the saddle. Yes, it was the main road. Ahead she could make out a procession of stately persons, some nobleman no doubt, was en route to Greenwich, the royal palace which abutted the grounds of Coudenoure. Great torches mounted on sturdy poles were carried by horsemen at each corner of the entourage. An additional one walked slowly some paces ahead while another brought up the rear an equal number of paces behind. Between these light posts were armed men in a livery of silver and blue whose function was to deter the marauders who frequented such roads at night. The effect was a resplendent show of light but also of power, for no one save the truly wealthy had either the men or the torches for such a heavily guarded evening ride. She watched from a distance, hidden by the dark, as a high lord and his lady passed on. She noted the flowing crimson robe of the woman, the elaborate and bejeweled caul which held back her hair and wondered briefly who she was. In the end, however, her thoughts returned once more to her own situation, and she let the party pass well on before gently nudging her mount into the road some distance behind them. She could follow this group safely all the way to Greenwich, and beyond that she was certain she could ride undetected and unmolested. There would be no one to come after her until the morning. And by then…by then she would be securely away, acting on the plans laid down years earlier by her mother, the Lady Elizabeth.

The scheme was a good one she hoped, and as the last torchman passed under the great monolithic arch of the outer battlements of Greenwich Palace proper, she kicked her horse into a steady gallop. It was long past Matins when she reached Woolwich. A lone torch lit the quay and she pulled her reins taut, wrapping their whip ends around her left hand while reaching behind her with her right to pull forward the bundle secured there. The horse settled, and she quickly opened the outer bag. Three items met her probing fingers: a hard, stone object; a bag of coinage, and a folded paper. She opened the paper and began reading by the flickering light of the low torch. She looked up after a moment, confused. Again she read the note and looking about her, tried with growing desperation to orient herself in a way that would fit the directions she was being given by the letter. Giving rein to her horse she trotted to the end of the quay, looking for a house with a blue door. Quietly and determinedly she examined each in turn until finally, she pulled to an abrupt halt. She dismounted and knocked quietly on the door. Silence. Once again, a quiet knock.

After what seemed an eternity, the door creaked and an old man with a stubby candle appeared. A woman's face could be seen over his shoulder. The man peered at her through the dark, keenly eyeing the quay as he did so.

"What is it, child? Who are you?"

She paused. Would they remember Elizabeth and her careful plan for her daughter's safety? And if they should remember, had they been recompensed adequately to see it through?

"I am Constance." She spoke simply. "And I am here at my mother Elizabeth's demand. She has directed me to say the word, "Bucephalus" in order that you might know 'tis time to aid her daughter."

The old woman drew a sharp breath but never hesitated. She stepped forward into the flickering light.

"Come, Constance, we must hurry if we are to defeat that evil witch and see you safely gone."

She pulled the younger woman through the door. The man glanced guardedly once more at the dark quay beyond. He passed the candle to Constance, and pulling the door behind him, stepped out into the dark, gathering the reins of her horse in his hand. Silently, he walked the sweating beast into the ebony gloom and away from their door.

*****

The sun was almost upon the horizon by the time Constance stood at the prow of the ship, feeling the salty sea air beat against her face as the wind pushed the vessel ever farther from England and danger. She held tightly to a heavy object with both hands, feeling her tears mix with the spray until she was one with the misty, rosy pre-dawn. She held the object up and placed its bottom on the prow's railing in order to stabilize it and stare at it.

Carved from the most flawless white marble she had ever seen was the face of a woman turned slightly away from the viewer. Her hair flowed out behind her in a great wave, and her right hand, so delicately carved that a single breath might cause it harm, reached gently out towards the viewer. The beautiful face, carved in such exquisite detail as to be almost ephemeral, caused her tears to flow anew, for it was that of her mother, Elizabeth de Grey of Coudenoure.

Chapter Two

September 12, 1560

But it was not Hatfield. Queen Elizabeth lay in the bed chamber which formerly belonged to her father. She lay beneath the same soft down covers and looked out the same window upon the same great lawn of Greenwich Palace. The branches of a giant tree, perhaps an elm, occasionally scraped noisily against the leaded diamond panes of her window. Someone would need to trim that, she thought lazily. Pulling the covers higher she sank deeper into the warmth they offered and sighed. Greenwich was lovely and palatial and majestic but it was not home. It was not Hatfield.

She studied the grand bas reliefs which decorated the canopy frame of the bed. Had her father really been that obsessed with the Lancaster and York feud? She doubted it. The more she looked at the carvings of Tudor roses and battle scenes from Bosworth, the more convinced she became that her father had inherited the bed from his father, Henry VII. The carving was blunt and marshal, not at all what she had come to yearn for from her Henry. Her Henry – what a strange appellation for one's own father, particularly a father barely known! Her mind drifted back in time, to an era when Henry was still alive. As always, she struggled to find memories of him that were not of the king but of the man. She knew the king well enough – from his political machinations to his religious designs to the fateful decision that had denied her the warmth and presence of her own mother. Yes, she knew that king as did everyone else in her realm. But the man...was there anyone left who had known Henry and could tell her of him? What were his private thoughts on love? On music? What was his favorite color? His favorite pastime? She had inherited his flaming red hair and his famous temper, but really, what else? Perhaps her love of language? Or perhaps her insatiable appetite for sweets? As always, the line between what she might have inherited and what she had nurtured within her own soul just to please him became blurred. Likely, as with her mother, she would never know.

She threw back the covers and rose for the day. Immediately, three lady's maids appeared from the shadows. As if some silent cue had gone out through the stillness of the morning, a young boy began stoking the fire. A side door opened and Elizabeth saw two bowing and scraping scullery domestics pass a tray of morning food to yet another of her maids. A robe was laid across her shoulders and as one of the women tightened its sash around Elizabeth's slim waist, a brusque knock could be heard on the main door. Without further notice, two men entered her chamber.

"Majesty, you must hurry. The French ambassador wishes a word." William Cecil spoke harshly as he noted she was still dishabille. He could never move past the young queen's habit of spending, in his mind, an inordinate amount of time dressing in the mornings. Maids were filing in and out, each holding a gown draped over her person so that Elizabeth might choose her attire for the day. She ignored Cecil and spoke directly to them.

"Something to ride in – I wish to exercise before I meet that tiresome ambassador."

Before Cecil could speak she continued.

"He is here to discuss my cousin's approaching journey and her settling in Scotland. But Sir William, he is uncouth and makes it clear he does not appreciate having to discuss such state matters with a woman. Where is that delicious Monsieur de Castelnau, um? We will gladly meet with him anytime."

A wave of giggles passed over her maids, for the man she mentioned was the antithesis of uncouth and deeply appreciative of women. Cecil shifted on his feet and ignored her question.

"Madame, the ambassador is not uncouth. And as for his disdain of women, well, I say all the more reason, Majesty, to see him in a timely fashion, for to keep him waiting…"

"To keep him waiting, Sir William, is what we shall do. Send him a pretty maid, one with whom he may flirt, and a tray of scones – that will have to suffice until I am ready."

She smiled her peculiarly winning smile at him before finishing.

"Now if you and your young charge there do not mind…" she motioned at the young man who had accompanied Cecil into the room, "…I will be dressed and will see you anon."

"But Majesty, that is not at all what the ambassador wishes to discuss. He heard yesterday of Lady Amy's…"

Elizabeth turned on him in a fury, holding her hand up in a demand for his silence.

"Nothing! Do you hear me? We will not speak of it!"

She strode imperiously from the room, leaving Cecil shaking his head.

Not long after being suitable attired, Elizabeth found herself mounted on her favorite bay and with a retinue of courtiers, ladies, guards and horsemen she began making her way from the palace proper towards the inner gate of the palace. Both Greenwich and its fortifying walls were of ancient heritage and as she walked her bay she was caught by the timelessness of the place and scene, despite the constant building which had been its lot for centuries.

Whatever architectural scheme had dictated its original structure had long since been overrun by each generation's tinkering with its basic forms to suit their own needs. The result had been organic rather than planned growth and was reflected in the myriad wings and towers which seemed to have been added willy-nilly to any available free wall of the palace. Her own father had attempted to bring order out of the chaos but even he had only been somewhat successful. But as one moved from the walls of the palace itself to the interior wall of the great yard, a more stable view was met. The high-arched gateway set a more organized, patterned layout for the grand palace. As she passed through that gate the principal fortifications came into view. Beyond that, the high road to London and the woods.

The guardsmen who travelled with her had alerted their brethren at the gate, and they stood stiffly at attention as her entourage moved past. She nodded approvingly at the heraldic crest they wore

– a yellow phoenix, mighty and lion-like, rising from the red flames of her kingdom's past. It had been of her own choosing and clearly represented her own past and trajectory as well. She had held on through the muddled politics of first Jane Gray, then Edward and then her sister Mary. The tide of religious fanaticism and continental intrigue which had engulfed England upon Henry's death was only now beginning to settle. Glancing up, the pennants which waved gaily in the autumn breeze made her smile – the Tudor Rose, with its delicate, red petals surrounding four simple white ones, always brought back memories of her youth, a time before the death of her father. She must remember to tell Lord Cecil about her pleasure with them, for knowing that her chief minister was passionate about English heraldry it would please him no end.

They reached the outer gate of Greenwich Palace, set within the heavily fortified and turreted defensive wall of the grounds. On the other side lay the main road from the Thames estuary and the ports it supported to London and beyond. The arrangement meant that crossing into the Queen's Woods opposite required a stoppage of all traffic along the road so that the queen could pass unhindered. A great cheer arose when Elizabeth appeared and an almost circus-like atmosphere developed. Small children appeared from nowhere asking for alms; the heraldic horns, sounded to signify her approach and crossing, blew loudly and sweetly; the brave among the common came forward to bow and speak. Through it all, she smiled and spoke as though one of them – another trait inherited from her father, perhaps, for he too had the common touch.

With a final wave, she slipped into the dark quiet wood beyond. This was her respite, her temple sanctuary – the utter silence of the forest. No one clawing at her for answers or solutions to problems she barely understood. She raised her hand and immediately her retinue shuffled to a stop.

"I wish to ride ahead some ways." She waved away the concerned comments which came at her.

"You may accompany me, I did not say otherwise. But you will keep a distance. I wish to think."

She leaned forward and patted the neck of her horse while loosening her hold somewhat on the reins. It was their silent language, and she felt the great bay relax as it understood the signal and fell into a slow walk through the woods. Autumn had set in. The dank smell of rotting leaves mixed with the fresh, dry odors of those just fallen created a pleasant aroma which could only ever be autumnal. It floated upon the breeze, almost within reach but never quite. Elizabeth breathed deeply, enjoying the raw nature which provided such a refreshing change from the humanity of court. Her mount seemed to sense her need for meditative contemplation and was content to pick its way carefully along, past fallen trees and undergrowth.

Try as she might, however, Elizabeth could not stay focused on the primordial beauty all about her. Her thoughts were clouded by Cecil's morning message and again and again her mind circled back, refusing to release it.

So even the French ambassador had heard. How quickly such tales got about – if only, she thought wryly, her intelligence service were half as adroit at ferreting out information and passing it on!

Amy Robsart was dead. Word of the tragedy had reached Elizabeth at Windsor Castle two days previously as she was readying for progress to Greenwich. The woman had fallen down a flight of stairs at Cumnor Estate in Oxfordshire. Her husband, Robert Dudley, was with Elizabeth at Windsor when the news was delivered. But the matter was not simple, and everyone, it seemed, including the French ambassador, knew that. Dudley was her favorite. With his roguish charms, dark hair and eyes and exquisite manners, he had long since captured her heart, and her entire court was aware of his special standing. On the very day of her accession to the throne, he had travelled to Hatfield and witnessed the conference to her of the Great Seal of England. She had immediately named him her Master of the Horse, a greatly influential position at court due to its ease of access to the queen.

Tongues prattled on relentlessly about their relationship, but neither she nor Cecil had given much thought to the gossip – it was court, and there would always be rumors and innuendo. She was a virgin queen and it was only a matter of time before she would take a husband, so everyone said, but it would not be Dudley, for, though his wife seldom appeared at court, he was already married. This was a key assurance to her courtiers, to the foreign ambassadors who served their own continental masters, and to the country at large, for Dudley was not a popular man. He wore his ambition on his sleeve and had it been embroidered there in plain words it could not have been more evident: the man wanted the throne. And no one save him and possibly Elizabeth wanted him to have it. But now, Amy Robsart's sudden death put a new and alarming twist on the matter, for without her, Dudley was a free man, and with that freedom came everything that no one had ever had to consider seriously before.

When the messenger had delivered the news, Elizabeth had instantaneously understood its implications. But when the messenger had provided details of the death, Elizabeth had gasped. It seems the staircase down which Amy fell was shallow with few treads. Additionally, the treads themselves were deep, allowing the entire foot to rest comfortably on the step; how she had fallen, then, was a curiosity. But there was more. According to the coroner's initial report, the cause of death was a broken neck. Again, the angle, length and make-up of the staircase seemed to make such a fall well-nigh impossible. Finally, the coroner reported that there were two wounds of unknown cause on Amy's head. Elizabeth had barely had time to take in the news herself before it was being discussed by all levels of her court.

Had Dudley played a role in his wife's death? Had his ambition finally gotten the better of him? Perhaps he had decided to trust no longer to Fate to provide for his wife's demise and put him beside Elizabeth on the throne. So she had immediately sent Dudley away and he, in turn, had called for a full and open investigation of his wife's death. He could do nothing else if he wished to maintain a shred of innocence. Meanwhile, the scandal was hot and threatened to engulf Elizabeth's authority and virtue. She had no idea how to handle it, for the simple reason that she had no idea if Dudley had been involved. Like everyone else, she knew his ambitions, but she found it hard to think him capable of such a foolish and cold act.

She sighed deeply. So much had changed for her since the coronation, and now this. Robert Dudley was more than a friend to her, and their relationship ran deep and long into her past. With so many people demanding so many things and with her reign barely under way, she desperately needed the counsel of those with whom she shared some past history, and he was one of the few. And now. She had survived the tempestuous and stormy reigns of Edward and Mary, with all their fanaticism and paranoia. Would she survive this, she wondered? No, she sighed again. This was not Hatfield.

She realized that for some time her steed had been picking its way along an established path. When the wind reached beneath the trees and its gusts swept the forest floor, she could see it as well. It was an old one, worn almost to a rut, and narrow – it could not even support two horses abreast. As she began to pay attention, she noted that the trail was weaving its way to an open meadow nearby. Sure enough, within five minutes she had cleared the deep autumn gloom of the woods and stood in a pastureland bordered by the wood, the river, and a high ridge across the way. After a moment, more out of curiosity than anything else, she gave her mount rein and he once again began following an old, rutted and narrow track. The tall grasses and flowers of the summer, now dry and whispery, caught at her boots and skirt hem as she continued on. How could there be a path? This was the queen's wood and the queen's land. Neither Edward nor Mary had ridden. It could only be one that her father had used, and used often enough to have worn a familiar groove in the earth. But where did it lead – where did he visit with such regularity? She looked around as her horse continued across the field at a leisurely pace, pausing now and again to sample first this oat grass, now that dried flower head. An almost unconscious curiosity to see where it led set in, and, as the horse continued on, she returned to her mulling of the news of Dudley and his wife.

Once across the meadow her steed paused at a sharp bend in the path. Elizabeth glanced about.

She could continue on the same path which now began to hug the bank of the Thames as it meandered beyond a bend, or she could ride up to the top of the high ridge and see what lay beyond. Knowing that Cecil would shout if she stayed out all day, she decided upon the latter as a better course of action. It would allow her to see what was on the other side and that might possibly explain why her father had come along this way so often. No doubt she would be met by the sight of a forest where the hunting was fine. Elizabeth pulled sharply on the reins and began her ascent up the steep and craggy hill. Her retinue followed at a respectful distance, but as she finally crested the last knob she let out a pleased shout and called them forward.

The hill was not the highest, but its situation allowed a breathtaking view of its immediate environs. She could see the tops of Greenwich Palace, the woods through which she had just come, and she could trace the Thames along its wandering path for some distance until it was swallowed up by mist and hills and hamlets. It was a stunning view, and she believed she now understood why her father had so often come here. Why not, since it was quiet, scenic and laid the kingdom out before its sovereign like a rolling and bejeweled quilt.

"This is lovely!" she exclaimed. "I must ride here more often!"

"Indeed Majesty, I believe it is one of the finer views of the surrounding areas I have ever seen."

Elizabeth barely heard the courtier for she had noticed that on the far side of the hill were not the woods she had anticipated but a small manor house set some distance away. Smoke curled from its chimneys, and she noted the careful layout of the grounds which surrounded it. She turned to her retinue and motioned in the direction she continued to gaze.

"Tell me, what manor house is that? Is this not the Queen's property?"

The silence which met her question was deafening. She looked at her retinue.

"Did you not hear me?"

This time, coughing and averted gazes were her only answer.

"You there, Lord William, I am asking you directly: what is yon place? Now answer me!"

William, an older man with a graying beard and a dark cloak wrapped around his shoulders, responded.

"That is Coudenoure, my Queen, and it is not the Queen's estate. Indeed, I have heard that this hill upon which we now rest is part of Coudenoure – the Crown's land begins at the base which abuts the meadow."

Elizabeth thought for a moment. Coudenoure. Yes, she knew the name but she could not put it in context.

"Tell me more of this estate," she demanded.

William sighed but did as she wished.

"Madame, it is said that it was a favorite haunt of our late and good King Henry, your father."

"Go on, man."

William coughed again and continued.

"It is said that he spent a great deal of money on the grounds, and from here you can see much of his handiwork." William pointed as he spoke. "He employed your grandfather's architect, Robert Janyns, to lay out a place where a king might find respite. You can see the geometric symmetry of the place from here – 'tis lovely to behold, is it not?"

Elizabeth nodded.

"Did the Crown own Coudenoure at that time? Has it passed out of our possessions somehow?"

"No, Majesty, it has always been in the family of one Thomas de Grey, Baron Thomas de Grey. He served your grandfather with distinction at Bosworth. Indeed, it is said that he saved Henry's life. In return, your grandfather granted him the small manor you see before you."

"I understand, William, but why did my father spend money on an estate he did not own?"

William motioned for her to ride with him a short distance so that the others might not hear his words.

"Queen Elizabeth, I shall tell you all I know."

She nodded impatiently.

"There is a rumor, well, now more of a legend, concerning this estate Coudenoure. As you can see, it is hidden quite away from the road which passes Greenwich Palace and which leads on to London. Indeed, one must traverse the old medieval road by the river in order to reach its gate."

"And that is why my father spent his money on the place?" Elizabeth asked drily.

William smiled.

"It seems that in his youth, our good King Henry was pre-contracted to the only daughter, nay the only child, of Thomas de Grey. It is said that he loved her more than life itself, and that their love was of an uncommon kind."

"What kind would that be?" she asked laughing. "I want to hear you expound on the special love my father had for a child of his youth."

"It was a love that represented all that meant something to him in this world. The woman, and her name was Elizabeth as well, Majesty, had known him since childhood. They had grown up together and considered these woods…" he pointed to the forest on the far side of the meadow, "…to be their playground. Henry was treated as a son by the old man de Grey, and together, the three of them seemed to form some kind of familial bonds. You must remember, Majesty, that your father was a second son for many a year. Accordingly, until the death of our beloved Arthur, he was free to explore and mingle with others. And at Coudenoure, he was treated as the other children were – he was free to romp and play, and he knew that he was beloved for himself alone, not for his position."

Elizabeth looked at him and smiled wistfully.

"'Tis what we all long for in this world, is it not? Family, friends, security."

William nodded and continued.

"Indeed, Majesty, and at Coudenoure, Henry found his bearings. He came to manhood secure in the knowledge of the place and of the people who lived there. All of it – the servants, the grounds and Elizabeth and her father – all of it represented a world of peace and sanctuary to him. And in times of difficulty in his reign it is said he always returned to the place to re-orient and refresh himself."

Elizabeth was silent for a moment.

"And the woman? This Elizabeth? Clearly my father did not marry her. What was the outcome of that pre-contract pray tell."

"Madame, I only repeat the legend."

Elizabeth looked at him sharply. So there was more to the tale than he was letting on. She continued staring at him until he was forced to continue.

"Madame, a child was born to the woman, a child widely believed to be Henry's child."

"Why my father's? It could have been anyone's!"

"No, Majesty, it could not, for the child…the child…"

"Oh Lord, Mary and all the saints, man, say it!"

"The child, a girl, is so like unto our late good king that it could only be his. And remember, the love between the child's mother and Henry continued throughout his life."

"And what happened? Is she still alive?"

"No. Elizabeth died defending your father, Majesty, as her father died defending your grandfather. It seems the de Greys are loyal to the Tudors even unto death."

"And the child?"

"At the time of the crisis that cost her mother her life, the child fled. For many years it was rumored that she lived in Rome. Indeed, I believe that to be the truth, for your father searched high and low for her. Forgive me Majesty, but it seems he was at Coudenoure often enough and long enough for the child to understand, and just as he formed an unbreakable bond with her mother, so he did with his daughter. But the rumors and the legends. All of that was many, many years ago. I daresay she died in Rome for otherwise surely the rumors would still circulate."

"And this woman child had no desire to be queen?" Elizabeth asked guardedly.

William laughed.

"And that is why I believe the rumor to be true," he explained, "For it is said that court and courtly life were anathema to both the king's mistress and to her daughter. Indeed, 'tis why she fled, for there was fear she might be dragged hostage from Coudenoure in an effort to undermine your father Henry."

"I can see that, yes," Elizabeth said. "So now, why 'tis still standing? The old man is dead, the mistress is dead and the child disappeared long ago."

"Ah, and that is another reason why I say it was an uncommon love which your father found with Elizabeth. For even after her death, he kept Coudenoure as it had been during their years together. Even now, I believe, it is maintained by the Crown, though it belongs to the de Greys."

Elizabeth suddenly knew where she had heard the name before. In the account books of her myriad palaces, castles and manors, the smallest of them all was Coudenoure. It was one line at the bottom of the estate registry, and because it cost almost nothing, neither Edward nor Mary had bothered themselves with it. And if she had not come riding today, she would have gone that way as well. On impulse, she turned her horse and started back down the hill.

"We shall continue on to Coudenoure."

Chapter Three

The road which led to Coudenoure was ancient in origin and only used by locals travelling the backways around Greenwich Palace. It had never risen far above its humble beginnings as a cow path and followed the contours of the land rather than tracing out a straight line. Those with proper wagons and horses or oxen, vendors with wares and travelers en route to greater places all used the main road which abutted the palace fortifications. Only those born and raised in the nearby hamlets even remembered the track's existence. Despite its tortuous way, however, two small manor houses depended upon it for egress. One of these was Coudenoure, and the other that of the architect employed by Henry to shape its presence.

The turn which gave onto Coudenoure's long, straight drive was barely visible amid the brambles which threatened to engulf it on all sides. A wall of limestone, built to a defensive height, showed itself behind the undergrowth. No gate connected the two sides of the fence across the drive, but etched in bold letters upon each of the limestone fence-posts which set it off, in large letters, was a message written fairly recently, for the moss and lichen had yet to settle in upon its surface:

To Queen Elizabeth We Pledge All

Elizabeth stopped and looked for a long time at the words. Whoever lived in this out of the way place proclaimed to the world their allegiance to the new queen, a brave move considering that some believed her hold upon the throne to be tentative at best. Perhaps William was right – perhaps this family, or whoever was currently living on the estate, did indeed give her support in her early going. She turned to her retinue.

"I shall proceed from here alone. You are to wait for me and I shall return when I am done."

An uneasy glance passed among those with her. One of the guards jumped from his horse and spoke.

"Majesty, we do not know who or what lies beyond this fence. Surely 'tis a better plan to take cavalry with you?"

She shook her head vigorously.

"You have heard my decision. I shall join you anon."

Using her riding crop to beat back the tallest of the briar bushes, she fought her way through the thicket. So intent was she on getting through the entrance and onto the drive proper that she failed to notice the view. When she looked up she smiled.

What a place! At the end of a long straight drive sat a perfectly proportioned and symmetrical manor house. Its large, limestone blocks shimmered in the morning sun while its diamond-paned windows caught each ray and reflected it back like a rainbow. Contrary to the exterior of the estate, the grounds within were pristine. The drive must have been raked that very morning for the sunlight had yet to dry the newly turned gravel. A low ha-ha separated the grounds immediately adjacent to the house from those farther out nearest the fence. Elizabeth rode slowly up the drive, drinking in the visual beauty of the place. An orchard was laid out with geometric precision on the west side of the house, but beyond that the ruins of an ancient sanctuary caught and held one's gaze. High gothic windows graced the aged façade of what must at one time have been a truly marvelous church. Now, sunlight poured through the empty windows and what remained of the stone outline of the once grand structure was gray and weathered. Gone with time were the end walls and the interior – nothing was left but the skeletal ruins of two side structures.

As she studied the aged sanctuary, Elizabeth noticed a low stone barrier adjacent to it which enclosed an equally archaic cemetery. Her gaze might have continued on but she noticed a figure sitting within its bounds. On impulse, she steered her horse across the great lawn and rode to see who might be keeping the dead company on such a fine day. She dismounted and approached.

An old woman sat on a small bench near two headstones. She was speaking in a low voice and occasionally waved her cane at nothing in particular, and Elizabeth had to cough to make her presence known. The old woman turned and watched as Elizabeth approached but made no move to stand and bow before her sovereign.

"Good morning, old ma'am," Elizabeth said, deciding to ignore the lack of protocol on the old lady's part. "'Tis a lovely day, is it not?"

The old woman glanced up at the sky. The red scarf which had draped her hair fell backwards, and Elizabeth noted the white, sparse hair which it revealed. The face was refined, but like a looking glass dropped on a stone floor its quiet countenance was broken by a hundred lines and creases. After a moment, the old lady spoke.

"Aye, you are right, young missy." She patted the stone bench beside her as she looked at Elizabeth.

"'Tis a very fine dress you have," She eyed Elizabeth up and down. "You must be from the court at Greenwich."

Elizabeth smiled gently. The old bird had no clue to whom she was speaking and the novelty amused her.

"I am indeed," Elizabeth responded. "I had had enough of the palace this morning and wished to breathe some fresh air."

She pointed at the distant ridge.

"I rode to the top of that hill and saw this lovely place and decided to see who might live here."

The old lady nodded appreciatively.

"Well, you have come to Coudenoure, the estate of Thomas de Grey." She raised her cane and rapped it sharply on the top of the nearest tombstone. "Thomas died some years ago now. It was that terrible day the northerners tried to steal Constance and do Henry harm – can you imagine such a thing? Thomas blocked the door to give young Charles time to get away with the child. They struck him down, they did, but Charles got away. You see, Thomas had indeed bought him enough time. "

Her voice cracked and she closed her eyes as though remembering the moment from so long ago.

What had begun as a lark of a conversation for Elizabeth was now becoming quite interesting. She spoke quietly to the old lady to encourage her to continue. After a moment, the narrative resumed.

"Well, you see, as Charles bolted the stable, Henry came with his men from around that corner."

She pointed back to the manor reliving the scene.

"Charles knew at once that he must first protect the king, and so he threw Constance to our servant Prudence and told her to hide in those woods."

She smacked her gums together and nodded.

"Yes he did. And young Charles turned and defended Henry and together they killed the rebels."

A long silence ensued. Finally, she tapped the gravestone again.

"Aye, Thomas was a fine man. His love of books was a sin, but he would never hear me on that subject."

Elizabeth was intrigued. She had no clue what event the woman was remembering, but clearly it was still vivid and had etched itself in stark detail in her aged memory. There was no account of such a confrontation in the court records that she knew of, yet there had been many skirmishes with rebels from the north. Her thoughts were interrupted by the gentle rustle of an autumn breeze. It caused the dry grass which covered the graves to whisper their own version of the past. Elizabeth felt it pull a wisp of hair free from its netting and she settled it back in place as she spoke.

"Madam, a wind is coming. Shall I accompany you back to the manor? I would love to hear more of Coudenoure."

The old woman shook her head.

"No, no, I wish to speak to Elizabeth." Now she stretched and tapped her cane upon the next gravestone. "Elizabeth too died defending Henry. Such a good king he was. And a good man."

She looked directly at the queen.

"Go to the manor. Constance is in the library and can tell you about Coudenoure. It is hers now."

"Tell me, what is your name?" Elizabeth asked.

"Agnes, my lady. I was born before Bosworth, if you are familiar with that battle. And I have been at Coudenoure since that time."

Elizabeth's face broke into a smile.

"Aye, as you say," she replied. "I am deeply familiar with that battle." She turned to go.

"And you? What is your name, child?" Agnes called out.

The queen turned.

"I am Elizabeth."

As she walked away, Elizabeth heard the old girl mutter to herself, "Poor child, she thinks she is Elizabeth when we sit in front of Elizabeth's grave. Tut, tut, poor child."

Elizabeth stifled a laugh and walked on.

She led her horse across the great lawn, piecing together the tales of first William and now of this aged creature Agnes. Saints in heaven, she reflected, the old woman did not even recognize her own queen. And who was this Constance that she was about to meet? Her father's love, perhaps?

The dry autumn breeze felt good against her skin, and she looped the reins of her mount through the iron circle of a hitching post near the front door. Before she could knock, one massive side of the double door creaked open. An older woman stood before her in a simple dress with a cook's apron and cap. This one, too, looked at Elizabeth without recognition.

"Madam, I am Prudence." An inquiring look met Elizabeth's steady gaze but there was no curtsey or bow, only simple civility such as one might extend a neighbor.

"I am here to see Constance," Elizabeth said. "Agnes stated she is in the library."

"Oh, aye, then if you have seen Agnes." The name "Agnes" seemed to serve as a password for entry, and Prudence pushed the heavy door open further. "Come this way, madam. Shall I tell her your name?"

"No, that will not be necessary." Elizabeth was entranced by the situation and the place and wanted no hint of her position to break the spell. She looked around in wonder at the great limestone walls and floors of the manor house. Stained glass from some earlier century sparkled on either side of the front doors, and a high vaulted ceiling gave an ethereal quality to the great hall through which they proceeded. With its monastic plainness, the place was the antithesis of modern, yet the tapestries and rugs gave it a warmth seldom found even in the oak and elm paneled rooms of her own palaces. Surely, her father had felt the same, for why else would he have protected the place and built upon it for so long? But even as she admired the long hall, Prudence knocked and opened a side door. Elizabeth entered and could barely stifle a gasp.

Before her was a room of such simplistic elegance that it took her breath away. A medieval fireplace tall enough for her to easily stand in its chamber graced the middle of the outer wall. Its mantel was of polished but uncarved marble. Above it hung a great sword. But the mantel paled in comparison to the wall upon which it stood.

Great solid shelves, each four inches thick, stretched from floor to ceiling along the entire wall. They were polished to a high gleam and supported by even greater beams which ran vertically between them every five feet. It was a masterpiece of symmetry, beauty and organization. But even that was not what took Elizabeth's breath away – it was what lay upon those shelves.

In neat rows and carefully placed stacks, in scrolled papyri set out one at a time upon various shelves, in vellum pages and bound books was the greatest library Elizabeth had ever seen. Silently, she walked slowly to one end of the wall and gently traced her fingers along the spines of the volumes set there. She paused before the shelves which housed ancient scrolls, so ancient that even she had never beheld documents of such antiquity. Illuminated pages lay singly upon some of the shelves, so fragile that their owner had not wished to place even a single page on top of them lest damage be done. On and on she walked, lost in the vast and ancient collection. Twenty minutes or more had passed before a polite cough behind her caught her attention. She returned to the great hearth and for the first time noticed the arrangement of chairs in front of it. In one of them sat a middle-aged woman who might once have laid claim to great beauty. Her face was square and her eyes gray. Her hair was streaked through with white but even so the flaming red of its original color still caught one's eye. As Elizabeth came near, she rose and bowed with difficulty.

"Majesty."

Elizabeth looked at her and knew that William's tale was true, for she was looking at her father in female form. A heavy cough caused the woman to sway slightly and Elizabeth realized that not only must the woman be ill, but she was also lame, for she stood upon one leg.

"Sit." She ordered her. The woman fell back into her chair and looked up at Elizabeth.

"My Queen, we are honored."

Elizabeth sat in the chair next to her. Her head was spinning.

"Madam, you look very much like our like great king, Henry."

A crooked smile creased the woman's wrinkled countenance as she studied the face before her: Red hair and gray blue eyes set against an alabaster complexion. The face had the fullness of youth but promised to give way to high cheekbones and an aquiline nose in old age. And there, yes, there was the narrow chin much like her own. She continued to gaze at Elizabeth and looked beyond the physical attributes of the woman. Here was an intelligent being, but one who was terribly guarded. Her eyes were watchful but gave nothing away, as though a lifetime at the whim of conspiracy, fear and chance had taught her well. She trusted no one. That much was certain.

"Majesty, you have nothing to fear from me or from Coudenoure, for that matter. We support you and your court unequivocally."

Elizabeth interrupted. "I am sure you do since the crown pays for the very roof over your head, madam." She heard her own voice, harsh and strident and wondered why she had said such a thing. But the woman next to her seemed to understand Elizabeth's need for supremacy and control. She looked down as she countered.

"Majesty, you are right of course. But whether our small household lived here at Coudenoure or in some hovel in a faraway village, you would still have our undying support. The de Grays have always been thus."

Elizabeth nodded.

"Yes, I have heard. But you have yet to answer my question concerning the resemblance between you and my father."

A long pause ensued.

"Majesty, with all my scars and missing limbs…" she nodded towards the footstool, "…and with my breath which is slowly leaving me, yes, I am your sister."

Elizabeth sat quietly, stunned by the simplicity of Constance's answer. So she had a sister. Her only experiences of near relatives were not happy ones, and her immediate instinct was to flee and formulate destruction before it could be visited upon her. Yet the face before her defied such an interpretation of the situation. It echoed the simplicity and innocence of the answer provided to her question. This woman was helpless, and surely if she intended harm to Elizabeth she would not be living in complete anonymity and isolation at Coudenoure. She would be raising an army or consulting with rebels and Catholics. Elizabeth remained silent, considering the situation. She was in no immediate danger and her guards waited at the end of the drive should trouble erupt. What to do? Every fiber in her being shouted that here was yet another threat to her own person, yet another pretender to her throne. How many, she wondered, must she endure? Was her life always to be full of such turmoil? Why had God given her everything only to allow it to be threatened at every turn? And yet, Constance did not convey such evil purpose or the cunning required to achieve it.

Her thoughts of schemes and intrigues and counter-moves were pulled back by the patient, intelligent face before her. It watched her with nothing but kindness written across it.

"You wonder whether to trust me, do you not?" Constance asked. "Indeed, I suspect your entire life has been one long struggle: to please, to stay alive, to succeed, to protect yourself, your crown and your kingdom."

Elizabeth waved her hand for silence.

"Who are you? What is your name?"

"Constance de Gray." The woman waited.

"If you are as you say then your mother was my father's mistress."

"Initially, Majesty, that was so. But my mother respected the sanctity of marriage and once Henry was married to Catherine, they no longer shared carnal pleasures. Their love for one another was bound up with their shared past."

Again, what to do? She knew instinctively the woman before her told the truth, but she knew from sad experience that nothing but grief and trouble came from those who might also have a claim to her throne whether they pursued it or not. If she exposed this Constance, and if she did it would end badly for the woman she was certain, then she was denying herself the one thing she had never been able to find, even at her own court when the crown of England was finally hers: someone who knew her father.

All his friends had passed on long before Elizabeth came to the throne. And it was only then that she was in a position to ask and to seek answers. But by then it was too late. And now, like a gift from God himself she had stumbled across a place her father obviously loved deeply and had devoted himself to in no small measure. She had accidentally found the one person who could tell her of Henry, of what he was like when he was not king and on his guard. Who was the man? This woman knew, and held perhaps the last key to understanding him. If she destroyed her and Coudenoure, she would lose forever the opportunity to know her own father. She took a deep breath.

"Constance, who knows of your heritage?"

"No one", she replied. "I lived abroad for many years, and when I returned, I wanted nothing more than what I had left with – Coudenoure and all its memories."

"Did you know our father?"

"Aye, I did. What a fine and funny and kind man he was."

"Kind and funny?" Elizabeth laughed. "Madam, I do not believe I have ever heard him described thus."

It was Constance's turn to laugh.

"My good Queen, can you not tarry a moment? Prudence, my friend and cook, can make us a light repast. You see, I have no one with whom to share my memories."

"What of Agnes, the old woman whom I just met?"

Constance laughed again.

"Lady Agnes lives with the dead. She has no need of my memories for she has her own of this place, of my mother and father. No, she cares not for mine."

She hesitated.

"Agnes knew your grandfather, Majesty, did you know? She has tales she would wish to share, if she knew who you were."

Elizabeth rose and warmed her hands in front of the fire. After a moment, she turned.

"Tell me, do you ever leave this place? Do you have visitors who come?"

The questions seemed pointed, as though Elizabeth were making a calculation of some sort.

"No Majesty, I do not. Tradesmen come to the backdoor and are managed by Prudence. The servants who manage the fields and stables deal only with her. I am here, with my books and my things only. No one here would speak of you, nor will anyone beyond Coudenoure know of your visit."

A long pause ensued. Elizabeth saw a flicker in Constance's eyes, but it passed before she could identify it.

"Very well," Elizabeth finally spoke, "'Tis nothing to me, but I will nevertheless hear your tales of our good King Henry."

She picked up her riding gloves from a nearby table.

"But not today. I shall return when I am able."

Constance attempted to rise and Elizabeth was once again struck by the frailty of the woman. Her sleeve caught on the chair and revealed an arm so thin as to be bone and skin only.

"Sit. We will meet again and in the meantime, this meeting does not leave Coudenoure."

Constance lay back in the chair and wheezed, but raised her hand to acknowledge Elizabeth's command. With that, the queen strode from the room. She mounted her horse and galloped quickly down the drive to her waiting courtiers.

"Majesty?" William asked once she appeared.

"Sir William, you have led me astray, for this place is nothing of the Tudors. There is none of what your legends and tales speak of. Let us not worry with this place again, but leave it in its isolated splendor – there is no one there but an old servant who has never been turned out. We shall leave the place as we found it."

They turned for Greenwich, and Elizabeth rode amongst the others without joining in their chatter. She was turning events over in her mind. She knew she could trust Constance, but she also knew that the flicker she had seen in Constance's eyes indicated that the woman was hiding something. Perhaps it was immaterial, perhaps not. Time would surely tell.

At Coudenoure, a young woman and man crouched in the yew hedge which extended from the east corner of the manor house.

"What do you think?", the young woman whispered as they watched Elizabeth ride away. "Do you think perhaps…"

"…it is in connection with the mystery of Coudenoure?" the young man ventured.

"Quinn!" came the exasperated reply, "There is no mystery of Coudenoure. 'Tis my mother's estate and a very pleasant one. That is all."

"Aye, but the rumors, Bess. My father tells me king Henry loved this manor above all others."

"Did he say why?" Bess whispered.

Quinn chuckled under his breath.

"He said it was because of "the great Robert Janyns" vision and talent in renovating the place. Others, however, do not give my father credit, but rather lay it at the feet of one Elizabeth of Coudenoure."

As the queen disappeared from sight, Bess rose and looked at Quinn in anger and amusement.

"Elizabeth of Coudenoure was my grandmother, and you will quash such rumors as come your way. I will not have my family maligned by my own pre-contracted husband."

Quinn attempted to speak. Bess cut him off, but the wounded look on his face caused her to reassure him.

"Do not worry so much, Quinn dearest."

He perked up once again like a puppy given a treat.

"Leave now, and I will go see my mother. Anon."

Quinn watched as she ran lightly through the heavy front doors of Coudenoure. His eyes, dreamy pools of ebony, looked upon her in silent admiration and love. How had he been so lucky, he wondered? He stood to wipe the grass from his stockings, tripped on the end of his own scarf and fell headlong into the hedge. He ignored the setback and rose again, this time traipsing across the great lawn towards his own neighboring estate. The fall was not necessarily a surprise. Quinn knew his inherited talent in architecture was unmatched, but he also knew that once outside that comfortable realm of models and geometry and planes and space, he was frequently a victim of his own clumsiness and inability to organize himself and his surroundings. He spun through life leaving a trail of debris through which he had to continuously backtrack to find the necessary bits and pieces he needed to move forward again.

But Bess. She suffered from no such calamities of nature and nurture. He was certain that if she so desired, she could order the very stars in the sky to do her bidding and they would float across the vaults of heaven in complex patterns of beauty and light, steered by her will and desire. After all, he mused happily, she ordered him about thus and he found it comforting, maternal. Or what he imagined to be maternal: his own mother had died in childbirth leaving his aged father to raise him alone in a world with a marked absence of the fairer sex. The result was a boy, then a young man, who had no knowledge of women and their ways. They seemed to him mysterious creatures with almost prescient knowledge of the world around them and how to make it right and good; born of a tribe with secret, cultish ways that men could never understand, only appreciate and need – desperately. His childhood with his father had been joyous and carefree, but in addition to leaving him with only a loose definition of chaos (and a looser one yet of its origins), it had resulted in a distinct awkwardness in the presence of women. He had always come away feeling bruised and generally off-kilter – until Bess.

As Quinn larked across the lawn, Bess joined her mother in the library.

"Who was that?" she asked as she stood before the fire. "Quinn and I saw a woman leave just now."

"Oh, just some lost soul who turned up from Greenwich Palace," replied Constance, "– no one you need worry about, dear."

She paused.

"Shall we have some tea?"

Chapter Four

Elizabeth rode out with only a minimal escort the following morning. Even for a woman who required little sleep her evening's rest had been brief. She had always imagined that should the crown ever grace her brow she would be able to breathe freely. The frets and terrors which had defined her until that moment would melt away and she would be at her leisure to think, to act, to live. Thus far, however, that had not been the case.

The business with Dudley and his wife had served to push her to the breaking point. Dudley had retreated to Yorkshire, to the estate of his beloved sister Katherine. The investigation was ongoing, but nothing seemed to slow the gossip at court. The death had rhyme and reason for everyone knew of Dudley's ambition and almost no one liked him. Her evening had been spent with her court, but as she ate and danced, she felt the eyes upon her in a way she seldom did. She was being watched now, not as queen and sovereign but as the possible mistress of a murderer. Gone was all talk of the good work she and Cecil were doing with the coinage of the land – giving it a solid weight and thus ensuring its acceptance for trade at home and on the continent. So too her subjects had ceased to discuss religion and her move towards practice as dictated by conscious. All had been swept aside by Robert Dudley and his scandal. There was nothing she could do until the coroner's report was put abroad and like so many other times in her life, she struggled to compartmentalize the angst and uncertainty of the situation by maintaining some semblance of normalcy.

And Coudenoure. She hardly knew what to think of the place with its ancient walls and ruins. An estate, albeit a small one, full of old women who talked serenely to the dead, who limped around alone in a library God himself must envy, who treated their servants as friends and who had no recognition of her or the times they lived in – what manner of place was that, she wondered? The house and its inhabitants seemed barely tethered to the earth, much less to her own life and reign. It was as if she had stumbled across a schism in time that allowed her to leave her own troubles in the here and now and float away into a past filled with her father and those he loved. People who did not fear or envy him, or covet his favor, but who simply loved him as he was. They knew nothing of Dudley and her trials and she was certain that had they known, they could not have cared less. Good Lord, she thought savagely, I understand why my father hid the place away from the world and those who might destroy it, and I have only been queen for a year. How much more so must he have guarded such a refuge as the years upon the throne took their toll?

Dudley had sent frantic messages to her all evening, and she had resolutely ignored them. Their situation had moved from intoxicatingly and romantically dangerous and amusing to something far more serious – something that could have consequences beyond her control were she not careful. She suspected that Coudenoure might provide a tiny sliver of relief from the strains of court. And that tiny ray of sunlit distraction, divorced from anything that might be considered relevant or that might haunt her, could prove to be a dose of tonic against the stress and anxiety she felt otherwise. As she had galloped away down the long, straight drive the previous day, she had found herself energized by the place's dream-like quality, and felt herself now better able to deal anew with her real-life problems. Somehow that moment of respite in such an utterly simplistic and quiet place had given her enough reserves to continue on. But the rest of the story was that of her father. She could not go back in time, but there was no need for that since Coudenoure seemed to bridge the two worlds of past and present. Between knowledge of her father and respite from her growing concerns, the place and its proximity was a most welcome discovery. She had decided on impulse to ride out that morning and revisit it. Perhaps the strain of the past few days had imbued it with more charm and grace than it actually possessed. Another trip would tell the tale.

She left the guards at the end of the drive and once again rode the great drive alone. No one appeared to meet her or assist her dismount and she smiled to herself as she pulled the rope attached to the ancient bell on the door jamb. What a place, she thought. Who are these people. After the second clanging ring, a loud racket could be heard on the other side of the door. It took a moment for Elizabeth to realize it was a voice.

"Settle down, do you here? You will wake the dead. Aye, you will if you ring that infernal bell again."

It was the old woman from the cemetery, Agnes. She looked at Elizabeth suspiciously as she wagged her cane.

"I know you, young lassie – you were here yesterday. Or the day before." She paused. "Was it last week?" Elizabeth moved to answer but was met by more cane waving.

"It was definitely of recent times, so what matter." Agnes satisfied herself with that answer and moved to let Elizabeth enter.

"Old ma'am, you are right – I visited with you…" Elizabeth hesitated and then decided to be bold, "…and Thomas and Elizabeth yesterday, remember? You sent me here to talk with Constance."

Agnes smiled.

"Oh, aye, I remember now. You were confused about your own name." She reached out and gave Elizabeth a reassuring pat on her arm while winking at her. "No mind, no mind. We all have our moments, do we not? Now, we will go have breakfast with Constance and Prudence, but dear, try and remember that Elizabeth is dead for otherwise you will be thought a nit." She pointed to her own head with a knowing look and nod.

Elizabeth had never been referred to as a nit, but Agnes continued on oblivious to her guest's surprise.

"Yes, yes, let us go to the library. Come."

Elizabeth stepped into the cool interior and was once again escorted into the great room which ran parallel to the hall. Constance, the servant Prudence and a young woman were seated before the fire – a table was drawn close to it for warmth. Elizabeth spoke before Constance could say anything.

"I am Colleen, from Greenwich Palace. I was here yesterday."

"Well done, dear, well done," Agnes whispered in her ear.

Constance smiled at the deceit.

"Please join us, Colleen."

The young woman rose and pulled two chairs to the table for Elizabeth and Agnes. Elizabeth studied her carefully for she had not seen her on her previous visit to Coudenoure. She was tall with deep set gray eyes. Her hair was an uncontrollable riot of rich, black curls which escaped the netting set in place to give it shape and form. Instead, it flowed around her like a halo and framed her face enchantingly. She was not beautiful, but she was arresting and very interesting.

Constance saw Elizabeth studying the girl and spoke quickly.

"This is my daughter, Bess."

"Ah," thought Elizabeth, "That was the look which crossed her face yesterday. The shoe drops – she has a child and was concerned about me knowing."

Bess offered a plate of fruit to Elizabeth, smiling and chatting with Prudence the entire time.

"No, you do not understand. Marble has veins which the sculptor ignores at his own peril, for if you work against the stone it will shatter."

"Child, why not paint? 'Tis much easier and cheaper."

"Dear Prudence, an artist does not choose her medium, it chooses her. Now, I must go to the studio and plan – you know I have a new piece of stone coming sometime in the next three months. My father said he would send it."

Before she could leave, the door opened and Quinn appeared. He looked around the room and almost fainted. It was his worst nightmare – a room full of women and nary a man with whom he could stand. He wanted to impress his beloved, and so with what he hoped was a courtly, gallant smile, he bowed deeply. It was a grand gesture. Had it not been for his cap falling off, it would have been grander still. As he picked it up Bess moved to his side.

"Lady Colleen, this is Master Quinn Janyns, from Tyche, the estate which bounds Coudenoure's far side. He is a fine architect."

Elizabeth said nothing, studying the boy and his dress. He was tall and athletically built, with dark curls and ebony eyes. His dress was that of a dandy and the simple linen frocks worn by the women in the room made him stand out like a peacock. An awkward silence set in as she continued to stare at him in an imperial manner and he continued to shuffle on his feet.

Bess broke the spell by kissing her mother, grabbing a plum scone and moving towards the door. Quinn followed obediently and gratefully.

Agnes looked at the two of them with sharp, knowing eyes and believing them out of earshot, spoke authoritatively.

"That young woman will never find a husband if she continues being so bossy and that young man continues following her about."

Constance patted her hand.

"She says she will not marry, that her work is her calling."

Bess was grateful that Quinn was too wrapped within himself to have heard the remark. She had not informed them of her contract with Quinn. It was a small deceit, and a necessary one, she assured herself, for they would surely say she was too young to know her own heart much less pledge it in marriage. She pulled the library door behind them.

Before Agnes could wave her cane and commence pontificating on young women and manners, Constance spoke.

"You must forgive my daughter. She was raised in the studio of her father and thinks of nothing but art day and night."

"'Tis not that simple." Prudence laughed. "She thinks and speaks of it in five different languages."

"So she is gifted with language abilities, is she?"

"Indeed," Constance chimed in, "They seem to run in our family. And you, Colleen, you have the gift of speaking in foreign tongues?"

Elizabeth smiled with pride.

"I believe I may match her in those abilities, for they run in my family as well." The double entendre was not lost upon Constance.

The breakfast was finished and Agnes and Prudence left them alone before the fire. The two women sat in a comfortable silence for some time taking each other's measure and considering their unique situation.

Finally, Constance spoke.

"Majesty…," she began, but Elizabeth cut her off by gently patting her hand. She looked her sister in the eye and a small chuckle escaped her lips.

"Call me Colleen."

Constance laughed as Elizabeth continued in a more serious vein.

"'Tis a simple matter," she stated matter-of-factly. "If you, or your daughter betray me, there will be consequences."

"How would we betray you?" Constance asked incredulously. "Surely you must realize that

Coudenoure stands with you, and if you are worried about my daughter – "

"Yes," Elizabeth interjected bluntly, "I am. For she could be a menace to the stability of my kingdom if her heritage became known."

"Majesty…"

"Colleen."

"Yes, well, *Colleen*, the only person outside of you and me living who knows my heritage is Agnes, and I believe we can both agree that knowledge is safe with her. And as for me, if I wished to be connected to the court or the throne I would have made that clear years ago. Surely you must see that."

"Indeed."

"And as for my daughter, she believes her father is Roberto Ransdell, an English artist who lives in Rome, and that one of her grandfathers was a tradesman and that the other died at sea."

Elizabeth noticed the careful phrasing used by Constance.

"You say she believes – 'tis true?"

"Well, mostly."

"A convenient answer."

"'Tis long and complicated, Colleen, and to understand your father you must understand his circumstance here at Coudenoure."

Elizabeth leaned back in the chair and waited. Constance suddenly shouted for Prudence and as she appeared in the library door, called out to her.

"Prudence, my friend, would you bring me the lockbox from my bedroom? I have need of it."

Prudence disappeared and again the two women sat in silence before the fire. Prudence returned shortly with a smallish box which sported a significant lock. She bowed and left the room, pulling the door behind her.

Elizabeth watched as Constance fished for a necklace from under her over blouse. At the end of a long, gold chain were two objects: a key and a gold cross set with rubies. Constance pulled the box closer and leaned towards it at the same time. The key fit neatly in the lock and as she carefully opened its lid, she finally spoke.

"If we are to start, we shall begin at the beginning. This is the first item I own which indicates the love and collaboration between our father and my mother. 'Tis the document which set the renovation of Coudenoure in motion. It was drawn up when my mother, and our father, were young." She paused as she continued fidgeting with the lockbox. "Young indeed."

"There are others, here, but we shall begin with this."

Elizabeth gasped.

"You have documents? In our father's hand?"

"Yes. Some letters, some songs and poems. Some schemes in which they conspired together for projects at Coudenoure. There is a rather large piece of paper, drawn in my mother's hand, which served as the plan for the original renovations of the estate's grounds. Yes, this is what I was looking for. "

She began unfolding the page as she spoke.

"And here, see this? That is your father's annotation."

Elizabeth clasped the paper and read slowly.

"Bucephalus?" she asked curiously. "Alexander's horse? I do not understand."

Constance pointed at the page.

"Ah, read this."

Elizabeth read as instructed.

"For Elizabeth and our chipmunk Bucephalus."

She looked at Constance.

"Apparently, when they were quite young, your father and my mother Elizabeth would sit under yonder tree." She leaned and waved her cane in the direction of the window. Elizabeth moved quickly to the window and saw an ancient elm on the far hillside beyond the perimeter wall. Constance went on.

"They called it Bucephalus, for Henry declared that such a small inconsequential creature should at least possess a grand name. They trained it to eat from their hands and apparently referred to it humorously as their first born."

Elizabeth laughed and read her father's note again – it was light and playful, a million miles from the world that awaited him as king. It pleased her to touch it and run her fingers gently over its surface. Her father had written it so long ago. She glanced at Constance and saw that she, too, was being drawn back into the past. There were tears on her cheeks, but whether of fond memories or sorrow Elizabeth could not tell. She folded the paper and returned it to Constance.

"You know, this place, this room, 'tis very peaceful."

"Yes," Constance agreed, "I believe they planned it that way. They would sit here, where you and I sit now, for hours upon hours, chatting, writing and dreaming. Sometimes Henry would compose upon his lute while mother tended to her needlepoint."

Elizabeth leaned back and closed her eyes. The warmth from the fire smelt of burning wood and ash, while the light from the window etched patterns across the floor and bookshelves. Their chairs were deep and soft, and without realizing it, she dozed off. When she woke, someone had placed an old shawl across her lap for warmth.

She awoke not with a jolt, but with a strong sense of relaxation and refreshment. She sat up and looked about. Constance was tatting quietly exactly where she had been before.

"How long was I asleep?" Elizabeth asked.

"'Tis almost noon, Majesty. Shall I ask Prudence to prepare a meal?"

Elizabeth shook her head and stood.

"No, no, I must get back – I will be missed otherwise."

She smiled at Constance.

"I shall be back when my schedule allows." she stated, "And we have much to talk about, and not just our father. I am curious about your daughter, Bess – you must tell me about her, and how you came to be lame."

Constance smiled in return as Elizabeth swept from the room. She listened to the horse galloping down the drive and wondered what would come of the sudden connection between Coudenoure and the new queen.

Chapter Five

Elizabeth de Grey was named after her grandmother, but she had never been called Elizabeth, only Bess. She was tall, as was her mother, but not lithe. Strongly built like a Grecian goddess from long ago, and with warm honey-colored skin, she had presence. Intelligence shone forth from her ocean gray eyes like those of her mother, and passion radiated from her like light from a flame. She was not a fussy woman, nor was she overly feminine, but a woman's grace permeated her every move.

Constance had worried about telling her daughter of their impending move back to Coudenoure. After all, Bess had been raised in Rome, in an open, artistic manner, one which had allowed her great freedoms. From an early age she had spent her days first in this studio, now that one, absorbing the lessons and language of art. Her world was one of color and form, not of protocol and ritual. Roberto, her presumed father, had once told her of her grandmother Elizabeth's predilection for dressing as a boy in order to travel the streets and galleries of Rome unimpeded by the rules which governed the behavior of the female sex. Bess had immediately fallen in love with the idea and not soon after could be seen in the market place or the Vatican or on the wharves of Ostia also dressed as a young man of the Roman middle class. Constance had finally tumbled to how her daughter was spending her days when she showed up at Roberto's studio unexpectedly and Bess ran in with new canvases tucked under the man's shirt and vest she was wearing. Despite her best attempt at feigned apoplexy, when Bess cited her grandmother's behavior and Roberto had laughed, Constance lost the battle – she came to learn that with a head strong daughter one must choose one's fights carefully.

When she learned of the impending move back to England, Bess had surprised Constance with her enthusiasm for it. It would be an adventure, she declared. Like her mother and grandmother before her, she would sail the world and meet interesting people. Constance thought of England with its heavy mists and rolling wooded hills, so different from Rome and the Italian countryside. She thought of her own sojourn into uncharted lands and the bitter lessons she had learned about living one's life through the imprint left behind by one's parents. It was dangerous to expect a common outcome from similar experiences in separate lives – the most one could hope for was a deeper understanding of oneself and one's inheritance. But Bess was young and like all those who are young believed that life's problems could be solved by moving on. She was immune to the descriptions of England intended to prepare her for the different climate and different life she would lead there. Constance explained that there would be no fusion of cultures as there was in Rome – Rome was a bustling metropolis, but England was an isle, far from the East and Africa, and more importantly far from Coudenoure. There would be no merchants from Cathay, no Moormen with their strange tongue or Africans with their exotic spices in the marketplaces. No invitations to warm southern villas in the rolling hills of Italy would come their way at Coudenoure.

When day of their departure finally arrived, Bess had appeared from her room at the Ransdell house dressed in boy's clothing. Constance had not been prepared for it and had explained yet again that England would not look upon such behavior in the same way as Bess' friends and mentors in Rome did. Bess shook her head and declared her indifference. She explained to her mother her intent to make the voyage as a man, thus freeing herself to learn sailing and cartography and wayfaring. It was late, the ship was leaving, and Bess won.

As on her voyage to Rome so many years earlier, Constance suffered from constant seasickness. She could not adjust to the rhythmic rolling of the ship's hull and the constant sound of the sea sloshing and battering its sides. She spent her days in their cabin, her head in a bucket. Sea spray misted the air like fog on the Thames in the pre-dawn hours and her leg ached with the damp chill of it all. She remembered the voyage out to Rome, leaving Woolwich and believing her life would unfold as her mother's had when she left England – an exciting adventure through which her own passion and personality would shine forth. But it did not turned out otherwise. Now she wanted nothing more than to return to her childhood home and pick up where she had left off. She knew instinctively that such a thing was not possible, but she yearned for it nevertheless. She wanted home. Desperately. She no longer knew what such a place might look like, but Coudenoure had sheltered her for her entire childhood, and even with the changes which must surely have beset the estate in the intervening years, it was all that came to mind when the word "home" hovered on her lips and in her thoughts. She would take it as a beggar might take a crumb from a passing stranger. The ship shifted beneath her and she rolled onto her back, clinging to the brace which ran above her bunk. Coudenoure. She hoped it would provide what she needed, and getting there was simply to be endured, not enjoyed.

Bess was solicitous of her mother, and secretly worried about her constantly. The loss of her lower leg had cost her dearly, and even now her recovery seemed less than certain. Her cough had always been with her but it seemed to increase in depth and frequency since the accident. Bess wanted to do what she wanted to do, but she also wanted her mother's approval and love. She split her spare time between trimming the sails and cleaning the decks with caring for Constance. Each day after dinner, she would curl up beside her and read to her from one of the many books which were making the journey home with them. Once Constance dozed off, Bess would go to her work above deck, returning with supper in the early evening. She played cards with her, told ridiculous stories to make Constance laugh, and hugged her when the roiling of the ship proved to be too much and emptied the bucket. She listened to her mother's stories of her own youth at Coudenoure and built a picture of the place in her own mind. To pass the time, she purchased charts from the captain a large page of paper intended for nautical. As her mother described Coudenoure she began tracing out the manor on the page. The exercise proved to be a tonic for Constance, for it made real what she not seen in more than twenty years. For Bess, it gave her a clearer picture of the great unknown which awaited her.

Roberto and Michelangelo, along with other artists in Rome, Florence, Paris and beyond, had wide networks which they used to procure pigments for their paints, stone for their statues, and canvases for their work. Never rising to the level of major sea-lanes but nevertheless worn and certain, merchants of all manner of goods had plied these secondary routes, searching and bartering over vast regions in the Far East, Africa and the lands north of England to obtain everything in demand. Early on in her Roman sojourn, Constance had begun using this tenuous means to transport letters to and from

Coudenoure. It was through this method that she learned of her mother's death, of her father's search for her, and of the upheavals which accompanied his death. As the years had crept by and she had become ever more disillusioned with her life in Italy, Constance had likewise used this channel to communicate her own discontent and finally to tell Prudence of her decision to return to Coudenoure along with Bess. Prudence, in turn, had learned of the arrival of their ship through their contacts at Woolwich, and had hurried forth from Coudenoure to meet them. Constance was overjoyed to see her.

In November of that same year, Mary died and Elizabeth ascended the throne.

Chapter Six

True to her word, Elizabeth began visiting Coudenoure on a regular but erratic basis. Greenwich Palace and Whitehall served as her major seats of governance and prior to her discovery of Coudenoure, she had used river transports to travel from one to the other. Her subjects had become accustomed to seeing her in glorious state as her retinue came and went between the two on royal barges. Once she became aware of the treasures that Coudenoure held for her, however, she began alternating such transport with horseback rides along the Thames and backroads which still connected Greenwich to London proper. As her father before her, she learned that such rides necessarily took longer and generated a much more fluid time for her expected arrival at the other end. This, in turn, allowed greater windows of opportunity for discreet stops at Coudenoure.

Elizabeth no longer wondered about Coudenoure's hold over Henry, for it had become a magnet for her as well. She would leave her guards at the end of the long drive and along with them her cares. She found in Constance and her small household the same respite from the throne that her father had relied upon for so many years. She and Constance would sit before the great library fire, as their father and Constance's mother had done as well. Constance taught Elizabeth bezique, a card game she had learned to play and love in Rome. In turn, Elizabeth told Constance of life at court and her own transition from bastard princess to queen. The exchange allowed the two women the opportunity to breathe freely in a world which they had often been denied such honesty.

"So, Constance, you rode that night to Woolwich and boarded a ship bound for Rome?"

"Yes, you see, my mother had planned such an escape for years should I ever be in danger."

"Ah, and so you repeated your mother's own life?" Elizabeth sighed. "I have always wanted to please my father and to rule as he did, but 'tis difficult to know the answers to many of the problems presented to me."

Constance poured Elizabeth a cup of tea.

"Are you sure this is healthful?" Elizabeth asked cautiously. "It is used for medicinal purposes only at court."

Constance waved her hand to dismiss the concern.

"I have been drinking this delightful beverage ever since I lived in Rome and I believe it to be beneficial. It provides me energy when I am feeling fatigued."

She laced her own cup with honey before continuing.

"And as for pleasing your father by emulating his reign, be careful my friend, for I sought to do the same with my mother's life and adventures, and it ended not well."

"Tell me."

"I believed that by going to Rome and living as she had lived when young, all my own questions and problems would be resolved. I was terribly wrong. What I found was that I although I am the daughter of two passionate souls, I myself do not possess such passion. It took many years for me to see that and to learn that I must betray my own identity."

"I do not understand."

"Elizabeth, as I have told you before, when my mother was in Rome she knew the great artist Michelangelo. I, too, knew him, but in a different way. The man trained my dear friend Roberto..."

"Dear friend? I thought he was the father of Bess."

Constance shook her head and smiled.

"No, her father is Michelangelo, although she does not yet know that."

Elizabeth put honey in her tea and considered what she had just been told.

"So what is this about you and passion?"

"Michelangelo told me much about my mother – about her creative spirit and that it was matched by a passion that time would never quell. He was right, for she loved Henry until the moment she died, and likely even now beyond the grave. But he also told me frankly that I did not have that same passion. I am creative and learned, but creativity without passion produces only small finite creations, creations that only live and breathe for a moment.

"It is only when creativity is married to passion that great loves, or great works of art are realized. Michelangelo is blessed with both, as were my mother and Henry."

Still Elizabeth remained quiet.

"Roberto Ransdell had known my mother since she left England as a young maid. He had great talent but no passion – his work is valued and certainly treasured, but it cannot compare to that of Michelangelo."

Constance poured more tea and honey before continuing.

"At any rate, Roberto and his wife sheltered me when I arrived in Rome. Shortly after that she died of the plague and Roberto was left with two small children. I served as their mother until he remarried. Michelangelo loved my mother as a father does a daughter, and when he learned I was in Rome, he insisted I come to his studio and work beside his students. After a bit, we became lovers, for he was in between mistresses, as he said, and I was eager to know carnal love."

Elizabeth gasped.

"You are very open about such matters, sister. Some might call you…"

Constance laughed.

"Call me what, sister? A whore? Perhaps, but I have always gone my own way, and you must remember, I was not a young maid when I reached Rome."

"And so you were with Michelangelo, the great artist?" Elizabeth leaned slightly forward and her voice invited Constance to say more.

"I was." Constance's eyes twinkled with the memory. "He was kind and passionate and gentle and taught me much. But it was not to be a long affair and we both knew it. In a way, I believe we both got what we wanted. He was desperate for female companionship at the time, and I confess I wanted a child regardless of the circumstances of conception. It had begun to drive me in ways you may not yet understand."

"No, I understand what you say, for I myself have felt such stirrings."

"Roberto and his new wife took me in..."

"Do the people of Italy treat such matters lightly?" Elizabeth's voice was laced with incredulity.

Constance laughed.

"Perhaps not the people of Italy, but the people of the art world are not so bound to custom and tradition as we are, sister. Roberto took me in and for some years we all lived happily."

"What happened?"

Constance shrugged.

"I missed England. You know, you might think that a warm climate and a beautiful city would replace such a musty and damp home as our little isle but it will not, I assure you. I began to long for the smell of peat upon the snowy winter path, of lavender mixed with the scent of roses in the spring, for the sight of the muddy Thames flowing slowly onwards."

"And you never contacted our father?"

"I dared not, for I knew that should my heritage become known, I would be in danger of being pulled into intrigues against him for the throne, intrigues in which I have no interest even now. I waited for an opportune time, and after your brother Edward and your sister Mary died and left the throne to you, it seemed safe to return."

Elizabeth nodded understanding.

"Also, Elizabeth, you must realize that my daughter and I are Protestant in our beliefs, while Agnes clings to the only faith she ever knew – the faith that Thomas and my mother died in, and which she will die in as well. It would have been difficult had I come home and the rift which was playing itself out in the realm then been reflected within my own household."

"Yes," Elizabeth responded slowly, "I can follow your reasoning. But were you ill and lame when you left England?"

"No, the cough which robs me of breath came upon me late in my stay in Rome. I visited numerous doctors, but none had an answer for what caused it, much less a cure. But I am fortunate for it grows no worse as time passes. It is only when I exert myself that it causes me harm."

"And your leg?" Elizabeth asked gently.

"That happened in Rome as well. After the birth of Bess, while I was living with Roberto, I continued working and studying in Michelangelo's studio..."

"What! You continued working for the man even though you had his child and were no longer his mistress? What manner of relationship allows such behavior?"

"A relationship with a great artist who lived among other great artists," Constance laughed as she spoke. "It was not the model of courtly behavior to which our class usually subscribes, but artists are not like us – they have their own code of conduct and their own sense of morality which only occasionally intersects with that which exists at court."

"But as you can imagine, I did not want Bess to be labeled as I had been, a bastard child."

A bitter laugh escaped Elizabeth.

"I know all about such labels, Constance."

"So Roberto agreed that I could claim that he was her father, and that we had been married."

"And Michelangelo?"

"He was appalled that I would want to return to a place where our child might not be beloved, but in the end he accepted it and understood that she would be raised as I had been – outside the strictures of the court but with paternity rather than without."

Constance coughed a deep wheezing breath.

"My leg – you asked about my leg. During my last months in Rome, we were supervising the moving of a great slab of marble and one of the tethers broke –" Constance made two fists and a snapping motion with her hands.

"The marble fell on my leg."

Elizabeth listened in horror.

"I was lucky it did not fall on my person proper. My only hope to survive was the sacrifice of my leg. I did not hesitate to allow it for I desired rather to live crippled than to die whole. It took some months at death's door even so, but my will to live prevailed."

She coughed again.

Elizabeth placed a shawl around her sister's shoulders and looked around for her riding gloves.

"Enough for today," she exclaimed. "We will talk again."

Constance lay back, exhausted by her own memories. She listened to the slowly fading sound of hooves beating down the gravel drive and knew that the sound had marked her entire life at Coudenoure. She remembered her father Henry on his mighty destrier coming and going. Strange how patterns repeat, she thought as she dozed off, and how sounds can pull and push memories at will.

Chapter Seven

Autumn turned cold as winter drew on.

As always, old Agnes refused to wear more than her thread-bare shawl over her head when visiting the cemetery. It had been her habit for years and no one save those willing to risk the random thrashing of her cane suggested she might benefit from additional clothing on her daily outings. She adamantly refused to hear the warnings of her loved ones about the effects of winter cold on old bones and continued her daily treks to convene with those in her past wrapped only in her thin garments.

Constance's cough, which had shown signs of improvement in the summer months, grew worse as the damp and clammy air closed in around them and the light faded to a glow on the horizons of the late afternoons. With each waning day, she seemed to cough more and sink deeper into her own sad thoughts. No funny stories from Bess or cakes and scones from Prudence could free her from the clutches of her own disaffected and mordent reflections. They held her as a hawk might hold a helpless mouse in its talons as it flew high above the earth and traced its way homeward. Even on sunny days, when Bess placed her chair in the library window so she could enjoy the bright winter sun, her melancholy remained acute.

The change of seasons seemed to have triggered the reflections, though she knew not why. She realized that her life had always been lived in the shadowy reflections of others' thoughts, others' wishes and others' existence, and this knowledge suddenly seemed to drive a depression she had never felt before. Had she ever known happiness, she wondered, or was she simply one in a great chain of beings whose lives have no outward purpose? But even as her thoughts darkened with such conjectures, she knew it was not true, for she had Bess. She would gladly live it over again if it meant she once again had such a light in her life.

Visits from Elizabeth became more and more routine, but even as they did so they became less about Coudenoure and more about Elizabeth's troubles beyond the gates of the small estate. Were her sovereign's calls at the heart of her own discontent? Early on, Elizabeth had demanded deep and intimate detail of Constance and her life. She seemed to feed on the knowledge it provided her about their father and like a young child at its mother's breast she could not get enough. With each revelation about Henry and his personal likes and dislikes, she would lean back and close her eyes, fitting the detail into some overall mental image she obviously held of the man. On and on Constance talked until finally, Elizabeth was somewhat sated. But the endless talking had brought back endless memories for Constance, and with them came a sense of an unfinished and quite useless life. It might not be true, but she remained its prisoner nevertheless.

It was on one of Elizabeth's visits that Constance was simply too tired to talk or play cards. Secretly, she acknowledged that it was not fatigue but a weakness in her chest. To ward off questions and concerns, she suggested Elizabeth walk with Bess, and learn more of Coudenoure in that manner. Elizabeth was at once amenable to the suggestion, for despite her frequent trips, she knew little of her niece, save that apart from Constance she was her closest living relative.

"So you sculpt stone, I understand?" Elizabeth began chatting as they pulled the heavy wych elm door of the manor house behind them.

"Yes. And you?"

Elizabeth chuckled.

"No, I have not the time nor the talent. But I do enjoy painting, and languages."

"We must set you up here with paints and canvases," Bess insisted. "Then, when you come and mother is too tired to talk, you may keep her company and paint. 'Tis very soothing, you know. Your father and my grandmother spent many happy days thus."

Elizabeth stopped, horrified at the implication of what the young girl had just said. She turned and watched her warily. Bess met her gaze with a tranquil and wry smile.

"How did you know?" Elizabeth asked.

Bess shrugged.

"Are you familiar with the word "eavesdropper" Majesty?"

Elizabeth smiled.

"Ah, indeed. And yes, I am familiar with it. In fact, my father…"

"And my *grandfather*…" It was Bess' turn to smile.

Elizabeth waved her quiet.

"At Hampton Court, in the Great Hall, Henry had small figures carved to peep out through the high rafters."

"Eavesdroppers!" laughed Bess. Elizabeth nodded.

"He wanted to remind everyone that the throne knows all and hears all. And so I am to assume you...overheard...others speak of your heritage."

Bess giggled.

"Yes, and of course, there was Roberto."

"Roberto? I do not understand!" Elizabeth was becoming alarmed – how many others knew of the young girl's bloodline?

"Roberto, Majesty, in Rome."

"And how did *he* know? Saints alive, does the entire world know of Coudenoure and the lineage of its owners? It seems I was the last to learn of it."

"Roberto knew my grandmother. His father was a sea captain who was married to Agnes."

"Agnes was married?"

"Why not?"

Elizabeth considered for a moment.

"Well, she visits the graves of Thomas and Elizabeth, not of her husband," she said.

"Yes," agreed Bess, "I have noticed that as well, but I think 'tis because her ties to Thomas and Elizabeth were life long, whereas her marriage to master Ransdell was brief in comparison."

Elizabeth nodded and Bess continued.

"Roberto was Ransdell's son and when my grandmother and her father left Rome, Roberto stayed behind to apprentice with Michelangelo. The talk amongst the family was frequently of Elizabeth and her love for Prince Henry."

"I grew up in Roberto's household, and naturally, he came to tell me those tales. And, I must say, Roberto believed that a secret was something you told one person at a time, not a thing one kept to oneself."

"But your mother believes you do not know."

Bess laughed.

"Funny, is it not? She has always told me that when she was young, king Henry and my grandmother never told her of her father. She found it out from others and always resented their not telling her themselves. And yet she repeats the same offense with her own child! It seems, Majesty, that generations repeat patterns, do they not?"

They walked in silence past the brown and lifeless stalks of winter's kill.

"And you, Bess? What are your plans?"

Bess immediately blushed.

Elizabeth stared her down as they walked.

"I just mentioned that generations repeat."

"Yes, well, what of it?" The reply was short and pointed.

"It seems I may be pre-contracted to Quinn Janyns from the neighboring estate." She pointed vaguely westward.

"It *seems*? I do not understand. Did you accidentally take part in a marriage ceremony? Did you drink too much mead and lose your senses? Did you... "

Elizabeth was warming to the subject and continued on in the same vein.

"Did you fall from a tree and temporarily lose your mind? And what on earth makes you think that you are repeating the patterns of a previous generation?"

"My grandmother was pre-contracted to your father and no one knew."

"Good and kind Lord. You know, niece, I am constantly amazed at what I find when I come through the gates of Coudenoure."

She paused as the implication of Bess' statement became clear.

"Let me understand. Your mother knows not of your engagement?"

Bess nodded warily.

"And your mother believes you to be ignorant of your relationship to me?"

Bess gave a nervous giggle.

"Tell me, how many other secrets do you people keep from one another?"

"Not many."

"'Tis not the answer I was hoping for."

"Well, Majesty, all of us have skeletons, do we not? Some haunt us, some help us, but we all live with the past."

"'Tis the first sensible thing out of your mouth on this walk, child," Elizabeth replied. "Now tell me of your young man. He seemed a clod when I met him."

Bess ignored the observation and sighed with bliss.

"Where to begin? He is as warm as the sun on a summer day. And bright? Oh Aunt, he is the most intelligent man I have ever known. Kind and good, honest and true…"

Elizabeth waved her hand laughing. She loved the way Bess threw herself into whatever life presented, heart and soul. Where she was cautious and closed, Bess was carefree and open. Had the girl received such a wonderful gift from Henry? He, too, was known for meeting life head on. Over her time at Coudenoure, Constance had repeatedly expressed concerns for Bess – such a naïve trust in the fates and assurance in oneself was not common among women of any age, much less in such a young girl. Had she herself ever been like that, Elizabeth wondered? Was it events which had stifled her spontaneity or was it her own nature? She reined in her thoughts and returned to the conversation.

"Kind and good, honest and true…Stop, please. Next you will tell me his second name is god."

"No, but do you not agree that he is very handsome in a dark and smoldering manner?"

"He forgot to take his own hat off when he bowed." she replied somewhat dryly. "Handsomeness can only take a person so far."

"Quinn is awkward amongst women. That is all."

"Indeed."

Bess ignored her.

"He is an architect and so he understands me as a fellow artist. When we are of age, we will live happily and create beautiful art, beautiful buildings and a beautiful family."

"Well, no one ever sees the dark clouds on their own horizons, do they?"

She patted her niece's hand. Constance was right: love for such a child so full of joie de vivre and concern for the same were impossible to separate.

"And 'tis a good thing we do not," she continued, "...for we could never make our way through it all if we knew our troubles in advance."

As she spoke, Elizabeth's thoughts again turned from Bess to herself, and she seemed to withdraw as she spoke. Bess noted the sudden sadness in her voice and squeezed her hand warmly.

"Do not fear, you will be fine now that you are queen. The past is behind you."

"Perhaps, child, perhaps."

Still the sadness.

"Aunt, you must stop, for if one more person on this estate begins to talk to the dead or mope in the corners I shall lose my religion."

A smile played around Elizabeth's lips.

"And I tell you further, Aunt, that you will be happier indeed when we set you up with paints and brushes. Just wait!"

"Ah, so that is all it takes to shake this suspicion towards the world that I have, is it? Then let us return to the house and share the knowledge with your mother so that perhaps she might shake her weariness and be happy once again."

They walked arm in arm back to the manor, Bess chatting happily about her plans with Quinn. As they came within sight of the front door, it flew open and Prudence burst forth and ran screaming towards them, her face contorted by fear and grief.

"Hurry! Oh God, hurry! Constance is dead!"

Bess gave out a shriek, abandoned the path, and made a swift dash across the intervening field, ignoring the seeds and mud which stuck to her dress and shoes. Elizabeth's guards, hearing the alarm, mounted their steeds and rode furiously towards the manor house. Elizabeth ran to keep up with Bess.

In the library, as if from a great distance, Constance heard her child screaming for her mother. She closed her eyes and her own mother appeared to her as in a dream. It was warm and light there, where she was. Her leg tingled and as she looked down she was made whole once again. Constance could feel the warmth beginning to envelope her and she gave herself over to it. Such love, such tenderness, and yes! Just behind her mother was Henry, a gentle smile on his face. She rose from the chair and ran towards them and into the light, and as she did her sadness fell away as surely as the dark of night is banished by the breaking dawn.

Agnes died the following day. They found her as always sitting on her bench in the cold sun of winter. Her cane rested on Thomas' gravestone and her head was bowed. She, too, had gone home.

Chapter Eight

Bess had known loss but never death. She had left Rome behind for the great adventure of a future in her mother's homeland. Gone were her friends, her studios and family. So too the warm climate, the oleo of cultures, and exotic beings from faraway lands with strange tongues and manners. As she settled into Coudenoure, that sense of sacrifice and occasional homesickness had made her feel more mature, somehow, as though she too knew what it meant to suffer loss.

But her mother's death. And Agnes' following on so quickly. No. It was not loss. It was fire raining down from heaven. Bess' self-assurance deserted her and she was left a falling leaf in a vast and windy sky.

News of Constance's death traveled fast and by sunset Quinn was at Coudenoure. The queen had left with her guards and he found Prudence sobbing in the library. There was no sign of Bess. As he swept into the room, she only glanced up.

"She is not here, young Janyns." Prudence always referred to him by his last name. "She has gone out and I know not where. Try to find her for night is falling."

Prudence returned to her tears leaving Quinn wondering what to do. He guessed Bess would retreat to her studio and as he hurried out the back kitchen door of the manor house, he heard the distant sound of hammer hitting stone. She was there. Early on in her tenure at Coudenoure Bess had recognized the small stable at the very rear of the yard as a place in which she could work. Situated at the end of the small avenue of cottages set aside for the estates' crofters and servants, it caught light from all directions. She had torn out the exterior walls and replaced them with glass. Gone were the individual stables and the great feeding troughs, leaving the building with nothing but a high ceiling and a wide-open floor. An ethereal sense of space and light permeated the small building and both Bess and Constance had immediately fallen in love with its simple utilitarian beauty. They had hung art tools on the walls and had scattered old tables with paints and canvases all about its capacious interior. It was a mirror version of the studios they knew in Rome and provided a strong sense of continuity for them as they transitioned back to England and Coudenoure.

Roberto had made good on his promise to send marble and in the center of the room stood the most recent arrival – a huge block of stone wider than it was tall. A shaft of light shown upon its face, revealing the beginnings of a street scene carved in exquisite detail in bas-relief. The cold immutable power of the white stone stood in sharp contrast to the emotional scene being revealed as its layers were chipped and smoothed away: a beggar with his hand outstretched sat upon a low curb; down a little ways was a vendor with a cart piled high with tomatoes and eggplants; and there, in front of a row of buildings were two young boys playing hoops. Had anyone asked, Bess would have told them it was the street of Michelangelo's studio and next to it, Roberto's house – her home. The unfinished stone behind the carving rose above it like a protective cloud.

As he slid the door open, Bess' pounding became louder. She was working not on the street scene but on a smaller piece of marble sitting in a far corner. There seemed to be no plan in her approach to the stone as her hammer laid vicious blows upon its surface. Huge chips flew from the resulting planes and cracks. She looked up briefly as he entered before continuing. He went to her, putting his hand gently on her shoulder. She threw her tools down and turned, sobbing, into his arms.

On the surface, they were an odd pair, Bess in her plain linen dresses and Quinn in his usually mismatched vests, trousers and stockings. She was shorter than he and sturdier as well. But it was not only their physicality and mode of dress which marked their personalities as distinct; their emotional makeup was noticeably different too. Whereas Bess was given to defiance in the face of social mores, Quinn tended to conform if for no other reason than for ease of passage; Bess wore her emotions and opinions on her sleeve; Quinn was not uncertain so much as disconnected, something most put down as his being circumspect.

When he had stumbled upon her one day, painting alone along the great ridge which separated her estate from that of Greenwich, she had seemed like an angel sent from heaven to inform his life and work, one sent to save him from his own imploding chaos. He had never known a woman who expressed herself in anything save needlework and Bess' fearless approach to life and art had left him gasping for breath; he was certain her organizational skills were God's own rules. In turn, his rambling and chaotic approach to life and architecture was one she understood from her days spent among other artists in Rome.

As she sobbed in his arms, Quinn had been uncertain how to comfort his love and had given her what he knew he had so often wished for in the face of tragedy – a pair of strong, loving arms. The night was long and he spent it with her and Prudence in the library, discussing arrangements and other practical matters. It seemed to be the best way to occupy her mind. The following morning, Elizabeth had returned.

"Who are you?" She had swept into the hall of Coudenoure and past him.

"I am Quinn Janyns. We have met several times. Colleen, why are you here?"

Elizabeth ignored the question but noted that Bess had not given her identity away.

She strode into the library and gathered Bess into her arms. The previous day had been a raging firestorm for Bess and Prudence. For Elizabeth, however, the trauma extended far beyond the immediate events.

Prudence's screaming and Constance's sudden death had brought back memories of her own mother's death, memories she did not even know were there. She had long ago buried the agony of that day but now bits and snippets kept rising to the surface of her consciousness unbidden, but not necessarily unwelcome. Her night had been spent pacing in front of the hearth in her bedroom, drinking the tea Constance had introduced to her and remembering.

They were in bright sunshine in a garden, she and her mother. Anne feigned fear as she, Elizabeth, chased her about. Elizabeth closed her eyes, remembering their laughter, feeling the memory of that happy day. Her mother's gown – was it green? Yes, or perhaps it was blue, the color of the sky, and her own little dress had been green.

The game ended with her mother hugging her close
– Elizabeth could feel Anne's warm breath on her
cheeks when she closed her eyes in front of the fire
that evening. But with the unexpected flood of
happy memories came the haunted whispers, those
memories with the power to terrify her even now.

She knew her mother was executed in May.
What a word, she mused – executed. So clean and
antiseptic and dispassionate; so much more
acceptable and objective than the word which truly
applied: murdered. She had been at Hatfield, a
child of but three when the news arrived. Nanny
was with her. A letter had been delivered, and with
it came screaming and crying and terror. Endless
terror. Nanny held her close and whispered kind
words in her ear, but others did not. She could not
remember who told her the news or why, but she
was told all the same.

She rose from her chair and threw her tea in the
fire. Why could they not have kept it from her, if
only for a little while? She had been so tiny, such a
small child! So fragile. In the small table near the
window she kept a lockbox and she opened it now.
A small, secret panel in the back gave way to her
prying fingers revealing a ring which lay within.
Elizabeth held it gently and returned to her seat in
front of the fire where she gazed intently at its ruby
set in a largish pearl face. But the ring held a secret,
one she had always loved. She slid her nail deftly
between its surface and back and it sprang open
revealing two miniature portraits: one of her

94

father…and one of Anne. She must have gazed upon the faces a thousand times since the ring had been given to her by Anne as a child. They seemed so happy, her mother so vibrant – Holbein had performed a miracle by capturing not just their likenesses but their essence.

She held it to her lips, remembering. After some time, she rose – I am no longer a scared child, she thought, nor an imperiled princess. She placed the ring on her finger and held it out to the light of the fire. She might continue her practice of never speaking of her mother, but she would be forever close now, giving others the same comfort Elizabeth herself had felt that day as she and her mother had romped in the dazzling sunshine.

The next morning she had returned to Coudenoure, determined to spare Bess the traumas of her own past. A surge of maternal feelings for her niece drove her decision.

Her sudden appearance caught Quinn by surprise.

"Madam," Quinn's puzzlement was obvious in his voice, "…Madam, why are you here?"

"Saints in heaven, man, I am Elizabeth, your sovereign."

Quinn suddenly remembered a conversation he had had with Agnes and shook his head vigorously.

"No, I remember now. Madame, you are confused. Elizabeth was Bess' grandmother. Kind lady, you must sit and rest while I send for your family. I am sure they will come for you."

Elizabeth looked at Bess. Bess looked at Elizabeth. The sorrow, the lack of sleep, the odd situation, Quinn doing his kind best to aid the person he believed to be a touched stranger in their midst, all of it came to a point and the two of them began to laugh hysterically through their tears. Quinn rubbed his forehead, for the situation confirmed him in his beliefs about women and their utterly enigmatic ways.

Through her tears and laughter, Bess explained that Elizabeth was indeed Elizabeth R. Quinn, now thoroughly confused, bowed deeply. Once again, he forgot his cap. Bess and Elizabeth broke out in fresh peals of laughter.

"Fetch some tea, young Janyns. I must talk to Bess and Prudence."

She dismissed him curtly and she, Prudence and Bess sat before the fire together, remembering Constance and Agnes. The conversation was short, however, for Elizabeth had already determined what would happen next.

"You will come with me to court, child," she demanded.

"No, Aunt, Coudenoure is my home – I cannot allow anything to happen to it."

Prudence patted her hand.

"I am here, Bess, I will see to the place."

"But my work, my library…"

"Nothing will be touched, but a young maid cannot live alone."

"And I know nothing of the ways of court, absolutely nothing! And further, I do not care to learn the ways of the place!"

Elizabeth knew Bess spoke the truth. While she was mannered and aristocratic, her particular ways were not those of the court, and she would stand out not so much as a ruby but as a quaint artefact from another place and time. Prudence provided the answer.

"Bess, hear me – do you not speak as many languages as God? Do you not paint like a master? You may go to court and continue your work there until you are old enough to return to Coudenoure. You may be a tutor to the young women in her Majesty's retinue!"

"Prudence you are clever," Elizabeth smiled at the old woman. "Indeed, I see why my father felt it as well."

"*And* he loved my spice cakes too." Prudence shook her head proudly with a satisfied air.

Quinn returned, clearly unhappy delivering tea. Before the new plan could be spoken of he drew himself up and declared himself with authority.

"We shall have to sell Coudenoure, Bess, for what good will it be when we are married? Of course, this library will fetch…"

A wave of feminine will smacked him as three women cut him off as one.

"I live here Master Quinn," protested Prudence, "and will always do so!"

"No – 'tis my home!", said Bess with distinct resolution.

"Silence, idiot! Nothing will be touched at this estate, for it was a favorite of my father's and is now a favorite of mine. Do you understand?" The queen's words left no room for further discussion.

Quinn felt his face flush and his knees weaken. What he learned of women that day would stay with him. Bess pulled a chair and invited him to sit. He looked at Elizabeth and began bowing and mumbling incoherently. Elizabeth was not accustomed to holding her tongue.

"For the love of God, man, just sit. And remain silent."

He did not need to be told again.

*****

The day after Constance and Agnes were laid to rest in the ancient cemetery, Bess moved to court with Elizabeth. She was introduced as an artist from Rome whose role it would be to teach the young ladies of the court Italian and painting so that they could entertain Elizabeth with learned talk.

The evening prior to her departure, she and Quinn had discussed it at length in her studio.

"My hat! She thinks I am a clod!" Quinn spoke through wounded vanity.

"My love, she is the queen…"

"Yes, and you never told me that, Bess. I thought we had no secrets!"

"'Twas a secret but not," Bess hedged. "No harm was done."

Quinn scratched his head and looked at her keenly.

"What is this interest she has in you and Coudenoure? I do not understand."

Bess gave the answer she had rehearsed many times in her mind.

"Coudenoure was King Henry's favorite estate…"

Quinn cut her off.

"Yes, but her interest extends to you, personally. Why? Is there a connection there I know not of?"

Bess winced internally and spoke even as she prayed for forgiveness for the lie.

"What connection could there be? I have only just returned from Rome…"

"Yes, but your mother grew up here. Is there a reason the queen shows you such favor, a reason beyond Coudenoure being an estate she enjoys from time to time?"

Bess looked him in eye.

"No, Quinn, there is no reason."

She left for the court the following morning.

Chapter Nine

Fall 1561

Like her father before her Elizabeth loved spectacle and understood its use as a tool of power and authority. Intrigues, parties, balls, art – all of it swirled about Elizabeth as she moved from palace to palace. Her court consisted of layer upon layer of courtiers, ladies-in-waiting, servants, administrators, ambassadors and clergy. In turn, each of those came and went with their own small stables of staff and friends and family. The gates of her palaces swarmed with vendors, stockmen, the poor and every ilk of the simply curious hoping for a glimpse of their young queen. For every person around Elizabeth there was a separate story, an individual thread woven through the fabric of the court. The tapestry was rich and layered and gave an optimistic view of England's future. After all, Mary was gone.

Queen Mary's rule had mirrored the end of Henry's with its deathly fears and arbitrary dictates.

One had never known from one minute to the next who would survive. She had wielded her power as a blunt instrument of death; commoners and noblemen alike had shuttered their lives against her prying eyes and those of her watchful minions. Her marriage and false pregnancy had only exacerbated her suspicious mind. The Spanish influence at her court ran deep and Englishmen of all stations quaked when she turned her wrath upon them, knowing that even a sure and innocent step could spell death and ruin.

But with Elizabeth now on the throne, the very air they breathed seemed imbued with youth and openness. The young queen was every inch King Henry's daughter and as she paraded daily through the streets of London and its environs the people turned out in droves to inspect her and admire her. The old were astonished at the physical similarity between the two while the young commented upon her fine clothes and regal bearing. She stopped frequently to talk to her subjects and proved herself able to relate to commoners in meaningful ways – with each exchange, a love of her kingdom and its people bled through her entire speech and manner and seeped into the fabric of all England.

Elizabeth did not just employ pomp and spectacle as a necessary evil – she truly loved it. Her morning ritual of spending time in her private rooms and picking over which dress to wear and with whom to hold state became the part of her day which allowed her to order the remainder. Cecil never understood this and their clashes over the loss of so much time were nitpicky but constant. She ignored them.

As she had relied upon Constance as an outlet for her private thoughts, so now she relied upon Bess. Under the guise of consulting about the weekly progress of Bess' pupils, they would walk and talk. Elizabeth was careful to stage these meeting in the open grounds about her palaces, for even hedges and trees seemed to hide those who would know her innermost thoughts and spread them abroad. When she had discovered Bess' ability to keep a secret – after all, she had never even told her beloved Quinn of their shared heritage – she knew instinctively she could trust her niece.

"So how is Dudley?" Bess frequently referred to the courtier by his last name.

"Sir Robert is fine as is the mill which grinds the gossip about him."

Bess laughed.

"Will you ever marry the man?"

Elizabeth smiled and passed the end of her walking stick over the tops of nearby flowers.

"I cannot, Bess, for his wife's death has changed everything. The queen can hardly marry a man suspected of murdering his wife."

"The coroner's report found him innocent of wrong doing."

"Yes, well, I am sure there are those who felt Brutus had done no wrong."

"And yet he still…" Bess searched for the right word, "…hovers."

"Indeed", came the thoughtful reply. "I rather like Sir Robert's *hovering*, and now that the door to marriage has been locked and sealed, I see no harm in it. Let the court prattle on – there will be no wedding and therefore I shall continue to enjoy his company."

They walked on in amiable silence.

"And your young man? Quinn? Is he still the nit he once was?"

"He is still awkward around women – I do not believe that trait will ever leave him."

"What thinks he of your time at court?"

"He thinks it unnecessary. Since he is older than I, he feels he would be my good shepherd should I marry young."

Elizabeth snorted and pulled her wrap about her.

"Indeed. Why do men always feel we need shepherding? And that they are just the ones to do the shepherding?"

Bess giggled.

"I do not know, for truth be told Quinn is in desperate need of...not so much shepherding as organizing."

"I suspect you are the stronger of the two, are you not?"

"Yes, but do not think that I do not need him too, Aunt."

"In what way do you need him? It seems not that way to me at all."

Bess thought for a moment.

"He understands me, but that does not create my need. It comes from his ability to anticipate with intuition what I am thinking and feeling. He is an artist who attempts to understand nature, not just to paint it or to build upon it or to portray it somehow. He..."

"You know, Bess, each time I ask you about Quinn your words never end. Perhaps it is just best to say, 'I know not why I love him but I do, um?'"

She held up her hand as Bess tried to start again, and laughed wryly.

"Men."

After a time, Bess glanced up at the sky, gauging the time by the sun.

"I must go," she begged, "For I am to give your ladies a lesson in Italian this afternoon."

"Ah, yes – and tell me, how do they progress?"

"Majesty, I hesitate to answer that question."

Silence.

Bess knew that Elizabeth could wait her out – she had never been able to best her on remaining silent until an answer was forthcoming.

"You see, Majesty, some of them are clever. Very clever indeed. And some of them are almost clever which is close enough in most cases."

"And the rest?"

"Donkey brains."

Elizabeth roared with laughter.

"You cannot say that, Bess. You have been brought here to tutor these young women…"

"I thought I was brought here to alleviate your concern over my being alone at Coudenoure with nothing but my grief."

"It was not you being alone with your grief that worried me – you are young and will survive. No indeed. It was you being alone with that young man of yours. That is why you are here. And of course to teach languages to my ladies and to instruct them in the fine arts."

"I promise you, Majesty, for some of them that instruction must begin with which end of the brush it is one paints with. And by the by, who is it that puts those ridiculous partridge feathers on her bodices..."

They had completed the rectangle of Hampton Court's outer yard and Bess knew she must hurry. She bowed and traipsed lightly across the lawn. Elizabeth watched, amused by her niece and her utter refusal to fit into the court. Bess had not changed her way of dressing when she left Coudenoure. The simple plain frocks and kerchiefs for her hair allowed her to roam the halls and backways of Elizabeth's palaces almost unnoticed. Her anonymity reminded her of her days in Rome when she had wandered the streets in boy's clothing soaking up all the city had to offer. She had no inclination to make friends with those around her for she considered her life at Coudenoure far superior. She served her aunt and no one and nothing else and her reserve in all matters of the court eventually assured her invisibility even amongst the ladies who were her pupils. Above stairs, she walked in the shadows of the great halls, taking her meals alone or with Quinn when he was able to visit. Unseen. She had made friends with the kitchen staff for she missed Prudence's cooking and the camaraderie which existed below stairs. Over time, she came and went seamlessly between the two worlds.

Bess was now late for the afternoon lesson in Italian and had prepared nothing for the class. She felt frantically for her book in the small pocket of her apron and drew up behind a tall, marble support pillar to collect her thoughts before entering the room where she would instruct. As she flipped through the pages of the Italian grammar she intended to use, a whispered male voice, barely audible, caught her attention.

"You have it?"

"*Oui*, but she has not seen nor approved the plan."

"Then ride north."

The conversation was in French and clearly intended to be private. Bess heard the clicking of heels receding and waited until they were gone before stepping out. She saw no one.

She wondered momentarily about the conversation but she still had no lesson plan for her pupils that afternoon. She tucked the knowledge away intending to revisit it and walked on towards her class.

Chapter Ten

October 1562

"Majesty."

No response.

"Majesty, we need an answer, madam."

Lord Cecil's tone was weary and carried a note of frustration. He sat at a table to her right, plume in hand ready to record her answer and begin the drafting of a response. Elizabeth sat upon her morning throne, the large, heavily carved and bejeweled chair she had inherited from her grandfather and father before her. She presided over morning court – the time she chose to deal with the more mundane issues of her reign – under an elaborate canopy of Flemish tapestries. A raised dais elevated the chair and Cecil's table, thus allowing the queen to see and be seen.

All morning, Elizabeth had ducked and dodged giving answers to any of the myriad problems laid out before her on that particular day. She had drunk too much the night before with Robert Dudley, and as a result her head ached dreadfully, particularly when she turned it. She felt scratchy, as though she were somehow off kilter with the world by several degrees and the friction thus created made even the slightest irritation monumentally annoying. Moreover, she decided ,her dress was too tight.

She wore a flounced blue silk with white panels of damask. The tailored bodice, also blue, rose from a pronounced v-shape at her waist and extended to a large, white ruff of a collar which covered her throat. The entire business made it difficult to breath. A necklace of pearls and large rubies hung in multiple strands around her neck and draped the front of her gown, but rather than making her feel regal and queenly, they clicked together each time she drew a tortured breath and the dull aching in her head had now developed a rhythmic pulse which beat merrily along to each click of the jewels. As an additional misery, her feet rested only minimally on the floor -the throne had been made for her father and his father, men who were obviously much larger than she. To have it cut down to size would make her appear less than they. As a result, she could not lean back but had to sit forward in order not to look like a child sitting in an adult's chair with legs and feet dangling. She longed to close her eyes if only for a moment, but she also knew that such a thing would lead to napping, something not done during morning business, not even by the queen.

"Majesty." It was Cecil again. She floated briefly back into the moment, answered his question, then promptly turned back to her own thoughts.

Mary, her cousin, had arrived in Scotland the previous year. Mary's grandmother was Elizabeth's own aunt, Margaret, Henry's elder sister. The woman had spent her life primarily at the French court, but when her husband had died – killed in a jousting tournament – she had immediately begun to meddle in Scottish affairs. Elizabeth had been forced to make peace with her through the Treaty of Edinburgh but to Elizabeth's horror, Mary refused to sign the treaty, signaling her belief that not only the Scottish throne but Elizabeth's English one as well were *both* rightfully hers. Elizabeth was apoplectic, but beneath her public fury lay the old nagging fears of her childhood.

She would be queen or she would be dead: her heritage did not allow alternatives to that reality of stark alternatives. There could be no retiring from public life for her. She was Henry's daughter and even if she abdicated her throne, moved to Cathay and joined a convent there they would seek her out, use her to play games for their own ends, use her until her usefulness had passed. Then they would kill her as they had killed her mother. This was the dark side of power. She secretly laughed at her courtiers as they jockeyed and danced for her favors and her throne. They did not know what they were about, for only the one who ruled could ever understand the perils and nightmares which accompanied power: behind every conversation, every sunrise and every event she clearly saw the horsemen of death, their white steeds chomping furiously at their bits, eager to get on with it. Only to the strong goeth the crown? She smiled inwardly. No. Only to the one with absolutely no other choice save death. She knew her cousin Mary felt the steeds' hot breath as well, and guessed that her cousin's behavior was calculated based upon the same sure and certain foreboding as her own.

She sighed and rose. Perhaps it was not the wine causing her fatigue and ill-feeling. Perhaps it was her worry over Mary in her northern kingdom. Or, perhaps it was the sudden progress from Whitehall two days earlier. Smallpox had begun to settle in upon London and Cecil had insisted that she decamp to Hampton Court for safety. Perhaps the suddenness of that move had affected her condition somehow? It made no sense, but then neither did her increasing sense of fevered short-temperedness.

Her headache had become a thundering roiling noise in her brain and she could no longer deal with the court. Cecil had been speaking and she waved him silent as she abruptly rose and passed out of the hall. Men and women alike bowed deeply and behind her rose first a hushed whisper then a cacophony of voices. Whom had she heard that day? Which cases had been settled, to whom had she granted favors or shown signs of dislike?

Enough. She would retire to her rooms, change out of the restrictive clothing she currently wore, and go for a walk to clear her head. Perhaps Bess was available to entertain her with gossip and straight-forward and thus amusing repartee. But even the thought of her young niece's ability to find humor in the day-to-day goings on of the court did nothing to alleviate the fatigue. She paused to catch her breath at the large window on the stairwell which looked out upon the great lawn. An ancient oak sheltered the eastern portion of the yard and beneath it she saw Quinn and Bess talking and eating from a basket which sat nearby. She watched them for some time: Quinn gesticulating wildly while Bess nodded. What would she do, she wondered, when the time came to release her niece and send her home to Coudenoure? Since her arrival at court, Bess had become Elizabeth's fondest and most trusted confidante. How could she give that up? To whom would she turn for such trust, such family? There was no one else, and so she had decided to keep Bess at her side. She watched another moment before continuing on up the stairs – she would think about it tomorrow, perhaps. The idea of a walk no longer seemed appealing. A nap was called for. Yes, that would refresh her.

*****

Quinn and Bess sat happily together in the shade of their favorite oak. It provided a vantage point for observing the comings and goings on the palace's main drive, which in turn provided the two young lovers with entertainment. Bess had used the sudden progress to Hampton Court as an opportunity to visit Coudenoure briefly and leave a message for Quinn. He had arrived that morning.

Bess missed Quinn and Coudenoure terribly. Life at court had initially been enthralling, amusing, – an endless curiosity for her. And the progresses! Elizabeth used them to show herself to her subjects and inevitably rode a great steed and dressed in her finest clothes as she moved from one grand palace to the next. She insisted that her courtiers and ladies ride behind her in their finest, and that even every animal in the procession be marked by her Tudor arms, indicating to one and all her great wealth and power. For everyone else, however, the monumental labor involved in moving so much and so many was tiring and tedious. Everyone and everything had to be taken along and the ox-driven carts which trundled behind the initial, glittering parade were always laden to the hilt. For those who served, there simply was no settled place to call home, and yet no one seemed to mind.

Bess marveled at this time and again, for her own nature called for home and family and like a swallow beating ever northwards her heart had begun to turn towards the peace of Coudenoure. Elizabeth needed her desperately though, and Bess was keenly aware of the attachment. They were for each other the closest thing to family either of them had. Bess sighed.

"What is it, my love?" Quinn paused in his explanation of the geometry of conical structures and turned his loving face to her. Bess brushed the crumbs from her lap as she responded.

"Elizabeth. She needs me, and I must say, I need her – she has become a mother for me in so many ways. But when will the day come that I am released to return home?"

Quinn threw a piece of bread and they watched in silence as a fat squirrel promptly carried it away.

"The day will come, dear. Do not worry. She has many things on her mind and you have told me often that you are her sounding board."

Bess nodded.

"'Tis true. There is Dudley, always Dudley, and of course that woman Mary."

"Mary?" Quinn did not follow court intrigue or politics of any kind. Unless the word architecture appeared in a sentence, he skipped along in his own world oblivious to the greater environment.

Bess laughed and patted his hand. Her physical touch was heaven, and he froze his hand lest he cause her to move hers. He closed his eyes, enjoying the moment.

"Mary, Quinn."

"What?"

Bess pulled her hand in feigned exasperation.

"The French woman who is a pretender to Elizabeth's throne. Really, do you listen to what I say?"

"Sometimes." They both laughed at the frank admission.

"Well," Bess suggested after a moment, "You could come to court, you know – that way I would not feel so bereft of home and hearth."

Quinn laughed.

"And what, pray tell, would I come as? The queen's nit?"

"She no longer calls you that," Bess assured him.

"Not to my face," Quinn replied. "But no matter. Bess, there is no place for me at court."

"You could be a courtier – you are a knight after all."

"Ah, a courtier, right until the moment I split my pants bowing or dropped a stuffed pheasant into William Cecil's lap at table."

"He does not eat with the queen."

Quinn ignored the correction.

"Or perhaps I could be a char boy? Hmm? Burn the place down?"

Bess caught his playful mood and giggled.

"Or a chef! I hear that on the continent royal courts routinely employ men as their premier cooks!"

Quinn rolled on his side with laughter.

"Madame Queen," he pitched his voice.

"Majesty," Bess again corrected him.

"Madam-We-All-Do-Your-Bidding," he started again, "I have prepared a special treat for you this evening. It begins with grouse feathers arranged smartly in a sauce of oak leaves and spring saplings!"

"Never mind," Bess gave up.

"Talk to her about coming home," Quinn suggested and stood. "Now, I have to go for there is a minor baroness on the south coast…"

"*I* am a minor baroness! How many of us are there?"

"…who wishes to have a glass house for her peacocks. She tells me they do not like the sea breezes but need the sun."

He made a show of taking off his hat and bowing to her before disappearing towards the stables.

She picked up her basket and walked on without him, deep in thought as to possible solutions for her love life. It took a moment for her to realize that two men walked behind her at a more rapid pace and were slowly overtaking her.

"Careful, she is the tutor for the queen's maids." The words were French and Bess attuned herself to them as the men approached.

"Do not worry, she speaks Italian badly and no other language save English."

She bristled at the insult but remained quiet, being careful to give no outward appearance of comprehension.

"We must act quickly, for the queen is impatient."

"Not too quickly, for we must have a papal blessing lest we risk our souls."

"But the Yuletide comes quickly, and we must be ready."

The men tipped their caps as they passed her and walked on, their voices fading on the breeze. Bess watched them curiously. Their manner of dress marked them as foreign – huge plumes in their velvet caps and pantaloons and vests embroidered in gold in a heavy, continental style. She did not recognize them and initially thought perhaps they served one of the various ambassadors which advocated for their own masters at Elizabeth's court. But only two days earlier, just as they were planning to quit Whitehall for healthier quarters, there had been a masked ball. Bess was fairly certain that all of the ambassadorial contingents had been present, and she did not recall seeing the two men who had just passed by her.

Had their tone been conspiratorial or were they simply passing tidbits of court gossip confidentially? As they turned sharply and disappeared from sight she remembered the quiet conversation she had overheard earlier. The men were not familiar to her but then, she reasoned, she surely did not know everyone at court. Yet the conversation was disturbing in a way that Bess found hard to pin down. Elizabeth was head of the Church of England – what need had she of a papal blessing for any undertaking? She pondered the matter as she returned the basket to the kitchen and on impulse went in search of the queen. With quick steps, she crossed the inner courtyard leading onto Elizabeth's private quarters hoping to find her there. Luck ran with her, for Elizabeth was in her room, resting by an open window. She smiled when she saw Bess and dismissed her maids, beckoning Bess to come close.

"You have seen your young Quinn, I see."

"How did you know that?" Elizabeth was uncannily good at knowing when Bess had had a rendezvous with Quinn and she was puzzled by her aunt's ability. It had become a game between them with Bess slowly working her way through whatever clues she thought Elizabeth might be picking up on. "I am not blushing, nor am I particularly happy with the meeting, so it can be nothing in my demeanor which tells you that."

"Settle down child," Elizabeth chuckled. "I saw you out the window."

"Oh."

A deep, hacking cough rose from Elizabeth's chest and Bess immediately voiced concern.

"Have you a cold? I will send for Huicke at once." She rose to summon the doctor but Elizabeth bade her sit again.

"'Tis a small cold, nothing more."

"Still…" Her words trailed off as she felt Elizabeth's forehead. Concern began to write itself across her countenance.

"Bess, 'tis nothing," Elizabeth insisted, "Robert Huicke has been my physician since Hatfield and he trusts my judgment in these matters. He will tell you the same. And since when are you my nanny?"

"Since you are the only relative I have in this world, since that is since when." Bess answered curtly.

"Grammar grammar grammar. Your last sentence was rubbish."

Bess ignored her and pulled a satin coverlet off the bed, placing it gently over Elizabeth's legs.

"I will send for some hot chicken broth and the doctor will be here shortly."

Elizabeth wagged her finger at her niece but did nothing to stop her. It was comforting to know that someone wanted nothing more than her well-being. Indeed.

*****

Elizabeth was seldom alone, and as Bess hurried from the room, she decided against ringing for her maids. Solitude was a luxury now, one she could not purchase nor demand nor barter for. It had to find its way to her through the crowds who wanted bits and pieces of her, always wanting more and always crying her name. The autumn breeze brought the sad, sweet song of a whippoorwill through the open window, and she closed her eyes and listened to its mournful melody. It matched her mood. So much to do today, she thought, and so little energy.

Dudley had stormed off to Kenilworth Castle, his northernmost estate, that morning, ridiculously angry at what he knew to be the only path open to her. She could no more marry him than she could swim to the moon and yet he finagled, schemed, and plotted constantly towards that goal. Had he become more insistent, she wondered, or was she just tiring of the constant thrust and parry of his conversation. He was the only person in the entire kingdom who counted his wife's mysterious death as naught against his desire for the throne. Long ago, she would have believed he wanted her and her alone and that the throne was only a secondary consideration. Now...she smiled to herself as she waited for Bess to return with the doctor. She was still not immune to his charms, but the years had taught her well: power was never a secondary consideration and those who considered it thus did so at their own peril. Such a sad situation, she thought, for she would have been happy with him on the throne by her side – he had much good judgment and she had been confident she could manage him. But all that was gone now.

She watched the singing bird as it continued to trill its melody just beyond her window. So much to do today. And yet she felt such fatigue.

A knock on the door interrupted her reverie. The doctor had arrived.

Bess waited in the hallway with Elizabeth's maids, listening to their chatter and speculation about the queen.

"She is pale of late – I am certain."

"Perhaps it is more than a malady..."

"Perhaps she is..."

On and on they went with their idle chatter until Bess was ready to scream. But she had learned to hold her tongue and be invisible – much gossip came her way as a result.

An hour later, the doctor appeared in Elizabeth's door and singled Bess out to enter the room.

"Child, she wishes to speak to you in private. Afterwards, you must come see me immediately. In the interim, I must gather some things."

The court ladies fanned themselves furiously, feigning not to listen or care. Both Bess and the doctor knew far better.

He walked away but turned back.

"And Bess," he whispered to her alone, "...take care."

He left.

*****

Bess entered the room tentatively. Elizabeth had moved from her favorite chair in front of the window to the bed. The room was stiflingly hot and Bess noticed Huicke had built a blazing fire and closed the window. Elizabeth smiled wanly when she saw Bess and propped herself on several pillows. As Bess adjusted them for her, she coughed and finally spoke.

"Oh, my friend, it seems I have a disease."

Fear was written across her flushed countenance. Bess dipped the corner of her apron in a nearby pitcher of water and wiped Elizabeth's face before she continued.

"I have the pox, Bess. Smallpox."

Bess instinctively hugged her tightly. Elizabeth clung to her and sobbed. After a moment, she lay back.

"So the rumors will come true at last – I will be the old virgin queen."

"Auntie, you may marry anyone you wish! Any man would be thrilled to have you as his wife!"

"Before, perhaps. But not now with the scars and pocks and savage inflammation of such. Now they will only want me for my throne."

She adjusted herself, blew her nose and looked sharply at Bess.

"You think it is just vanity on my part, do you not?"

Bess shook her head vigorously.

"No, I do not. I think 'tis the woman speaking, not the queen of all the land. What, do you feel that because you are sovereign you should welcome such scarring as may come?"

Elizabeth smiled, relieved to have Bess at her side. Bess eyed her speculatively.

"Do you think your father welcomed his ulcerated leg because he was king? Hmm? Or perhaps my grandfather, Thomas, thought happily upon his useless leg – after all, he gained it in battle."

She adjusted Elizabeth's covers.

"No, you see, 'tis about courage and the will to live in the face of fear – the outcome will take care of itself."

"The doctor seems to think I will survive."

Bess reached beneath her undershirt and pulled out a gold cross set with rubies. She carefully removed it and hung it gently about Elizabeth's neck, tucking it securely beneath the queen's nightshirt.

"What is this?"

"Well, I will tell you: when your father and my grandmother became pre-contracted, Henry removed this fine piece from *your* grandmother's jewels."

"Margaret Beaufort?" The beginnings of a smile appeared on her face.

"Indeed," laughed Bess. "He gave it to my grandmother, but I give it to you now for a special reason. You see, when my grandmother Elizabeth's ship sank in a great storm in the Mare Nostrum, she was wearing this cross. My namesake and yours believed it saved her, for it carries Henry's love within it."

"My mother, too, was wearing it the day the great stone fell, and she believed this cross to be the reason it fell only on her leg, but her life was spared. 'Tis a talisman against any evil which might threaten she who wears it. And so today I give it to you for I know it will protect you and see you through this ordeal."

Elizabeth coughed and clutched the ruby cross tightly beneath her clothing.

"Dudley." Elizabeth spoke with longing. "He will no longer desire me. I will lose him."

"Majesty, I have something I must confess."

The tone in Bess' voice and the look of contrition on her face caused Elizabeth to forget her melancholy and sit up.

"What is it, Bess?"

"For some time now, I have been privy to information I have not shared with you."

"Go on."

"I have undeniable proof that Sir Robert Dudley…"

"YES?"

"…that Sir Robert Dudley is a vain nit of the first order."

Elizabeth fell back giggling with relief.

"Do tell."

"Well, I have personally seen him adjusting his hosiery, and combing his beard, while viewing himself in a secret looking glass he keeps tucked within his purse."

Elizabeth, too, began to giggle.

"And Majesty, 'tis a famous fact that he has more articles of clothing than you, me and all of your ladies combined."

"My Robert may be vain," Elizabeth acknowledged.

"*May*? And Majesty, you run circles around the man intellectually. Why, my horse can calculate an arithmetical addition faster than his lordship."

Elizabeth howled with laughter.

"You know, Bess, your ridiculous twitter does not change the fact that he may not want me with the scarring."

"Who knows and who cares? First, let us focus on winning this battle, then you may decide on how best to keep him, if that is your desire. And truthfully, I believe beneath his lust for the throne he loves you as a woman."

A knock on the door interrupted them. Huicke appeared and behind him a small contingent of servants. Bess leant low over Elizabeth, held her gaze and spoke.

"I will not leave you, Aunt, not until this is done. We will see it through together."

"But you, Bess. If you contract the pox, you too will be scarred."

"Pish," she said with disdain. "What do I care? Quinn loves me regardless, and even if he did not, I will still stay with you till it passes."

"You must leave, now, child, for the queen must rest." Huicke spoke with authority.

"No, I will stay."

Elizabeth nodded her consent.

"Bring in an extra bed for the tutor – she will read Dante to me in Italian while I fight this battle."

Huicke passed a concerned look over Bess but seeing her defiant gaze he shrugged and directed the servants to their tasks. Great swaths of red cloth were hung over the windows and the fire stoked even higher. Red cloth was placed over the queen's bed and the canopy frame as well.

While the doctor oversaw the changes and monitored his patient, Bess wrote a quick note to Quinn.

As the char boy tended the fire, she approached him.

"You, William is it not?"

The child smiled shyly.

"Tell me, do you know Catherine in the kitchen? The undercook?"

Again he smiled shyly.

"Leave the fire, and take this to her. Tell her that Bess begs her to see that it goes to Coudenoure at once."

"Couden-what?"

Bess quickly wrote the word on the outside of the packet.

"Here, tell Catherine she must get this to *this* place immediately." She pointed at the word. William nodded and ran quickly from the room.

Bess gazed out the window while the doctor finished his ministrations. She thought of Quinn, of Coudenoure, of the marble upon which she worked when she was home. She thought of Prudence still baking Henry's favorite cakes in the great medieval hearth in the kitchen.

Would she ever see them again?

Chapter Eleven

Quinn Janyns liked to putter in his garden. His passion for the natural world had begun as a child, when he would collect beetles and give them all names, his favorites being the Johns. He had discovered early on that not all beetles cared for captivity and he had grown tired of the frequent need to remember new names. Accordingly, all June beetles were Johns; he favored Edward for crickets, and the lovely caterpillars – whom the Johns and Edwards courted in his make-believe world – were Lady Blossom.

Robert Janyns, his doting father, suspected the names stemmed from being an only child on an isolated estate with no other children nearby, but since there was scant he could do to alter the situation, he had left him be in that regard. His own obsession with architecture had been passed on to Quinn and the older Janyns took great pride in his son's mathematical abilities. Their time together was spent in endless discussions of geometry and planes, arches and aesthetics until eventually, the language of architecture became the language they used to communicate with one another regardless of the topic at hand. It was an easy childhood, and Quinn was quite old before he realized that the name of his constant companion was loneliness. But Bess had changed all that.

Today, he was collecting seed heads from the meadow near his house when the ground shook beneath him. He turned to see a rider thundering furiously in his direction. The horse reared, the rider threw himself off and ran the rest of the way.

"My Lord," he said panting, "You must come at once to Coudenoure. Prudence says it is Lady Bess."

Quinn dropped the seed sack, commandeered the horse and gave it full rein. Prudence was waiting for him on the drive of Coudenoure.

"Young Janyns, come quickly, for I have had a message from Bess." She was frantically waving a small piece of paper.

Quinn grabbed it and without bothering to answer her or go indoors read quickly aloud.

"Dearest Quinn,

Our great sovereign has been visited with smallpox. She is feverish but mercifully the spots have not appeared. We must pray for her recovery.

*Stay well clear of Hampton Court and its environs.
Do not allow those who have visited the court recently
to set foot upon either Coudenoure or Tyche. Above
all, protect yourself and Prudence for you well know I
have no other family."*

*"My love, I shall remain here and care for the
queen. Should I be scarred, I hope you will see past it.
Should you not be able to, I will forgive you but never
forget you. Should I die, pray care for Prudence as she
has done for me and mine."*

I am always yours,

Bess"

Quinn began pacing furiously back and forth
before the heavy doors of Coudenoure. He was
seldom faced with the need for immediate decisions
and such urgency always made him queasy. But
Bess' face rose in his mind. He remembered the last
time he saw her and the flutter the touch of her
hand had created within him. There was no
hesitation.

He remounted the sweating horse and spoke
quickly to Prudence.

"I go to her now."

"But young Janyns, you put yourself in danger
should you do so. Better to do as she asked."

He smiled as he turned the horse.

"No, you see I cannot, for if she is scarred, then I too will be scarred. If she dies, I die too – for I cannot live without her."

He left Prudence staring after him, crossing herself as she called upon Jesus, God and Mary to save them all.

Chapter Twelve

The news spread through court like fire in a tinderbox: the queen had smallpox.

It was said that when Cecil heard the news at Whitehall, he fainted. He had suffered from the pox as a child and was immune now. As Elizabeth's courtiers fled to the farthest corners of the kingdom, Cecil had ridden post-haste to Hampton Court and now danced worried attendance on Elizabeth every thirty minutes. His reason, he always stated, was the business of the realm, and in proof of that he carried countless folders and papers. But his true purpose was revealed in the worried looks and glances with which he inspected Elizabeth with each visit. And with each visit, as Elizabeth's condition worsened and Bess' refusal to leave her side became more apparent, Cecil's curiosity about the young girl began to grow.

"So how is Majesty?" he asked officiously.

"Since your last visit? Eh? Not an hour earlier?"

Cecil ignored the tone and turned to Bess.

"And Lady Bess? How is your humor?"

Bess curtsied sweetly and retired to a chair by the fire. She began embroidering and pretended not to listen.

"Majesty, these are the letters from Scotland and the northern territories. They require your attention."

Elizabeth waved her hand to indicate her lack of interest. Bess had kept a steady watch upon the sovereign, but she could not attend to the many duties required to nurse the queen alone, and Robert Dudley's sister, Lady Mary Sidney, had joined her as a helpmate and nurse.

*****

The following day, Bess stood at the window in Elizabeth's room and watched the mass exodus of lords and ladies fleeing the pestilence. Gone was any pretense of courtly or stately manners in their bearing. Instead they ran pell-mell, screaming at servants, carrying their precious objet d'art and clothing in their arms as they threw it all in their carriages and sped away to places yet untouched by the disease.

Bess regaled Elizabeth with a blow by blow description of the tumult taking place on the drive below.

"Ah, here comes Sir Edward Belknap – by god, the man must have arms of steel – he is carrying his entire silver plate and cutlery service by himself."

"What does he think will happen to it should he leave it behind?" Elizabeth asked weakly.

"Oh, who knows – when panic sets in people do strange things."

"They do strange things always," Elizabeth remarked. Bess stepped momentarily from the window to insist she take a sip of hot chicken broth.

"Tell me," she asked between coughs, "Has there been any sign of Lord Fitzwater? He is a fastidious little twerp who washes himself at least three times a day. Smallpox must surely make him quake."

Bess returned to the window.

"No, but here is Lord Hastings and Sir Nicholas Weston. Ah, and Lady Anne Herbert – I did not know she could move so fast. And just behind her Lady Jane Withering with that crimson damask gown you gave her last year."

Elizabeth sat up.

"I did not give that gown to her! I gave it to her cousin, Lady Margaret!"

"Yes, but Lady *Margaret* traded it for Lady *Jane's* pearl earrings – she says that with her white silk gown – the one with the bell sleeves – they make her *fine alabaster bosoms appear more desirable*." Bess pitched her voice on the last words, doing a fair mimic of Lady Margaret.

"Harlot." Elizabeth laughed. "Although I believe she is correct on that point."

She had given her courtiers permission to decamp from Hampton Court until the smallpox ran its course. Only Bess and Mary Sidney had demanded to stay on and see her through the course of the disease. And in truth, this suited Elizabeth – the rumors of her demise and the jockeying for her throne made her more than tired and even before Bess and Lady Mary had volunteered, she had determined to keep only the faithful near her. It was the third day since she had been diagnosed and thus far no spots had appeared on her body. She assumed a cavalier attitude towards the ravages which might yet come, but at night, when Mary and Huicke had departed and only Bess kept vigil, she could not hide her fear.

"It may not be untoward, Bess, but I prefer death to pox scars – how will I face my court? My Dudley?"

There was no easy answer, and Bess lay beside the woman, her sovereign, as the fever raged and the fears grew. She cradled her and stroked her hair as a mother would. There were no easy words to be given, but she tried to fill the void with tender care and love.

It was during the final flight of the stragglers, those who were not content to carry their pelf in their arms but felt obligated to pack before they deserted the court, that Bess caught sight of a familiar figure fighting its way through the steady stream of departures. Elizabeth caught the look of concern on her face as she stopped mid-sentence.

"What is it, Bess?"

"'Tis Quinn, he has come despite my orders."

Elizabeth's laugh caused a hacking spell, and when she had recovered, she spoke.

"As far as I know, niece, I am the only one in this kingdom allowed to give such orders."

There sounded a sharp rap on the door and Quinn blew into the room and Bess spoke.

"No, Majesty, any one may give them, but apparently yours are the only ones that are followed."

Quinn removed his hat and bowed to Elizabeth.

"I am here." He appeared nervous, tired and satisfied. In that order.

Bess seemed more concerned than grateful.

"How did you get in?"

"I uttered a simple sentence."

They looked at him.

"I have smallpox."

He was caught off guard by the look on their faces.

"No, no – I do *not* have smallpox – I only *said* I have smallpox. The sea of noblemen parted as though I were Moses on the shore of the Red Sea."

"Young Janyns," Elizabeth preferred Prudence's name for him, "Exactly *why* are you here? You have entered your sovereign's bed chamber and exposed yourself to smallpox."

Quinn drew himself up. He was shaking but spoke anyway.

"Beloved queen, my beloved is here with her beloved queen, and because my beloved loves her beloved queen I do as well because she is my beloved queen as well and so if anything were to happen to my, well, my two beloveds I could not go on and so I am here."

Elizabeth turned to Bess.

"You are right, dear. I have no right to call a man who can make such a heartfelt speech a nit. From now on I will cease and desist."

It was easier said than done.

"But of course, you must needs instruct him in sentence structure at your earliest possible moment."

"Majesty, of course but I was trying to express my deep love for my..."

"Let me guess," came the half-reply, half-retort, "...your beloveds? Bess, he is entertaining but I am tired. See that your young man has a room here in the court, for I declare that the two of you be the only subjects willing to risk it all with me."

Bess escorted him to the kitchen for food and then on to chambers. As she prepared to leave, she turned back.

"Quinn," she said shyly, "I am very happy you came."

"I would never not."

Her smile said it all as she pulled the door behind her. He was a happy man, for he needed Bess as the rain needs a rainbow, and it comforted him to know she missed him as well. He threw himself on the bed, grinning from ear to ear.

As Bess crossed the courtyard leading back to Elizabeth's quarters, William Cecil appeared from a side chamber.

"Ah, Bess. We never seem to have a moment to speak quietly together."

Bess began an excuse but Cecil would have none of it. His dark robes and darker yet cap made him a forbidding figure. He motioned her into the room from which he had just come while rubbing his hands together in a most satisfied manner.

"Now tell me, child, your heritage."

Bess stared.

"Come, come. Do not be shy. You see, our sovereign is ill – very ill indeed."

Still silence. Cecil began to tap his fingers lightly on the table at which they sat. His eyes narrowed as he realized that this was no simple country maid but a sophisticated intelligent woman who would say no more than she chose.

"Bess, I am an officer of the crown. As such, you must answer..."

"Why do you wish to know my background, Lord Cecil? It must tiresome indeed if you must do so for every maid at court."

A sour smile crossed his lips.

"Bess, I have heard chatter. If there be a relative of the queen's of which I am unaware, a close relative, I must know that. Surely you understand. Our Majesty is very, very ill. And I hear *many* rumors."

"I hear them constantly," she replied, "Do you know any *good* ones?"

She rose and before he could block the door she was gone. She turned at the first available corner and ran lightly down hall after hall seeking nothing but relief from Cecil's prying eyes. The palace was strangely empty and she found it eerily disconcerting. She finally paused to catch her breath but hearing footsteps behind her, she ducked quickly through an ancient, inset door. She pulled it behind her, listening carefully to the sounds beyond. The footsteps paused, then continued on until they faded completely. Only then did she turn. For a moment, she believed herself back in Rome, in the galleries, workshops and homes of the people she knew there. Not just artists but all sorts forced to live on the edge. They or their pursuits such as science or alchemy were frowned upon and so restricted to their own abodes. Magellan may have proved the earth round when he circumnavigated it in 1519 for the Spanish, but science was not accepted. Almost inevitably, such men and women maintained very private spaces similar to the one in which she now stood.

The room was large, but not spacious. Carpets of a high quality graced the many tables scattered about and various tools lay upon them. Collections of flower petals and insects and seeds and rocks were everywhere and reminded Bess of Quinn's own room at his estate, his constant work at mathematics and the universe. She loved him for his art, but she loved him more for his originality. Watching him always took her back to Rome, made her feel her childhood. She strolled slowly around the room, stopping at a large crystal prism which stood a full two feet high on a nearby table; she ran her fingers over its cold, sparkling surface – she wanted to bring Quinn here for she knew he would love it as he did his home. As she looked around she began to wonder who might inhabit such an unexpectedly strange place. But before she could pursue the thought she became aware of a vast niche filled with books and manuscripts. It was not apparent upon entering the main space and she ventured closer. As she ran her fingers across the volumes, she came upon a shelf with no books or writings of any kind. It held only a simple carving of a woman and young girl. The girl leaned against the seated woman as a child would its mother. The carving, exquisite in its detail, even captured the loving gaze of the mother as she her hand rested lightly on the girl's shoulder. Bess gasped aloud, for she had seen the beautiful sculpture before, but not here, not in England. She had seen it in her father's workshop in Italy. As she ran loving fingers over it, a memory floated free from her subconscious and came to her. She looked up at nothing, still rubbing the piece and remembering.

"Eleezabeth, be still. Constance, can you not make her still?" she smiled in fond remembrance of the moment. . . Michelangelo struggling with his art against the fidgety will of a small child. A flood of emotion welled up within her, for since her mother's death, she found herself in odd moments turning again and again to her past. This was one such moment.

But what was this piece doing here, in a little known corner of Hampton Palace? She looked about and suddenly realized she was not alone. In a dark corner, unmoving, sat a man. She turned quickly, unsure of herself, but it was obvious he was not a threat. He was old, with a great white beard which he stroked as he watched her in silence. As she approached him, he rose from the stool upon which he had been sitting. His eyes were intelligent, his face kind.

"Lady Elizabeth?"

She paused, curtsied deeply and remained silent.

"Daughter, I believe, of my good friend Michelangelo."

A slight tilt of her head indicated acknowledgement.

"And you are, good sir?"

As he bowed deeply, his long white beard looked as it might touch the floor.

"I am John Dee, madam, and I am your servant."

He indicated a nearby chair and she sat.

"I imagine you are here avoiding our good Lord Cecil, are you not?" He smiled and she noticed the deep dimples which creased his cheeks and a merry twinkle in his eyes.

"You and our Majesty are prescient, I believe, when it comes to my circumstances."

His laugh was gentle.

"I assure you, I am not prescient – I am simply familiar with his footfall, and I might add that you are not the first to use my hallway as an escape route from his ceaseless inquiries."

"If you know I am Michelangelo's daughter, then you likely know why Cecil takes such a sudden interest in my lineage."

He bowed.

"Indeed, I am familiar with your story and your family. Both the queen and your father have told me the details. Cecil, I must say, is late to the ball."

"'Tis one way of looking at it," Bess agreed and pointed to the statue she had inspected only moments earlier.

"My father, 'tis his work, you know? It is of my mother and me when we lived in Rome."

Dee nodded appreciatively.

"It is how I recognized you – 'tis an excellent likeness. The fineness of the piece is quite astonishing. He sent it to me with directions to seek you out and give it to you. All things come right."

Bess continued to look around the room.

"Michelangelo tells me you have quite a library – he states that he knew your great grandfather who collected obsessively."

Bess laughed, remembering the tales she had heard about Thomas and his bibliophilic ways.

"My betrothed would love this room," she commented as she looked around, "For he too putters about a bit."

"He is here, is he not? Bring him."

"How did you know he was here?"

"Ah, well, that was a bit of court gossip, child. No prescience there either."

They sat together in silence.

"I must go to the queen," Bess finally declared, "...for she needs me."

"She will survive, child, do not worry. And Bess...please visit again."

She bowed and was gone.

Chapter Thirteen

Elizabeth's condition worsened but Bess refused to leave her side. Even the courtiers who had sworn fealty until their dying day – the very same who had stated loudly and prominently they would stay with their queen or die – had melted away. Bess watched through the window in Elizabeth's room as empty carriages and rider-less horses appeared from the stable yards. They no sooner slowed to a stop than they were snatched from the servants by owners frantic to depart the pestilence they now found all about. Foreign emissaries from far-away courts rode to and fro upon the drive at breakneck speeds, and with each such arrival or departure the rumors rose and rose again until their pungent and bitter sounds became a palpable crescendo of gloom.

Dark rumors filled the halls and courtyards. Whispered treason crept and crawled through the eerily empty passageways declaring that all was lost: The queen is dead: the queen is disfigured beyond recognition; she liveth not. A ground swell of panic rode upon the white horse of death and even Bess could not escape the sound of its thundering and ominous hoof beat. Would she live?

Foreign ambassadors paid lavish court to Bess and the physicians, promising to fulfill their most ardent desires, their innermost wishes, if they would just pass information, even if only a tidbit, of news of the queen's condition. They gathered and clutched, gossiped and speculated in their dark and velvet robes; the prayers they sent heavenward were not for Elizabeth's recovery.

Bess found herself more and more isolated with the queen. Food and drink were now left outside the door for as she worsened the fear of contagion spread. Quinn remained at court and Bess introduced him to John Dee, knowing that not only would Quinn find the man and his science irresistible, but also knowing that such isolation might help save him from the pox. She had initially found her job to be mainly one of distraction – she drew comical sketches of courtiers and ladies maids, gossiped mercilessly and endlessly, and played cards until she thought she could no more. But despite her constant attendance and Huicke's ministrations, Elizabeth had worsened.

On day four, her breath became shallow and her cough deeper – it seemed to rattle her very soul and Huicke took constant consultations with other physicians on the royal staff. Robert Dudley's sister, Lady Mary, had not left court. She stayed behind to demonstrate loyalty on the part of her clan. But on this day, she too fell ill despite keeping her distance to the extent she had been able.

"I am not well, today, Bess," she said to her in the hall just outside Elizabeth's door. "I believe I must lie down." Thereupon she had fainted and had to be carried to her room. Shortly afterwards, Huicke confirmed that she, too, had succumbed to the dreaded disease. Elizabeth was too ill to notice, however, for late that afternoon she lost the power of speech. Bess was the first to observe the deterioration and tiptoed quietly from the room before running down the hall frantically. Huicke and a cadre of his fellow doctors came galloping and Cecil was called. That night, she sank into a coma. And as Bess lay on her cot beside the bed, Cecil awakened her, motioning her to follow him into the hall. Bess ignored him, refusing once again to be caught up in the schemes and machinations she knew must come if the queen perished.

And then it happened: the miracle. On the seventh day, Elizabeth opened her eyes and spoke. John Dee and Bess sat on opposite sides of her bed, taking turns wiping her brow. They had been keeping vigil for hours, talking quietly back and forth about languages, now libraries and rare books, now Dee's beloved alchemy.

"Sir John," Bess half-questioned and half-teased him quietly, "How is it that lead or other such minerals might be turned to gold? I fear sir that you are wasting your time."

Dee shook his head, smiling.

"Child, you are misinformed. Alchemy is not just turning materials into gold – it is the changing of their base characteristics. Why, tell me this: have you ever boiled water?"

Bess looked at him suspiciously while nodding.

"Well, you have changed the water somehow, from its natural state to a state of steam. And if you capture the steam, you may change it back again! 'Tis alchemy in its most simple form."

"'Tis nonsense."

Dee and Bess were caught off guard.

"Majesty?" Dee leaned towards her and wiped her brow.

"You are an old magician, Dee, but you have a marvelous library so I forgive you. Now bring me some of that water you just spoke of."

Bess flew across the room, returning with a cup while Dee supported the queen's back. She drank a sip and Bess adjusted her pillows.

"Majesty, Majesty, thank God!" Bess exclaimed, almost too happy to speak.

"I had to come back," Elizabeth said mysteriously. "I was being called, but I heard the two of you jabbering and you would not hush with your nonsense. How could I consider heaven with such silliness in my ears?"

She closed her eyes and squeezed Bess' hand before nodding off.

Chapter Fourteen

The weeks of recovery were long and arduous. Bess had not realized her own fatigue until she caught a glimpse of herself one afternoon in the queen's looking glass. Where had the young, fresh girl gone? Who was the sallow and wan woman who stared back at her? The woman whose eyes shone dully forth from circles of deep shadow, the woman who no longer showed signs of youth, but instead appeared as a survivor of some horrific event. Bess noted the grim lines which had set in about her mouth. When Constance had died, she had cried and sobbed unendingly. She had never faced death, and it had been difficult for her to comprehend the finality of the loss. She kept expecting Constance and Agnes to come through the door, or to call out to her from the library. Their deaths had marked yet another phase of her own maturation, that of the ability to accept death and move on, but such a revelation had not come easily. Some remarked on the coldness of Elizabeth's tutor maid who does not shed tears. Was she made of her beloved stone? Only Dee and Quinn had quietly understood that before them stood a woman whose compassion and love burned steady and deep, far beyond the places where grief and sorrow might touch upon them.

Bess turned and saw that Elizabeth had awakened and was studying her. She motioned feebly for Bess to sit beside her on the bed.

"You must go home," Elizabeth said quietly. She clutched the ruby cross Bess had given her to see her through. "You have saved me, and now you must rest and regain your own strength."

"Maybe later, Majesty." Bess plumped her pillows. "For if I go now, who will report to you about the traffic on the drive? And more importantly, who will give proper interpretation of your court's excuses for having deserted you and Hampton Court?"

Elizabeth smiled and played with the silken tassels at the end of the drawstring on her nightshirt.

"Go." It was simple yet commanding. "When I am sufficiently recovered, I will come to Coudenoure."

The queen would brook no refusal. Cecil entered with a knock and eyed Bess coldly. He had not been able to break down the wall of silence masking her heritage and he was unaccustomed to such failure, particularly in light of her being a mere maid. He was certain the connection between Elizabeth and the girl was familial, but without her assistance, he realized he could get nowhere. In true Cecil fashion, he had determined that bearing a grudge against the young woman would be an unprofitable waste of energy, and he now forced a kind smile in her direction. Bess in turn curtsied and left the room.

Two days later, when the sky was gray and a light drizzle fell, Bess found herself seated upon the solid wooden plank which served as a seat on the ancient wain sent from Coudenoure to fetch her. Norman, the stableman, had blocked traffic on the great drive of Hampton Court as he and his team of oxen slowly made their way to the main gate and then beyond to the front door. His look of complete disregard for the carriages and horses behind him was matched only by the serene plodding of his oxen. The entire ensemble was oblivious to all shouting and cursing pitched in their direction, and all else too save for the purpose for which they had been sent: they were to pick up the mistress and bring her home. And no one was going to get in their way or hurry them along.

Bess looked up and saw Elizabeth watching them from the window. In a moment of sympathy and solidarity, Bess raised her hand, fingers outstretched, towards the window. After a moment, Elizabeth placed hers on the pane and left it there as she watched the wagon slowly make its way against the steady flow of traffic and disappear through the gate.

*****

Bess slept for days. Prudence kept a watch over her, and fairly screamed each time someone suggested she be awakened. She made her special breads, broths and meats and allowed no one to disturb her while she recovered. It was precisely what Bess needed, for nursing Elizabeth in the face of the pox had sapped her strength. The atmosphere at court had proven nearly toxic to her well-being, and as she lay abed at Coudenoure watching the snow fall outside her window, she vowed she would find ways to avoid any attendance at court in the future. The movement from one palace to another, the constant threats and innuendos, the smallpox, all of it had left Bess feeling almost disoriented – it took Coudenoure and its silent peace to restore her equilibrium.

Winter came on, and as the Yuletide approached, Bess began to feel restored and refreshed. She commanded that great wreaths and bows of whatever greenery the season offered to be draped and displayed about the manor. Bees wax candles were ordered to replace the usual tallow, and Prudence directed their placement so that even the

darkest corners of the ancient abode were gaily lit.
Quinn had returned to Tyche but spent his days at
Coudenoure wandering happily about its halls and
yards and eating Prudence's sweetcakes and plum
jams. Comments about his waistline were met with
silent, reproachful looks directed towards the
speaker. And then followed up with more
sweetcakes and jams. There was a general feeling of
lightheartedness in the air, a sense of joy that Bess
had not felt since she left Coudenoure for court.
Even John Dee, now a frequent visitor, commented
upon the atmosphere on one of his many stops at
the small estate. They sat drinking tea in the library.

"I must say, you have created a wonderful place
here – it seems outside of time, somehow, and
beyond sadness."

Bess smiled happily, for that was her sense too.
Prudence appeared with more cakes and fruit and
sat with them in the festive air. Quinn could be
heard galloping up the drive.

"'Tis what I need Sir John, to be creative. I will
be returning to my studio work soon, once I have
my strength back."

He nodded appreciatively, and noted the
prominent placement of the mother and daughter
sculpture he had given her months earlier at court.

"Just focus on your languages, my lady,"
Prudence's voice was stern. "You must stay in and

not exert yourself. Why not translate some heathen Italian text into our own God-given English? Eh? Your mother loved such pastimes and I have heard many say your Italian is better than even the Italian ambassador's at court."

The mention of her abilities in Italian stirred a memory.

"Not everyone thinks my Italian is so fluent, Prudence. Just before our Majesty became ill, two foreigners who did not know I spoke French disparaged it in front me!"

"They were nits – like all Frenchman," came Prudence's calm reply.

Bess reached for another scone and carefully place a fig atop it.

"I do not know, for they spoke in ciphers about the north and the Pope's blessing. And the Yule season – they said it all in light of some Yule celebration perhaps – something to do with the first moon. Indeed, I heard another conversation in that same vein which I was not intended to be privy to as well."

She popped the scone, fig and all, in her mouth and chewed happily as she looked at them. But their reaction was not what she had anticipated. Dee put his plate down and looked at her with a seriousness she had never seen in him. Prudence did the same.

"Bess, what have you heard?" Prudence asked gently.

Bess became alarmed but before she could speak Quinn strode in.

"Good day, 'tis a good day!" he said, reaching for the tea and a plate. Dee waved him silent.

"Child, what have you heard?"

Bess slowly and methodically related the two conversations she had overheard at court. As she did so, she realized she had been a fool. She began pacing frantically before the fire.

"God in heaven – I was distracted by the small pox entirely, and never thought of what I heard. 'Tis about the witch of the north, Mary, is it not?"

She called out to a servant to saddle her horse and resisted Prudence's attempts to calm her.

"No, no, you do not understand – it must have to do with our sovereign's very life. She survives small pox only to fall to an assassin's blade? Dear God, help me, help me!"

Finally, Dee spoke loudly and authoritatively.

"Bess! Compose yourself! You will not help our queen by panicking, nor will we be able to formulate a plan!"

Quinn spoke quietly.

"My love, can you identify the men who spoke?"

"The second conversation, the one about the Pope's blessing, yes, I can."

Prudence and Dee conferred quickly in the corner. The atmosphere, so festive only moments earlier, was now filled with alarm. The warm light of the candles became a garish river of foreboding as the four of them conversed. A quick, mutual nodding of heads signified an agreed upon course.

"Quinn, you will ride at once to Cecil – he is at his estate in Stamford. Do not stop for anyone and do not deliver your message to anyone save him. Can you find him? "

Quinn nodded and was gone.

"Bess, you must ride too, child. Elizabeth is at Whitehall and she must be warned."

He paced before the great hearth.

"I will ride to Dudley – he will be able to help Cecil call the realm to arms."

Quinn in his haste had not bothered to close the great wych elm doors of the front of the manor. They heard the cling and clatter of bits and horses brought up by the servants at Quinn's command. Prudence ran from the room only to return momentarily with blankets and cloaks. As they moved en masse to the doors of the estate, Bess turned quietly to her.

"This is my fault. 'Tis all my doing – if only I had not been distracted by the noise and constant buzzing of the palace. 'Tis my fault!"

Prudence hugged her, and then spoke the words which would see her through the long night ahead.

"Look at me, Bess. 'Tis no matter in heaven whose fault it is. And 'tis no coincidence that God has brought us to this point. Coudenoure stands with our queen. Now get over yourself and your emotions and ride, child, ride, for our very kingdom depends upon it!"

Bess mounted rapidly, dug her heels into her mount's side and disappeared down the drive. Following close behind was Dee. Prudence stood in the cold, snowy air, and as always, said her prayers. But this time, they were accompanied by orders to the servants.

"You! Collect everyone on the estate, for we must prepare should we be called upon to defend ourselves."

She moved to the hearth, and lifted Thomas' heavy sword from over the mantel. Once again, she thought grimly, once again.

*****

She rode blindly, holding tightly to the pommel of the great steed. She used first the medieval paths and wagon roads and then joined the proper London Route which ran past Greenwich Palace.

Her horse knew the way well, and as she rode her thoughts too raced frantically, trying desperately to latch onto some plan or scheme which might have some chance of success. But there seemed to be no good way to protect the queen for she had no certain knowledge of who was involved in the plot or where they might intend to strike.

The Greenwich Road was deserted save for the odd scattering of old vendors and their older yet carts and oxen bedded down for the night on the sides of the road. Lack of a certain plan was producing a panic had just begun to envelope her when suddenly a mad galloping destrier passed her headed in the opposite direction. Bess slowed, willing her thoughts to do the same. As she did so, yet another man girded in armour swept past. What was this? Before she could think, a full contingent of armoured and heavily armed men swept towards her through the darkness. From within their midst a shout could be heard and the party halted uneasily. A white stallion appeared. Elizabeth rode upon it. Bess suddenly knew what she must do.

"Oh, 'tis the queen? Oh, Majesty, have mercy upon me for I have the pox!"

The men closest to her moved away. Elizabeth watched her intently, her face betraying nothing.

"Please, good and rightly queen, touch my sores s that I may be healed through your grace! I will show you my pustules…"

"Child! Fear not, for I will say a prayer over your blistering body, but you may not disrobe before these men – what are you? A wild animal?"

A chuckle went round the group and Elizabeth motioned Bess to follow her to the rear of the entourage. They dismounted. Bess was careful to shield them with the broadsides of their mounts.

"Oh, Majesty," she screeched, "…Save me!" Her voice lowered to an urgent, frantic whisper.

"You are in great danger – these men plan to assassinate you and put Mary on the throne."

A cough from one of the men ensued.

"Child, I cannot see through your undershirt – yet I smell your sore!" Elizabeth shouted.

Bess spoke again.

"Give me your cloak and your hat."

Elizabeth looked at her, fear written across her face.

"Give them to me now." The queen did as she was told.

Bess frantically donned the garments, pulling the cloak's hood over the hat. Elizabeth spoke loudly, calling upon God and all the saints to heal the child before her.

"Go to London, to Whitehall. Dudley and Cecil are marshalling troops. Take my horse and I will take yours. They will see me as you, and Auntie, you must ride hard, for the thing is most urgent and the time short."

"Oh, Bess! Bess!"

Bess pulled Elizabeth's hat low across her brow, and turned into the crowd of men. She gave the animal a vicious kick and yanked the reins tightly, causing it to rear violently. Elizabeth mounted the other horse and was gone in the night. Bess rode wildly through the men and they closed around her and swiftly disappeared in the opposite direction from Elizabeth. She soon outpaced her escorts, though none of them seemed to mind. Mile after mile she rode, putting all the distance she could between Elizabeth and danger. Her luck held until a sudden, sharp bend in the road forced her mount to rear once again. The cloak's hood fell back, taking Elizabeth's hat with it. The horse turned and Bess faced the assassins.

Their gasp of disbelief and fury gave her the little time she needed.

"You, grab that wench!"

"And you! Turn back and capture the queen!"

Amid the chaos and panic, Bess turned her horse into the thicket which enshrouded the side of the road. Her mount never hesitated, and she rode frantically, trying to orient herself to where she might be. A hundred yards on the briars and undergrowth disappeared, and she recognized the field abutting Coudenoure's great ridge. She was almost home. But the heavy hooves behind her sounded ever louder. Again and again Bess kicked her steed into a furious gallop towards safety. She cornered the base of the ridge tightly, knowing the small path which would allow her to cut across it as it sloped down to the river. It bought her time, and as she reached Coudenoure Norman appeared where the gates leading to the estate should have been.

"Bess, you must hurry on to Tyche! We have concealed the gates to Coudenoure with brush. You will ride to Tyche and they will not know the difference – they will believe it to be Coudenoure!"

"But Quinn's servants! His estate!"

"Quickly child – we have told them everything and they have seen to the master's most treasured belongings. We are all now at Coudenoure. Go! And once the men have turned in there, take the back route home – we have laid an ambush!"

Bess did as she was told, barely fifty yards in front of the wild and furious rebels who rode behind. One mile further on, she turned up the curved and narrow drive of Tyche. She knew the way by heart and expertly guided Elizabeth's horse onward. But so intent was she on reaching the house and the backway to Coudenoure she failed to see the two men who stepped in front of the horse. The animal reared and one of them reached high and dragged her from the saddle. They had cut through the woods to arrive ahead of her once she had turned onto the graveled drive of Quinn's home.

*****

"Madame, I know you, do I not?"

The man who spoke was short with a stocky build. His green eyes glowed eerily in the candlelight of Quinn's great hall, like those of a cat on its midnight prowl. His hair, blonde and unfashionably long, hung around his oval, red face. While his English was perfect, it was nevertheless of a dialect completely unfamiliar to Bess. He smiled at her wickedly.

"Oh, aye, I do indeed know you! 'Tis coming back to me now! It was you walking at Hampton Court that day, was it not?"

Bess' mind had been dulled by the repeated blows which came her way each time she refused to give them the answers they wanted; dulled, but not useless.

"I have never been to Hampton Court, sir, as I have told you repeatedly. I am a simple country maid…"

"Enough!" The man leaned close and slapped her again viciously. "A simple country maid out for an evening's ride on a moonless night, is that it? A simple country maid who happens to know that bastard queen Elizabeth?"

Bess arranged her face into an innocent mask.

"I know nothing, sir. She led me into the sheltered conversation we had and forced me to take her clothes."

The man stood, paced, and then consulted with the three others who had made the ride with him. Bess waited, trying desperately to control her rising panic. She had believed herself to be in the clear until the moment the rebels had pulled her from the queen's horse. She had not prepared a story, much less one responsive to the queries she knew would rain down upon her. With no one to help her, she had turned to the only rational thought she still possessed: she must buy time. However, wherever, through whatever lie or tale, buy time.

The plan had initially worked and Bess calculated that Elizabeth's men must surely be abroad in her defense by now. The clock at the far end of the room somberly tolled the hour for Matins. Please God, she prayed silently in rhythm with its heavy strokes, let them come for me soon. Even now, she thought, Dee and Quinn were riding to Coudenoure. If she could just hold on, just hold on.

The man returned to the seat he had occupied for the past several hours, a chair drawn up directly in front of the one in which she sat.

"This is your last chance," he spoke softly. "Either tell us who you are and how you came to know we would be on Greenwich Road tonight, or pay for your silence with your life."

Bess bowed her head, but not before she gave him an answer.

"You may go to hell."

"I thought you might say that, for you are a crude woman – why, just look at your plain frock, your simple shoes."

From the darkness beyond the great hall's door a voice spoke, clearly and simply.

"You heard the woman: go to hell."

The man in front of her jerked his head to peer through the darkened doorway. His companions drew their swords and all three banded together in the middle of the room.

"Who said that?"

Silence.

"A coward are you? Else you would come forward – show yourself!"

The ringing of a crossbow was his only answer. The arrow it released flew neatly past them and wedged its steel tip in a far wall. It missed them by at least two feet, but as they first ducked then turned to see its path, Bess seized the moment. She ran into the darkness screaming as she did so.

"Quinn! I told you to practice your aim!"

Quinn's face appeared from the shadows and he looked at her with an exasperated expression.

"Bess, I have come to *save* you! Now, stand aside – I cannot believe I missed the vermin." Quinn reset the bow and another arrow blazed forth.

"Damn," he declared as it too thudded into the wall behind the men, "… You know, my love, I believe this bow to be defective. It seems to shoot…"

Bess grabbed him as a heavy sword slice the air where only seconds earlier he had stood.

As they tumbled together to the floor, the giant oaken doors of Tyche flew open and Dudley roared past with the queen's men.

"I am here!" Quinn called gallantly and scrambled to his feet as a mighty clang of swords began to reverberate throughout the room. He glanced at his quiver, threw it aside, and began beating the nearest man viciously about the head with his crossbow. It broke almost immediately, and Bess in turn began passing him various weapons – vases, bowls, candlesticks – which he hurled at them with as much success as he had seen with his arrows.

"I came to rescue you, my love!"

He wanted her to know.

"And I love you for it, Quinn! Oh, quick, the vase!" He broke it neatly over the last man's head as Dudley skewered the traitor from the other side. It was over almost before it began. Quinn had the last word.

"I believe that bow…"

*****

Elizabeth had never ridden so hard in her life. She was unaccustomed to Bess' horse and its unwillingness to do as it was told. The animal wanted to turn for home and it was a struggle to keep it pointed towards London. After several miles, however, it seemed to give up the fight and from then on ran pell-mell as though enjoying the freedom of a night on the open road.

Elizabeth struggled with the knowledge and events of the past few hours. She had progressed to Whitehall, happy to leave Hampton Court behind after so many weeks there convalescing. It felt good to be out in the city, dressed as the queen and seen and acknowledged by all her subjects. When news of her survival had broken beyond the gates of Hampton Court, church bells in all of England's parishes had pealed the good news. A feast holiday was declared with great tables set and laid in town squares across the land – all at the crown's expense. It had seemed that for the second time, God had spared her life for some purpose yet to be revealed; otherwise, surely her sister Mary would have gone further than just imprisoning her in the tower – she would have taken the final step which Henry had shown her mother. But no, she had been spared then as she was now.

The thought had made her happy, and her courtiers reveled in her positive and optimistic mood at court. She awoke in the mornings grateful for her life and fortune, grateful to be alive. Food smelled better, the birds sang with greater clarity, the sun shone brighter – she could feel the beauty of the earth in every pore. When she had been approached that evening, then, about a matter at Greenwich Palace, the thought of treachery had not even entered her mind.

"A birthday surprise for our own Lady Jane!" she had exclaimed laughing. "How wonderful! And who are these?"

"They will accompany us, for the ride will be after sunset," came the smooth explanation from a guard she did not recognize.

"Then let us make haste, for we will have fun this evening! Imagine the good woman's surprise!"

She was in love with life – the feeling of rejuvenation after such a close brush with death was still with her, and she rode out in the joyous knowledge that her kingdom loved her and had rejoiced at the news of her recovery. So intense was her exuberance with life restored that she never noticed the guards had already saddled her favorite mare. Likewise, she failed to notice the absence of familiar faces amongst those escorting her, or the furtive glances thrown between them. It was not until Bess had appeared that she realized something was amiss.

Curse them. Curse them all, she thought, half-angry and half-terrified. She rode on through the night. As the lights of London grew in the distance, she slowed her panting steed to a walk. Keeping her head down, she made her way through the dimly lit streets and alleys to Whitehall. Should she go in? Should she ride for safety to some unknown place where she would be secure? There was no one to help her and no one to give her an answer. She steeled herself and approached the gate.

"Halt!" The guards pointed their lances menacingly in her direction. "This is no night to be abroad – go home and bolt your door."

One of them, however, suddenly gave her a keen look.

"Open the gate! Open the gate! 'Tis our Queen, her Majesty!"

As the gate rolled slowly back a great shout arose from within.

"Long live the Queen! Long live the Queen!"

Elizabeth breathed deeply to keep from sobbing and collapsing before such a display of loyalty and love. As she rode through the gate, throngs of guards, servants, courtiers and administrators greeted her, blocking her path, touching her gown. She reached out to them, feeling the warmth from the many loving hands.

"Back I say! Get back!" It was Cecil pushing through the crowd.

"You – we must get her safely inside. Bar the gate, do you hear?" He took the reins of her horse and led her up the drive.

"You are safe Majesty – the rebels were few and have been captured. They will be dealt with as we all feel, nay the entire kingdom feels, they should be. Rest, for the kingdom is in your hands and you are safe."

She maintained a regal posture as she made her way through the palace grounds to her own chambers. Once there, she demanded solitude. As she closed the door upon the last ladies maid and

Cecil, she slid down its smooth surface to the floor, cradled her face and sobbed.

Far to the south, a ship of unknown origin weighed anchor at Woolwich and turned for France.

Chapter Fifteen

Christmas 1562

Elizabeth di Lodovico Buonarroti Simoni, child of the great artist Michelangelo and Constance de Gray of Coudenoure, and Quinntius Robert Janyns of Tyche, were married on the third Sunday following the third crying of the banns announcing their betrothal. They married at sunset, amid the ruins of the ancient chapel which rose on the grounds of Coudenoure. The outcry over their choice of an outdoor wedding in December was immediate and prolonged.

"Outside? What? I have come all this way to stand in the cold?" being the most common comment.

Sir Robert Dudley, Earl of Leicester, had appeared at Coudenoure the evening prior to Bess and Quinn's nuptials. Quinn had opened the heavy door. A lone hiccough escaped his lips.

"Quinn, my good man, are you ready?" Dudley had asked cheerfully. His cloak was emerald green velvet with a deep brown satin lining. His silk hose were of the same green and, for his trunk hose and doublet, Dudley had again chosen emerald green but accentuated by cream panels sewn in. The colors were vivid and Quinn seemed dazzled, particularly when Dudley flourished the cloak and removed his cap.

"I say, are you ready?"

Another hiccough. Quinn took a deep draught of wassail from the cup he held and continued to stare while reaching out to touch the fine cloth. Another hiccough.

Prudence appeared, took Quinn's cup and gave a nod to Dudley.

"I see the Christmas season is already upon us," he observed as he watched Quinn disappear down the great hall and into the library.

"Do not encourage him," Prudence demanded. "We are a happy household, Sir Robert, but should Sir Quinn become much happier, he will pay on the morrow at his wedding."

Dudley chucked Prudence under the chin, laughing as he spoke.

"Every man should drink before his wedding! You know, even old maids may find a mate at such a happy time!"

She slapped his hand.

"Go on, you nit, and see that you look after that young man. Drink is the devil's brew."

"Poured from an angel's cup," Dudley observed, moving quickly to avoid the lecture which was sure to follow Prudence's glare and finger pointing. He joined the small group of revelers who had collected at Coudenoure for the wedding.

"Sir Robert!" John Dee tore himself away from his inspection of the library's great collection. "Tell these people they must be married in a proper church, particularly in December!"

"Why particularly in December?" Dudley helped himself to a cup of wassail.

"You do not know?"

Dudley took a long drink, wiped his mouth with the back of his hand and shrugged his shoulders with a quizzical look. Father Michael from the local parish church filled him in. His cassock of deepest black wool was stretched quite tight across his chest, and the red silk sash which adorned his waist had clear markings of having been tied further and further along its length as the years had passed. He popped a wine-soaked fig in his mouth and spoke while he chewed.

"Sir, they say they will be married in the ruins of the Coudenoure monastery's chapel! Out of doors in December! 'Tis impossible!"

"Outside? What? I have come all this way to stand in the cold?"

Before Quinn and Bess could respond, Elizabeth swept into the room. She, too, had arrived at Coudenoure that evening with a greatly reduced court. Only a handful of her favorites had been allowed to accompany her, and she had banished them to the upper quarters for the evening. She wanted nothing but family and cheer this night. All rose and bowed before continuing.

"What is the conversation?" She inquired. "I heard good Father Michael complaining I believe as I entered."

"Majesty," chirped Bess happily, "They disagree with our plan to be married in the chapel ruins. They cannot see the romance and beauty of the place."

"Not in December!" A chorus sang out.

Prudence entered and gave Elizabeth a cup. She sipped thoughtfully before responding.

"Tell me again, Bess, whose wedding is it?"

A great cry went up and round the room. Elizabeth waved and grinned.

"Prudence, have the musicians come in, for I believe we shall dance."

The evening was bright and Elizabeth noted every moment of it. She wanted to remember it forever, for she knew that the morrow changed everything. Bess was leaving court forever. The uprising of the previous month had never manifested itself beyond the craven acts of that one evening, and Cecil had refused to give it credence. He refused to mention it in the court records, and stubbornly did not pursue the matter further.

"Majesty," he had explained, "If you announce such a rebellion, you only inflame and inspire those who might have joined. Do not give them such an opening. Let the matter be dealt with quietly and in secret."

Elizabeth had responded heatedly.

"They were to assassinate me – they had me in their clutches!"

"No, Majesty, there was nowhere for them to go – they were a handful of Mary's men and they were killed or have now gone abroad. Do not give it legitimacy by speaking of it to anyone."

There had been no evidence that Mary was involved, but Cecil knew, as did Elizabeth, that the affair had been a bid to put Mary on the English throne. There could be no other purpose and indeed, long before that night rumors had flown through the court regarding such attempts.

Cecil was as good as his word: the number of guards at each palace had increased. All petitioners to the common court of pleas and appeals now had to be cleared before entering. Priests were watched more closely, the northern territories settled with more of Elizabeth's men, sea port activities more carefully scrutinized. Cecil was well aware of the danger the realm had been in that dreadful night, even though he chose to downplay the event with Elizabeth. There was no point in frightening the woman – the only point to be remembered was that the queen must marry and produce an heir. Now. All else was porridge.

Elizabeth sighed as the musicians filed into the great library at Coudenoure, for the rumors had continued unabated. Such was life at court, she thought ruefully. She looked around the room loving what it had become for her. Great candles burned even in the darkest corners, and the fire spit and crackled happily. Bess and Quinn sat shyly smiling at one another, suddenly uncomfortable in each other's presence, despite being joyfully pleased and happy with themselves and the world. There was Dudley, whom she leaned upon as much as ever. His curiosity about Coudenoure and Bess had never been satisfied. Nor had Cecil's. The secret made Elizabeth happy, as though court and crown had not conquered her completely. There still existed some small corner of her life in which her life was simplicity itself: Bess was her niece and she her aunt. The knowledge that Bess' loyalties had been tested and proved under the most terrible circumstances made her tender feelings towards the girl and her estate doubly important to her. This was her family. In that same moment, she had been forced to realize that the time had come for Bess to marry – she could no longer hold her captive at court to give her selfish comfort. No, the girl's own life cried out to be lived and she must let her go.

The music began and Dudley approached. Chairs and tables were put aside to create space and she closed her eyes as he held her tightly. Round and round they went, spinning together in a world that if only for this moment was devoid of all scheming and ugliness and doubt and circumstance. She lost herself in his eyes, giving herself over to him even as knew it could never happen save here while the music played. Oh Robert. My Robert.

John Dee watched them from a chair near the fire.

"They can never be, and they know it." he spoke sadly to Prudence who sat next to him watching them twirl happily upon the floor.

"I disagree, old man," was her response. "They are now, and sometimes that is all we get in this life."

He raised his glass in acknowledgement of her rightness.

"Shall we dance, Madame? It has been some long time, but I believe I can still manage it."

They rose and joined Elizabeth and Dudley on the floor.

*****

The air was preternaturally still, as though commanded to serenity for this moment. The cold stone floor of the old abbey was still in place inside its soaring, arching, skeletal walls. The servants had strewn it with carpets Prudence mysteriously produced from the attic spaces of Coudenoure. Tall spruce had been chopped from the estate's forest and stood banked in a semi-circle behind Father Michael. In front of them, in deference to the priest's age, a great fire had been built where an altar had once stood. Candles lit the scene and lined the makeshift aisle down which Bess walked. The small knot of witnesses gathered and as Bess and Quinn stood before Father Michael, she dropped her cloak to reveal a dress clearly from another age. It was a simple, velvet frock. A pale blue bodice, laced tightly beneath her breasts, revealed a finely woven linen underdress. A full skirt of the same blue was intercut with light velvet ivory panels, each adorned with intricately stitched bouquets of pale wild flowers.

Prudence began to cry. When she had first produced the dress, again from the shadowy quarters beyond the top floor of Coudenoure, the queen had questioned her insistence that Bess wear it at her wedding.

"'Tis the dress Elizabeth de Gray wore at her pre-contract to your father, Majesty. 'Tis her own dress, the very same."

The queen had touched it gently at first, then held it softly against herself. After a moment, she agreed.

"Bess, you must wear this dress, for it was your grandmother's at her pre-contract ceremony with my father."

Bess wore it now and its pale blue was picked up by the crimson pinks of the fading light off to the west. A sense of sacred purpose settled upon the small band gathered in the ancient sanctuary, and as

Father Michael walked Bess and Quinn through their vows, a gentle snow began to fall. Quiet settled across the fields and woods of Coudenoure. They were married that day in the eyes of God, of Queen and of family and friends.

The prior evening's treats and wassail had been only a prelude to the sumptuous banquet Prudence and the kitchen servants had prepared for the wedding feast. The doors of the great public room, the hall across from the entry and library, were thrown wide to welcome the wedding party upon its return from the chapel. As they stomped the snow off their shoes and boots and loosened their cloaks, they entered and gasped.

The oaken-arched ceiling, so high it seemed to reach unto heaven itself, disappeared into cavernous darkness. Medieval chandeliers of heavy iron, black from age and smoke, had been lowered and hung with fine and huge candles. The hearth, a relic of that same age, roared with a welcoming fire and almost drowned out the musicians Elizabeth had arranged for the party.

Tables had been put end to end and laid with festive foods: two stuffed peacocks decorated either end of the display, and in the center stood Quinn's favorite dish, mince pie of mutton, currants, figs and plums. Between the peacocks and the mince pie were innumerable coffins of various meats and delicacies.

The celebratory mood expanded and as the wine and wassail flowed, Elizabeth took Bess aside.

"Child, come with me."

Bess followed obediently. They slipped across the hall and into the library where a large wooden box, decorated with multi-colored tessellations of stars and squares sat upon a table. Around it was a wide, red satin ribbon tied in a pretty bow. Elizabeth nodded excitedly to her niece.

"Go on, open it!"

Bess giggled and slowly pulled the knot from the bow. As the ribbon fell away she lifted the lid and removed the linen cover. Inside lay yet another box and she carefully lifted it out and opened it. Inside lay a manuscript of such age Bess was almost frightened to touch it. Elizabeth lifted it from the box and Bess slowly realized what it was.

"'Tis the book grandfather longed for – the Latin Bible, the one printed by Johannes…Johannes…"

"Gutenberg," Elizabeth smiled and finished the sentence for her.

"And see here? An indulgence as well, and in Latin." She paused and counted the lines. "Some thirty lines I believe."

"When was it made?"

Elizabeth looked up.

"Before Henry VII came to the throne, child. The book is quite ancient, and Thomas, your grandfather, would have been proud to own it."

Elizabeth turned back to the box and from within it pulled another, almost paper-thin box.

"Incunabula," she said simply.

Bess turned and looked at her aunt.

"I do not know what to say, Majesty, for such valuable and rare gifts are surely out of place at such a small and unknown estate such as Coudenoure."

Elizabeth smiled and touched Bess' cheek lightly.

"Do you remember you told me about an inventory you had discovered one day among your books and manuscripts?" She nodded at the wall covered in books.

"Of course. Apparently my grandmother, at some point, prepared an inventory of her father's library. It seems it was terribly disorganized and unkempt."

Elizabeth nodded excitedly.

"If you look now, Bess, you will see that inventory lies upon yon table. I borrowed it some weeks ago and asked Dee to look it over."

"Why?"

"Bess, Coudenoure may be small, un-noteworthy and out-of-the-way, but because of your great grandfather Thomas and his obsession with books, it also boasts one of the great libraries of the realm. You must take care to protect it and add to it, for it shall be our legacy to our shared future."

Bess began to cry.

"Oh, Elizabeth, I wish they were here – Henry, Elizabeth, Constance, Agnes – to see this night, and the joy that fills Coudenoure."

Elizabeth looked beyond Bess into the fire.

"But they are not, child, and we go on."

A moment passed in silence before Bess spoke.

"I have something for you as well, aunt, but it is not nearly as grand as these." Bess spoke in an embarrassed but determined tone.

Elizabeth was touched and waited to see what Bess would produce. From a case near the window she took a large, rectangular package. A blue ribbon bound the linen cover neatly. Elizabeth noted a folded letter slipped under the ribbon.

"This is for you, aunt, so that you will not be bored without me. Now, you must bring your work to Coudenoure periodically so that I may instruct you."

Elizabeth smiled.

"Usually, Bess, gifts are given to the bride on her wedding day, not to her aunt," she observed as she tugged at the ribbon. It fell away, and she gently swept aside the wheat-colored linen. Beneath the wrapping lay a large sheath of fine parchment and paper, and two small boxes. Opening the first she discovered two rows of tiny pots of color – pigment Bess had mixed for her; the other contained brushes, two pots of ink and tools for drawing. She examined each minutely, picking them up, turning them and feeling their measure in her hands. After a moment, she turned and hugged Bess fiercely.

"Do you remember the jewel – the large sapphire – given me by Tsar Ivan Grozny?"

"The 'king'…"

Elizabeth interrupted her.

"Tsar – they call him the imperial *Tsar*."

"Yes, well, the man who stole the jewel from your ambassador to Cleves and then presented it to you as though it were a gift?"

"The man is troubled in his mind, no doubt. But that is not my point. Bess, that jewel and all my other wealth are nothing compared to this token of your love and devotion."

Bess considered before speaking.

"Whatever you do, do not ask your ladies maids for assistance."

"Why not?"

Another pause.

"Aunt, have you never wondered why they do not show you their work from my tutoring sessions with them?"

Elizabeth chuckled.

"'Tis true – though I had never considered it. I shall tuck that bit of fun away for a rainy day. Now, let us rejoin your guests, for I believe none of them have even missed us!"

As they walked towards the door Elizabeth stopped.

"Tsk! I almost forgot!" From under her gown she produced the ruby cross given by her father to his love so long ago. She placed it around Bess' neck.

"It did indeed protect me, and I thank you for your many kindnesses, child. Keep it safe."

They rejoined the party.

"Tell me," Elizabeth shouted merrily as they re-entered the great hall, "Who amongst you dares to dance with me?"

It was late indeed before they put the young couple to bed amid riotous laughter and innuendo. Finally, however, it was only Quinn, Bess, and a single candle burning on a table nearby.

They lay beside one another, covers drawn to their chins. Quinn finally spoke in a faltering voice.

"My love?"

"Yes?" came the whispered reply.

"I must confess."

"Yes?"

"I am a virgin. I have not done this before, and so I am uncertain…"

Bess rolled to her side and stared at him before breaking into a gentle, blushing smile.

"Put out the light, Quinn, and we will figure it out together."

Quinn did as he was told.

Chapter Sixteen

Summer 1565

Scents. They took Bess places. Places and times travelled before, places and times she had yet to know. Take for instance the lavender of the meadow on the far side of the ridge: it was Quinn. A peculiar dusky aroma she knew from his clothes when he collected seeds and insects from there. It was very different than that of the lavender which grew atop the ridge. In that place, the lavender was spare, growing among the rocks and clefts, keeping to itself, not mixing with the other wild and mongrel plants of the area. Its scent was pure – simple and milky in its ability to soothe. Like the feeling that flooded over her when she took her pots and canvases there and lost herself in the vastness of creation on display from such a glorious vantage point.

There was the sharp smell of the wild daisies which grew along the river bank. It mixed well with the pungent fragrances offered by the Thames, combining into the memory of a well-seasoned and good pot of fish chowder, or perhaps a halibut of the type Prudence used to prepare. Before Prudence became ill. Before she died. And in death, the smell of the white gardenias the old girl had loved since childhood, now planted round about her grave, contradicting the sad nature of death with their heavenly fragrance: defiance in its purest and most subtle form.

Of course, there was Rome. When she closed her eyes and remembered, the exotic nature of the scents she recalled were almost overwhelming. In the market, the day with her father when she had tasted the curry in the spice souk and cried for relief from its tingly burn. The smell of his hair and his clothes as he laughed and cradled her in his arms until the sting passed. The smell of sewage and the wharves of Ostia linked forever to the sight of her father and Roberto on the dock, waving farewell as they weighed anchor for England. The smell of cornflowers and Constance. Of grubby porridge and her son. The scents and odors that caused her to pause, almost but not quite catching a memory. Yes, scents.

Today, the sun beat down from a clear blue sky. A gentle breeze caressed the tops of the wild flowers and grasses planted in abundance upon what had once been the great lawn of Coudenoure. Quinn had seen no use for the neatly trimmed grass.

"It attracts no birds, no insects. Surely we must give them a home."

She had smiled and left him and his gardeners to their wild and grand schemes. The result was a harmonious chaos, choreographed color, shape and texture. The wind picked up all the scents from the happy madness – the good, the bad, the earthy and the fragrant, the sharp and the crisp and sweet – and rolled them into a powerful concoction of place and time and scent, and she knew that from now on, should such a potpourri ever rise again and be carried to her on some summer breeze, she would see Quinn in the distance with Michael on his shoulders and Anne with her butterfly net at his feet, happily waving it about as they tromped across the meadow-lawn of Coudenoure.

She raised her face to gather the sun's rays, feeling the intensity of their heat. Her hand rested on her stomach, and she felt the baby kick.

A perfect day.

*****

Elizabeth patted the neck of her sweating bay, and nudged it past the pillars of Coudenoure's gate. She had dressed too warmly for the day, and with her guards on the far side of the high wall, she impulsively unbuttoned her riding jacket, revealing the stiff front of the dress below. The patterned blue silk of the ensemble matched the sky and her mood, while the jaunty feathers in her flat cap of silk and wool completed the picture of queenly grace out for a ride on her favorite horse. What a lovely day. She dismounted and walked the drive to enjoy it more.

There was Quinn in his meadow-lawn with Michael and little Anne. Michael was singing some ditty atop Quinn's shoulders while Anne toddled along with her butterfly net. Anne. Elizabeth never knew a word which could encapsulate or fully express all of her feelings about the little girl. Borne on Christmas day, she had inherited the dark beauty of her great grandmother, Henry's love Elizabeth. Even at birth she had the sharp chin and dark almond eyes so characteristic of the woman in Michelangelo's sculpture which graced the library at Coudenoure. Her hair had cured into a warm chestnut over time and curled in ringlets about her face and down her back. But the physical traits of Henry's love were also the physical traits of his second wife, the queen's own mother. Indeed, Bess and Quinn had named the child Anne Elizabeth in celebration and remembrance of the two great women. But just as it had caused gossip and rife speculation in its day, so now the resemblance caused Elizabeth to catch her breath each time she saw the tiny toddler. Her familial love for the child became inextricably bound with her love and tangled, fragmented memories of her own mother, but with one obsessive distinction: her love for the child had no overwhelming loss and terror associated with it. As Anne grew so did Elizabeth's compulsive need to protect and nourish her against all that might come against her or harm her in any way. At some moment Elizabeth had realized she was heaping upon the child all the love she had never been able to express for her own mother – perhaps it was the moment she realized she unconsciously rubbed the portrait ring she wore each time she saw Anne, or perhaps the moment she realized that her heart lifted to a joy she had never known each time Anne appeared. She was never sure and she no longer cared or pondered the situation. Anne was for her all things happy and elating, and she reveled in the experience, knowing it was her only chance to know such unbound and unbounded love.

She saw Bess napping in the wooden chair Quinn had dragged outside for her on such beautiful summer days as this one. Her feet rested on a tuffet from the library, and Elizabeth walked her horse slowly up the drive to minimize the sound of crunching gravel beneath its hooves. She sighed at the picture of bucolic contentment the scene presented. Even knowing that such could never have been her lot and fortune, it yet caused a stirring for family and children within her. But it would not happen, despite her ministers and ambassadors continuing to harp upon the need for a successor. She was aging and with that age came a bitter maturity that now informed her decisions.

Her early intuitions had proven correct. Her life was best lived and protected with no king in her kingdom. One mistress and no master. To allow marriage to come between her and her people was tantamount to putting her own life at grave risk as well. She would become the pawn rather than the pawn's mistress, the queen jettisoned to ensure a more favorable outcome for someone else. Let them all rage and rant about continental politics and the advantage of this or that prince. She listened and pretended interest, nothing more, for even if one candidate should somehow managed to rise above her concerns for self and kingdom, none could temper her concerns about childbirth at her age. No, better to leave it all and enjoy what she had than to risk some unknown fate at the hands of someone who would undoubtedly place their safety and ambitions above her own.

In years past, she had questioned herself as to the validity of her fears. Were they justified or just goblins left under the bed from her terrifying childhood? But now those self-doubts and questions were laid to rest. Whatever their origins, the threats remained, but rather than fight demons she could never exorcise she chose to embrace them, realizing they would be with her regardless, even unto the grave.

She knew Quinn must have seen her by now for she was halfway up Coudenoure's long drive, yet he remained distant most deliberately. Again, Elizabeth sighed. He had never forgiven her for taking profit from John Hawkins' slave trade with the plantations of the new world. A man who could not bear to see a caterpillar harmed was not one to condone human misery in one of its most pure and debauched forms. She had tried to explain it to him, but he remained firm in his convictions that nothing justified such actions – all arguments in support of the policy were nothing more than irrational rationalizations in the face of moral absolutes. She knew him to be right, but she also knew the mounting pressures of continental politics and religious fervor – her establishment of the Anglican Church two years earlier would surely lead to her own excommunication with Rome, and such papal action would be accompanied by a rising fervor to see someone else on the English throne. Her enemies need look no further than her northern border to find that someone. Mary Queen of the Scots would happily take her place and see Catholicism restored. Elizabeth admired Quinn and even loved his innocence, but her profits from the slave trade must continue, for she needed to build a military which would give pause to all who might choose to confront England. It was not justifiable and she knew it but such knowledge did not stop her. Pray God he might forgive her.

She saw Bess stir and sit up and waved at her merrily. A shout went up and another chair was promptly brought from indoors.

"Bess, I declare, each time I leave and come back, you are yet again with child. Is there a connection?"

Bess laughed and began struggling to her feet to curtsey.

"Oh, what a sight," Elizabeth giggled. "I think, niece, we may forego the customary ritual for if you stand I fear the child may fall out. You see, you are quite, well, quite…"

Bess laughed.

"Fat? Huge? Yes, and then some! But 'tis my last time like this so I shall enjoy it and eat all the plum sauce I like."

"Ah, so we are still on plum sauce, are we. And the radishes?"

"No, mercifully I no longer desire them. Quinn would not kiss me when I ate them, you know."

"Clearly, Quinn has no problem kissing you. And yes! Here he is now! Sir Quinn, how are you today?"

Quinn shifted Michael from his shoulders and bowed deeply before disappearing indoors. Elizabeth gave Bess a frustrated look.

"Still he forgives me not?"

"Majesty, he knows, as we all do, the slave trade to be wrong, and that profit from such ventures will not advance England one whit."

Elizabeth sighed. When John Hawkins had first come to her with his scheme, she had known it to be wrong and repulsive. But the promised monies pouring into her eternally empty coffers were too much to resist. She knew it was wrong. She knew it to be morally reprehensible, but Quinn with his high-handed morality had at length got the better of her, and their many discussions had devolved into equally many quarrels. Were it not for him being Bess' husband and Anne's father, she would have put an end to the arguments. But she could not enjoy the relaxed and familial atmosphere at Coudenoure if she did so, and so she put up with it.

Bess watched her and then patted her hand.

"Aunt, Quinn does not understand the world you live in and navigate on a daily basis. He has no claim to know whereof you make your decisions."

"Tut," came the reply, "I would like to see him manage a kingdom as bereft of money as the one I inherited. Indeed I would!"

Elizabeth settled back in her chair and a table with tea, fruit and scones appeared.

A small voice behind her caused Elizabeth to grin and forget Quinn.

"Michael, curdy to de keen."

Michael and Anne appeared and Anne pointed a stern finger first at her brother then at Elizabeth.

"Dat is de keen. Now, curdy."

Michael attempted a curtsey and promptly fell over. Both children exploded in laughter and Michael, dark-haired, gray-eyed and ever mindful and delighted with an audience, repeated his performance. Anne spied the cakes and promptly climbed into Elizabeth's lap, looking with longing at the one Elizabeth held in her hand.

"Would you like a bite?" the queen asked.

Anne's eyes never left the cake. She watched in mesmerized awe as Elizabeth moved her hand closer. Carefully she leaned in and closed her eyes as she bit into the pastry.

"Mmmmmmmm." Both women roared with laughter. Bess passed a scone to Michael and he scuttled away.

"Now, tell me Anne, what have you been about?"

Anne considered the question thoughtfully.

"Well, keen, I must tell you dat de peacocks love der own feaders too dearly."

"How do you know this?"

"Because when I wanted some for de hat I am making Moder, dey screech when I try and get dem."

"What happened?" Elizabeth inquired with a smile.

"De bit Michael."

"They bit *Michael*?"

Anne nodded matter-of-factly as she took another bite of the heavenly cake.

"Cause he were holding dem still for me."

"Indeed." Elizabeth chuckled, "'Tis a good and intelligent division of labor it seems to me."

"I tink so."

"And how are your lessons coming? Are you working hard?"

Anne shook her head no.

"And why not?"

Anne grinned a toothy and gapped smile.

"Because der are too many butterflies I need to…to…dentify."

Bess passed her a scone and she, too, ran happily around the corner of the manor house.

"So you have not yet engaged a tutor, I assume?"

Bess nodded.

"I need to but I keep thinking of plums in all their many forms instead: sauces, fruits, tarts, sugared…"

"Yes, I believe I see your point. Very well, I shall engage a tutor for young Michael and Anne. They shall need one for language, and I shall get them one especial for science and nature – perhaps Quinn will then like me once more."

"'Tis not like or dislike, Majesty."

Elizabeth waved her hand to signal she was done with the conversation.

"They shall be here anon and Quinn and Sir John Dee shall be consulted in their hire. Now, what about your sculpting?"

The conversation turned to art, to the children's this-and-that, to court, to life. They were old friends now, and Elizabeth watched the colors in the meadows change as the sun rolled across the bright sky, happy in the present and the here and now.

Bess, too, was content with the lazy pace of the afternoon. Finally, however, Elizabeth rose and shook the crumbs from her dress.

"I will come more often, for today has been useful for me, Bess."

"'Tis good for me as well, Majesty. Since Prudence died, I have no women kin here about."

"She was not kin, but I understand the sentiment," Elizabeth mused. "We will see what we can do."

With that mysterious reference, she called for her horse and rode slowly down the drive now bathed in a dusky light. Bess called for servants to bring the furniture back inside and went in search of Quinn.

*****

"Are you coming with Papa or staying out with the ladies?" Quinn inquired of his son, looking down and smiling at the grubby little urchin. Michael seemed poised to enter the house with his father when the servants passed by with the table, tea and cakes. He never gave Quinn a second glance as he toddled back towards his mother and Elizabeth. Quinn smiled and closed the door.

Bess and he had settled comfortably at Coudenoure after their wedding. There had been flutter about what to do with Tyche: Quinn had insisted that while he would live wherever Bess desired, he would not turn the people who served him out to fend for themselves with no clear means for living. But Coudenoure was a small estate with no need for a doubling of its staff. Elizabeth had solved the issue for them when she suggested Tyche go to the crown, and she could reward a courtier with it in due time. In the interim, Quinn's servants had a home and could use the interlude to find other stations. It was a sensible solution, one agreed upon by all.

The only other issue with the happy couple taking up residence together was a space for Quinn to continue what had now become his passion: studying the natural world. He still spoke the language of architecture as his first tongue, but marrying Bess, having children and meeting John Dee had given him a second language with which to speak – that of the almost mystical world where God's plan was expressed through the rhythms, shapes and sounds of nature. His childhood delight in insects and their goings-on had developed into a mature study of their forms and habits. Tiny boxes with bugs, bugs with pins holding them to wooden planks, flowers carefully pulled apart and glued to whatever lay handy – all of these gave way to systematic and rigorous attempts to classify and understand. But where to house such activity? Bess and Quinn had stumbled upon the solution together.

The great hallway of Coudenoure stretched almost the distance of the house from front to back. Indeed, most assumed that the massive iron and oak door at its far end led to the outside world behind the house. It did not. Like so many other bits and pieces of Coudenoure, it was a relic from the medieval monastery which had once been the estate. Behind the door lay a large room once used by the monks as a public larder. Their ministrations to the poor had included herbal medicines, food and alms, and they had chosen to keep these wares in a central place. The hinges of the great door had rusted through and over time the space beyond it lay forgotten. Quinn had asked about it as they explored Coudenoure and at once they had determined to see what was shielded by its massive timbers. After much oil, muscle and the occasional whack of a hammer or two, the ancient door had yielded.

The interior was dark and gloomy, but large and with a high arched ceiling of the type so common at Coudenoure. Near the top of the outer wall a row of small, leaded windows afforded what little natural light was given to the room. Shelves and tables were filled with neatly labeled apothecary jars and in the corner, two huge barrels of flour, or perhaps oats, stood ready for handout to the poor. Record books, bound neatly, lay side by side with individual pages of the monk's ledgers which still covered one table – an ancient quill with a tiny ink well stood at the ready nearby. Quinn had immediately fallen in love with the space. Bess had not, and it took her new husband's architectural eye to see it as it might be. During their first year of marriage, Bess had been consumed with pregnancy and Quinn with his newly discovered study. The huge, limestone blocks of the back wall had been replaced with floor to ceiling windows. Shelves were built along the interior wall, and the tables were kept for uses such as might develop. The great fireplace and flue were cleaned and readied for use, and by the time their eldest child, Anne, was born, it had become for Quinn what Bess' studio was for her. Michael was born eleven months later.

Through John Dee and Elizabeth, Quinn became part of a rising group of English explorers and naturalists. It was a world which suited him and he never ceased to marvel at the sheer luck of his falling into a life which so matched his passions. Happy absentmindedness was his normal mode and as the children grew and his collections expanded, so too did the chaos of his life. He was thrilled as it all spiraled gently out of control.

Bess seldom interfered with her husband's daily routine, insisting only that his stockings match, his meals be eaten with the family, and that he and Dee cease all gunpowder experiments, at least in the house. The last one had rocked Coudenoure. When Bess, the queen, Dudley, the children and the servants had entered Quinn's study, they found him beating the right side of his head to put out the small fire which burned there. Dee's beard was half the length it had been moments earlier, and the room was filled with floating bits of papers, flowers, bugs and smoke.

"Quinn!" Bess had screamed. "My love, are you alright?"

Quinn and Dee had both blinked and stared at her without answering. Quinn continued to pat the side of his head absently.

"Quinn!" she screamed again.

"Did you say *again*, or *Quinn*?" shouted Dee over the ringing in his ears. "Because madam, 'tis not in anyone's best interest to do so. At least not until we have reviewed our methodology."

Anne had keenly observed her father's new manner of hair and had promptly taken Michael aside and cut his to match. They found her before she lit the candle.

During Bess' third pregnancy, Quinn had planned and begun executing the building of a small glass house attached to his study – friends were bringing strange seeds and plants from worlds Quinn knew he would never see himself, but might yet experience through the treasures they provided him. When Martin Frobisher had arrived with an eight foot specimen of a flowering tree which bore the precious lemon fruit, Bess had screamed with excitement – the tree brought back memories of Rome. It was the last such tree from Frobisher, however, for he was determined to find a northern route to the new world and had Elizabeth's backing to do so.

The only thorn which existed in Quinn's world was his ongoing displeasure with Elizabeth's taking profit from the slaving expeditions of John Hawkins. He could not reconcile such activity with that of a civilized nation. Time and again, Bess had tried to discuss it with him only to be rebuffed by his anger. But by late summer of '67, when Bess began laboring with their third child, she extracted a promise from him.

"You will stop the quarrel with our queen and my aunt," she had hissed between contractions, "...for I am tired unto death of the two of you. Do I think she should? No. Is it my choice? No. And just for you..." Bess sucked in her breath as another contraction hit, "...just for you she gives a portion of her profit to the poor."

"I am sure that makes all the difference in the world to the souls who are being traded like sacks of flour, dear."

He held her hand and she squeezed tightly before the midwife began hustling him from the room.

"Promise me."

"I promise, my love, I promise."

And that was that, for ultimately he could deny her nothing.

Catherine Jane was born the following morning.

Another perfect day. Another perfect year.

Chapter Seventeen

1573

"Quickly, Anne, before Nanny misses us."

"Nanny? Do not be silly, Michael. 'Twill not be Nanny who calls for us first and alerts mother."

On the banks of the Thames, Catherine threw rose petals from a basket all the while singing a sad, dirge-like melody which she made up as she went along. She was dressed in her finest blue silk dress, the one she had insisted must have purple tassels added to its waist for emphasis. The sleeves of the gown were cut with orange velvet panels, again of a fabric and color of her own choosing. On her head was the hand-me-down flat cap with peacock feathers given her by Elizabeth. Slightly too large and unwilling to sit on her blond curls, it was tightly secured by pins put in place by Anne. The overall effect was one of sumptuous elegance. In the children's eyes at least.

"Ah, he went to sea and was lost and dead," intoned the doleful lyrics…"Very dead indeed was he because he would not take his sister with him. And so to punish him God…"

"Catherine!"

She ignored Anne and continued to sing of her brother's impending fate since he would not allow her on board his ship.

Anne too wore her finest, a gown of dusky pink with tiny roses embroidered on its full skirt. Like Catherine's, the hem was blackened with mud and debris. Her hat had been lost in the struggle to mount the sail on Michael's rowboat. For the past two weeks, the two of them had carefully retrofitted the little craft with a rigging mast and rudder with cord controls. It had been arduous work, but the day had finally arrived when Michael would put to sea upon the Thames. Catherine was to be his lady fair waving her silken banner tearfully as her love pulled away. She was not inclined, however, to play the role of one who stays dutifully behind.

Michael wore black breeches with the silk hose given him by Elizabeth the previous Christmas. Anne and he had determined that the neckline of his nightshift most closely resembled what a pirate's upper garb would look like and so his breeches had an odd, stuffed quality to them. His hat was a wreath of laurel with feathers stuck round.

As the bed sheet rose upon the mast, Michael gallantly placed a foot on the plank seating of *The Pirate Man* and waved solemnly to his sisters. The tiny craft rocked and the sail almost billowed as he pulled away.

Anne pretended to cry.

"Farewell son! Bring glory to England. And loot! Do not forget the loot!"

"...and he pulled away and was dead at sea because I am going to tell Papa all about it..."

*****

Elizabeth was elated. Francis Drake had captured yet another trove of Spanish silver bound for the coffers of Spain from the new world. It was hers now, and in her mind she ran the calculations over and over again of what the windfall would mean for England. Even though she kept stringent control over the crown's resources, there seemed to be a hole in the bottom of her purse through which all her monies poured. She knew that keeping the Spanish treasure would create yet more problems in a relationship already strained by religion. With his new world wealth and resources, Philip was sure to one day to apply those means against the heretic queen of England. She knew it would come and had quietly begun to build a navy that might somehow outmaneuver the Spanish fleet.

But not today for such worries. Suddenly, she was a wealthy sovereign – surely she was entitled to one day's enjoyment of the welcome news. She leaned back on the lavishly upholstered seat of her barge and turned her face to catch the sun. As she did so, a small craft far across the river caught her eye. Too distant to read the name, she felt certain she had seen the sail before. She ignored it and directed her boatswain to stop at Coudenoure.

As they neared the small dock, Elizabeth caught sight of Anne sitting on its end, dabbling her feet in the water. Contrary to her usual ebullient greeting, Anne stood and shifted uneasily on her feet. She curtsied prettily as Elizabeth came ashore pretending not to notice the total wreck of her favorite's dress.

"Good day, Lady Anne," she called gaily.

"Majesty," came the slow reply as Anne looked down river nervously.

Elizabeth suddenly realized where she had seen the sail she had noted on her way up river. With a quick turn, she whispered to the captain of her guard. He nodded and smiled and ordered one of the barges back out onto the river. Its oarsmen turned the vessel towards Woolwich.

Anne looked worriedly at Elizabeth.

"Majesty, perhaps we should talk."

"I should like that very much indeed!" exclaimed Elizabeth. "But first, tell me, where are your siblings? Master Michael? Lady Catherine?"

"Oh, Catherine is fine, although the child cannot keep secrets, Majesty."

"Hmm," Elizabeth intoned thoughtfully. "And Michael?"

"The secret is about Michael," she turned her ebony eyes on Elizabeth and continued in a half whisper. "You see, Majesty, he is sailing for the new world today, and Catherine has gone to tell Papa. And, I must confess, I am not certain how sea-worthy his craft may be."

Anne pondered for a second. "But Michael is a fine sailor, and he promised, should I help him with the boat, that he would bring me treasure."

"My barge has just left for Woolwich, so 'tis likely they will pass Master Michael as he sets forth. I am sure they will inspect the craft and see to his safety."

A cloud seemed to lift from Anne's delicate features. She smiled and Elizabeth's heart skipped a beat, for the resemblance between Anne and her namesake had never lessened. For Elizabeth, it was as if she were looking upon the mother she had barely known.

They walked hand in hand to the drive of Coudenoure and then progressed along it as Anne pointed out the various flowers and grasses, proudly calling them by their proper names.

Bess opened the front door and waited for them with a stern look upon her face directed at Anne. As they drew closer, Elizabeth bent low and whispered.

"Perhaps, Anne, 'twill be best if you scoot round the corner of the manor, and I talk to your mother first. What do you think?"

Anne's grateful look was delightful. Impetuously, she reached her arms around Elizabeth's neck and kissed her heartily on the cheek before scampering away.

The two women settled, as always, in their chairs before the library fire.

Quinn joined them.

"Majesty, Drake and Dee are supping here at Coudenoure this evening. Will you not join us?

Perhaps we can find someone to play a tune and be festive?"

Elizabeth nodded in agreement.

"Michael has set sail today for the new world, Quinn."

"Ah, yes. Catherine told me all about it. The boy is mad about the sea."

He pointed to the hearth, where great fleets of painted, wooden ships battled royally against one another.

"Perhaps Drake can use an apprentice," Elizabeth suggested. Bess turned to her furiously.

"No, I am sure he may not. Michael is a child, not a man."

Elizabeth reached out and patted Bess' hand.

"Friend, today he is a child, tomorrow, no. You must see to his future and prepare to let him go."

"Not today. And have you seen what Catherine does with the gowns you pass along to be recut for her?" Bess turned to the servant and ordered that Catherine be produced. In good time, she appeared, still in the same garish, grubby costume she had worn earlier. Elizabeth stifled her laughter.

"Majesty, I see you smile. So you like my dress, do you?" inquired Anne.

Elizabeth nodded.

"Then I shall have one made for you as well!" She ran from the room, calling out to her nanny for help with the project.

A moment's quiet contentment settled upon the three of them.

"You have done well, Bess, and Quinn. Well indeed."

Bess nodded.

"My life is quiet and complete, for Quinn is my partner in all I do."

The two exchanged a loving glance. Elizabeth waved her hand and peered upwards.

"Wait," she said wryly, "For I believe I hear the sound of heavenly doves descending upon the two of you. Really. You should have the occasional fight just for form if for no other reason."

The afternoon drew on and as promised, guests arrived. Dinner at Coudenoure was a familial event whether guests were present or not. A hearty feast of lamb and pork with sour bread and fruit was laid before them, and the conversation rose to a merry babble. Afterwards, the children were put to bed and there was dancing and drinking. A fine evening.

Periodically, Elizabeth looked about her wistfully, absorbing the happy chaos that was Coudenoure: the toys on the floor; the packs of children running through the great halls; the servants who were as much family as employees; the constant projects of nature, architecture, art and music constantly engaged in by all who lived there. Her court by necessity was formal, and this place, these people, were the only ones with whom she might dismiss her guard and be carefree. Bess and Quinn were the happiest people she had ever known, and she wondered how that could be. Even her love for Dudley knew bounds and reached the end of its tether when they spent too many days in one another's company. But despite seldom leaving their estate, Bess and Quinn never quarreled and never engaged in harsh words. Their love seemed not passionate but deep, slow and ever burning regardless of the season of life.

Chapter Eighteen

The candles burned brightly at Coudenoure. True to her word, Elizabeth had provided tutors for the children. They had arrived with fear in their eyes and learning sputtering from their lips even as they stepped from the carriage, for they reported directly to the queen. They knew not the nature of the relationship between the strange family which lived at the isolated estate and the queen, nor did they ever dare ask. Cecil, now Lord Burghley in honor of his great service to Elizabeth, had vetted them carefully through layer upon layer of family, background, temperament and beliefs. Only then had they been interviewed by Elizabeth. She tested them carefully, for she had no desire to see the enthusiasm of her young kin dampened in any way – she merely wanted it augmented so that whatever road they chose, they would take with them a deep knowledge of the type she herself had always found invaluable.

Had her involvement ended at that juncture, their work might have flowed more easily. But it did not. Elizabeth found that in planning for Anne's, Michael's and Catherine's education she was transported back to the one area of her own childhood which was not tainted by fear and terror. The memories of primers, of practice pages and of hours spent learning everything from geography to mathematics made her happy, and she sublimated those memories to her efforts on behalf of Bess' children. It was demanded that each tutor present his lesson plans to her for review. She studied them assiduously, and was frequently heard cursing loudly at points which displeased her. Language lesson reviews in particular took years off their lives, and more than one of them lit a candle in the chapel before going in to see the queen at the appointed hour. Only after such study of the materials they presented and proposed, and with the tutor happily on bended knee – for it signaled the end of the interview was near – would she carefully re-write the curriculum to her satisfaction. She realized that had she not been fated to wear the crown, she would have been happy performing the task endlessly. There was a certain entrancing rhythm to the work. The entire exercise confirmed her in the knowledge that she was a stickler, and an unwelcome one to all but herself.

As Quinn chased butterflies, collected bark, boiled chemicals and wrote ever more esoteric monographs about his findings, Bess hammered her way through a small quarry's worth of stone. The children on the estate were fascinated by their mistress who turned ordinary, ugly rock into delicate renderings of the very estate on which they lived. Here was the façade of the manor house; here a bust of Quinn; there, perhaps a fragile depiction of the great elm which graced the hill crest just outside Coudenoure's wall. Occasionally she would have one of the children sit for her but they had soon learned to recognize the look which usually accompanied such requests as they had the tedious amount of time usually involved and the strict orders issued concerning fidgeting. Not even sugared scones were worth such torture. The result was an absence of children whenever Bess looked round for a new project. In the corner of her studio was a bust upon which she worked slowly and only intermittently. It was of a man with long locks and striking features. His head was turned slightly as though responding to some call from afar and his eyes, even cast as they were from marble, showed a man in search of a vision, one who was driven by passions and understanding that was rare if not unique. Quinn had questioned her about him one day.

"Should I be jealous, Bess, for I see you take great care and work with a loving touch upon your mystery man."

She only smiled. Quinn gave a nervous grin – he had never got over feeling that he would wake one day and find that such a creature as Bess loving him was only a fleeting dream. She patted his cheek.

"Do not be a nit, Quinn."

"Well, then…who is it?"

She had stared at the man emerging from her stone before answering.

"'Tis my father."

She said nothing further.

With the arrival of the children, the tutors, two new cooks (also from Elizabeth) and various nannies and workmen (to whom Quinn could frequently be seen giving direction in the construction of yet another outbuilding), Coudenoure had become a hub of bustling activity. The servants' cottages behind the estate were now full, and Bess had determined to make the estate self-sufficient. Norman, their stableman, had taken on two young apprentices, and a miller was hired to coordinate grain production and storage. Bess took inordinate pride when she walked through fields which had lain fallow since her great-grandfather's day. The ripe wheat heads waved gently as far as the eye could see. Field after field had been planted and Margaret, the new cook, had immediately commandeered Quinn's glass house when she realized it meant she could grow greens even in the winter. Quinn had easily acquiesced, which had initially puzzled Bess and the woman.

"Madam, I had thought he would put up a fight. 'Tis why I asked you to stand with me whilst I told him." She brushed flour from her hair with a hand smattered in flour. Her hair, a salt and pepper mix neatly tucked beneath a cook's bonnet, seemed the same as before.

"Indeed, Margaret, indeed." Bess was more than a little curious and a bit apprehensive, too, for Quinn's dislike of confrontation was not the same as an absence of backbone when something important to him was at stake.

Two months later, three large wagons rumbled up the drive – a master glazier had arrived with his crew to begin work on a second, yet more elaborate conservatory. Quinn had only smiled at Bess and Margaret and gone about his business.

*****

Christmas 1578

In the end, he left her.

Elizabeth hid her agony and heartache beneath a façade of furious wrath. Only she knew her heart.

Dudley had left her for another. Not just left, but left and *married* another. Why? The question refused to lie still within her mind, but pushed and shoved its way to the front of all her thoughts. Morning, noon and night it dug its talons into her consciousness, demanding an answer but receiving none, for she had none. He had left her and that was all she knew. He left despite the gifts she had insisted rain down upon him over the years. Why, his perpetual income from her own purse was no less than twenty thousand pounds each year! He left despite the titles she had bestowed upon him. He left despite the estates, the accolades from she herself, despite the protection she had provided him against all those who spoke in her ear with sharp vitriol against him!

He left her. In the end, he left her.

Her nights became tortured as she lay awake, trying to find within her memories the moment he must have begun the deceit. He surely had not married the woman with no planning and no foreknowledge. So there had to have been a moment in which he decided to go forward with the foul scheme. One moment he must have thought, "I shall not hurt my lifelong friend and queen", and the next, "Yes, I shall do it anyway". And afterwards, well, he had not even found the courage to tell her. She had been left to discover his falseness from rumors within her own court. She relived the day endlessly.

It was a Tuesday afternoon, quite leisurely. The winter rains were upon London and outside the world was dreary and damp. The malaise which sometimes settled in as autumn closed its shutters sat heavily upon her ladies that afternoon and their melancholy mood was contagious. She had no desire for work, and Dudley was not there to regale her with his endless humor and gossip. On impulse, she clapped her hands and demanded her musicians come forth.

Two hours later, in the great hall at Hampton Court, the furniture had been put aside, sweets and fruit such as might ameliorate the malaise were laden upon side tables, while Elizabeth and her women practiced their dance steps and invented new ones. The pensive gloom of the early day gave way to jolly glee as they pranced, ate and enjoyed themselves on the dance floor with no men to judge or assess their movements. The exercise and music seemed to relieve all but two of them of their moodiness. Lady Mary and Lady Beatrice of Riverstill stood aloof in the corner eating plums and whispering in one another's ears. But they were not whispering love secrets from this or that courtier, for Elizabeth noticed that no giggle or smile, nor even a blush, accompanied their talk. She stopped dancing mid-song and summoned them.

"I notice, my ladies, that you do not partake of our pleasure this afternoon, but prefer to closet yourselves away in a corner."

Both women blushed.

Hearing the tone in the queen's voice, her ladies gathered round and the music faded. But only silence met the queen's increasing curiosity.

"To resist such fun on such a dreary day, well, you must have something very worthwhile to discuss. Pray share it with us!"

She looked around and her ladies nodded enthusiastically. The blush became a crimson rose. Elizabeth grew tired of their silence.

"What were you discussing? Hmm? I demand that you tell me immediately."

Finally, both women began to stutter.

"You see, Majesty..." said Lady Mary.

"Majesty, it seems that Lord Robert..."

My Lord Robert?" Elizabeth exclaimed, looking around and laughing. "You have news of my Dudley?"

Finally, Lady Mary closed her eyes and blurted it out.

"Majesty, he is married. In September last, he married the Countess of Essex, Lady Lettice Knollys."

A great stillness settled upon the room. The musicians evaporated into thin air.

"I am sorry," Elizabeth spoke quietly, "But I do not believe I heard you correctly. You must repeat yourself."

And so hell had descended upon her.

*****

Bess was startled. It was the new girl, Jane, who had recently joined Coudenoure. Bess tried to place her as she spoke.

"Someone is here? To see me?"

Jane bowed again and shifted on her feet. Her cotton blue-print frock was overlaid with a cook's white apron. Her small white cap accentuated her pale features and light brown hair. Jane, Margaret's daughter – yes, that was it. Bess finally placed her in her mind. She had recently joined her mother at Coudenoure from some estate to which she had been apprenticed in the southland. There was a backstory of sorts – something about having failed to live up to the estate's expectations of a scullery maid. Bess was not sure about any of that, but she had noticed the child had a way with pastry.

"Who is it?" she asked, wiping her brow and putting down her mallet.

She repeated her question to the girl.

"'Tis a man, M'lady, 'tis a very short, but a not so round man."

Bess smiled despite herself.

"What else?" She was hoping for a name.

Thoughtful silence.

"Well, I must say, M'lady, he has a lovely hat. All nice and tall but not too tall. More round really."

Jane's voice faded as Bess walked to the manor house shaking her head. She tucked her hair haphazardly into its caul and opened the library door.

"Lord Burghley!" she exclaimed and bowed.

William Cecil turned from the window and smiled. His face had aged considerably since her time at court. His hooded eyes seemed darker but wiser somehow. He still wore his dark robes and ecclesiastical sash – Bess suddenly realized she had never seen him in anything but. He moved slowly from the window towards her and Bess noticed he favored one leg.

"Ah, yes, young Bess, you see my knee is quite stiff these days."

"Young Bess," Bess smiled and indicated a chair, "I have not been called *young Bess* in many a year."

"You are surprised to see me here?"

"Indeed."

"Madame, I have come on serious business."

Bess called for tea and scones and they settled in before the fire to wait. A few minutes later Jane appeared, placing a tea tray on the table between them. She stared at Cecil's hat in a fixed manner.

"That will be all, Jane," Bess repeated before the child collected herself and left.

"Bess, the queen is most upset."

Bess waited. She had heard a rumor from Margaret who had heard it from the cook at Greenwich Palace in the market, but she could not believe it. Cecil confirmed her worst thoughts.

"Lord Robert Dudley has seen fit to marry Lettice Knollys."

"Bastard."

"Madame!"

Bess looked him squarely in the eye.

"He has courted her all these years and now he leaves her? What is that except base behavior of the worst kind? Hmm? The most egregious form of devilry and for our Majesty to have to suffer it publicly at her own court, well..."

Cecil had to talk over her to gain a toehold in the conversation.

"Yes, yes, Bess, we all agree, but that is not the problem. The problem is that our Majesty has suffered a blow and it has brought her quite low. So low in fact that she is not herself."

More tea.

"You see, I believe a change of scenery would do her all the good in the world. But she mopes about, refuses to look at many items of important business, and does not enjoy her own exercise or meals. I am very worried."

"She must come here." Bess spoke more to herself than to Cecil. "Yes, here where she is beloved and can gain some respite."

"She will not, for I have given her the same advice."

Bess smiled.

"I am glad you thought of us."

Cecil sighed as he looked around the library.

"A brilliant library, a tiny estate, artistic children that babble artistic gibberish in six languages, an odd husband if there ever was one, servants who stare at my hat-"

"Yes, she was quite taken with it."

"What is there not to love about Coudenoure?"

"The Yuletide is upon us," declared Bess, "Let us, you and I, arrange a Christmas feast in her honor. We shall invite those who love her, Cecil, and who are sure to bring cheer to her sad heart."

"'Tis a fine idea," Cecil agreed, "And I shall also choose out those who will entertain – Frobisher is recently returned from one of his infernal and catastrophically expensive voyages – I am also certain he feeds his crew money rather than actual food. Did I tell you..."

Bess cut him off politely.

"The ball, Cecil, the ball."

"Ah, yes, well, I believe Drake is in country as well. There is also a young playwright recently trying to attain entry to court, one Christopher Marlowe – yes, 'tis a splendid idea, Bess."

"And musicians, Cecil, for dancing is a great remedy for a broken heart."

Cecil agreed, rubbing his hands together as though a great weight had been lifted from him. Bess poured more tea and they spent the next hour gossiping like old friends, for time had erased any differences they may once have had, and now bound them together in common cause. A sudden noise, not quite a scraping nor yet a knock, stopped Cecil mid-sentence. Bess smiled, put down her cup and moved to the door. The noise stopped suddenly and she returned to her seat.

"The children have learned of the listening post," she explained. "A piece of loose mortar in the wall yon," she pointed to the stone wall dividing the library from the main hall, "when removed, it allows one to listen to conversations here in the library."

Cecil smiled as she continued in a light vein.

"I know it has been employed since the time of my great grandfather Thomas. I shall leave them to believe they are the first to make its discovery."

That evening, the mince pie arrived on the dining table in a pastry shell exactly the size and shape of William Cecil's hat. But as either a fashion commentary upon what she believed Cecil's cap was in need of, or from pure artistic whimsy, Jane had added a lone, long peacock feather which rose and waved majestically from her creation. Catherine promptly grabbed it, shaved off the end originally in the pie, and put it in her hair.

"We shall have a ball and I will meet many courtiers who will fall at my feet." She waved her head gently to make the feather sway majestically.

"They will fall at your feet, sister, if you trip them. Perhaps that is your plan?" Michael spoke in answer to Catherine's remark but his eyes remained on Jane as she disappeared into the kitchen, only to reappear with yet another meat pie, this one in the shape of a ship, complete with stick masts and pastry sails. Even Quinn, in the middle of a lengthy explanation to Bess as to the rightfulness of the placement of bee's wings, paused and stared.

As she placed her work mid-table, she caught Michael's mesmerized gaze, blushed and retreated yet again. He sighed. He would be off to apprentice soon and if he did not find the courage to speak to her the moment might pass. Anne saw his look and squeezed his hand under the table.

"Courage, Michael, you must have courage. She is but a simple maid." She smiled at him, and as always, he took heart in her words. Catherine was not so kind.

"She made a meat pie in the shape of a ship, you nit. Do you think it was for Anne, or perhaps me? Um? You need not courage but a kick in the pants."

Bess looked at her sternly. Catherine smiled and bobbed her head again, enjoying the feel of the peacock feather as it waved gaily.

"Will the queen give us gowns? I have none suitable for such an affair."

"You have plenty, dear, as the queen has blessed you with many gowns already."

"But if I am to impress my future husband…"

"Put that peacock feather in your hair – that should tell him your measure." Michael laughed at his own joke. Jane listened at the door and smiled. He was such an interesting man. And such lovely hair, all thick and dark and curly.

While Anne, Michael and Catherine spoke of Yuletide events, Elizabeth continued listening to Quinn's talk about his latest project and the upcoming monograph which he planned to print and publish himself: *The Wily Bumble Bee and Why He Sees Fit to Buzz*. She patted his hand and smiled at him encouragingly as he waxed poetic about bee's legs and insect wings, but even the children's excited chatter and Quinn's earnest talk could not distract her from the afternoon conversation she had had with Cecil. Her heart ached for Elizabeth.

Bess looked at her beloved husband as he rattled on and tried to imagine her life should he suddenly decide to leave. Perhaps he would live once again at Tyche, or follow his heart to the new world and find there a new woman. Just the thought produced a terrified melancholy and she put it quickly from her mind. For Elizabeth, the devastation must have been near complete. Dudley had likewise been her companion since childhood. And he had not the courage to tell her himself.

"Mother, why are you so quiet?"

It was Anne, always alert to the feelings and moods of others. Always compassionate. Her resemblance to her great grandmother, Henry's beloved Elizabeth, obvious since childhood, had never left her, the dark eyes and raven hair most particularly.

"She is wondering how she and Papa may best defend me against so many suitors at the ball." Catherine, with her quick wit and sharp tongue, was always at the ready. With her blond curls and blue eyes, she was beautiful by any standard and she knew it.

Bess almost snorted.

"Child, do you think of nothing but gowns and marriage and men?"

Catherine pretended to consider the question seriously before giving her reply.

"No. I do not believe I do." More head waving with eyes turned upwards.

That night, as she lay next to Quinn, Bess reached out and held his hand under the covers.

"We are so fortunate, you and I," she whispered.

"I know it, my love."

"And Dudley did not even tell her – what a churl."

"Girl?"

"Churl."

"What is a burl?"

"Churl, Quinn! Churl!"

"Curl? Dudley is a curl?"

The soft shaking of the covers gave him away as Quinn stifled a laugh.

"Your wit – 'tis not what you think it to be," Bess smiled in the dark.

"Nit? Are you calling me a nit? Or a pit? Or a…"

Bess rolled over and Quinn threw his arm comfortably around her, pulling her close.

"Sit! You want me to sit? Or knit perhaps?"

Still smiling, Bess drifted easily into a deep sleep.

*****

They were awakened by a hammering coming from Bess' studio.

"Tell your daughter to stop, please!" Quinn's voice was thick with sleep.

Bess rubbed her foot against his leg before pushing it, albeit gently, towards the edge.

"*My* daughter! You were the one who told her that she had no talent for painting! Get up, man, and go tell her yourself."

"I do not understand – she is not painting, she is taking a marvelous piece of God's own creation and turning it into an abomination!"

They both giggled – Anne's decision to take up sculpting too had produced large piles of chips and flakes, a lopsided jagged stone which for some weeks she had insisted was "coming along", but not much else.

"Her talents lie elsewhere," Bess giggled again.

"Let us hope she finds them shortly."

And so began the day of the ball. Anne was still hammering away when Catherine joined her mid-morning. The two girls were as unlike as the sun and the moon, but fiercely protective of one another on a deep and invisible level. On a more superficial one, they could not have seemed to have cared less.

"Ah, I begin to see," Catherin opined as she walked round Anne's work space, carefully inspecting the stone and the artist at work.

"Yes?" Anne said excitedly. "It was just a matter of time, you see, before I understood the full scope of the project. Mother always says that one must see the art locked within the marble."

"Indeed, I *do* see. All of this time we have been thinking that the marble block was to be transformed – a figure released from it! From the confines in which it has lain for centuries. But no, sister! Clearly, you are focused on a pile of chips as art! That is the purpose of your work! How could we have missed it?"

Anne chuckled as she pushed a stray hair from her face. Silently, she raised an eyebrow and passed her mallet and spike to Catherine. In turn, Catherine raised her hands and backed away.

"I paint. That is what I do, not this. If mother and father insist that we all develop our creative talents…"

"If?" laughed Anne. "Sister, they are not normal, those two. I fear for our futures, I truly do. What man will want women who speak a thousand tongues and spend their days at such folly as this?"

She swept her arm to include the entire studio while Catherine nodded.

"'Tis why the queen helps us so much, I am certain – she feels sympathy for our plight. We are not even allowed to go to court by mother and papa. 'Tis shameful!"

Anne looked at her speculatively.

"Catherine, you have pronounced a problem which has troubled me for some time."

Catherine was pleased. Too often, she felt, she was viewed as flighty and inconsequential by her family. She knew that she was not, but understood that her rare good looks and timely wit frequently blinded even those closest to her true nature, which, in her opinion, was simply too complex and deep for almost anyone else to understand. She smiled happily as Anne continued.

"Why *does* the queen take such an interest in us? Hmm? She does not roam England, Catherine, seeking out maids with obscure titles and estates in order to give them gowns and tutors and royal attention."

"I suppose not," Catherine opened her eyes to Anne's pursuit of the mystery. "Why, just last summer she sat with you for hours as you practiced your writing."

"Exactly," Anne concurred, "And the two of us always discuss the library."

"Ah, well that. 'Tis because you love it so much and she sees that."

"But sister, think. I do indeed enjoy it. I love cataloguing the books and reading them. I hope one day to write of our vast collection. But why would the queen care about that?"

They remained silent, each turning their new enigma over in her mind.

"And something else," Catherine added quietly, "Why would the highest minister in the land call upon mother and ask her for advice about the queen and her mood? Why would it even be appropriate for Coudenoure to host a ball?"

Anne ran her finger over the rough surface of her marble without answering. Catherine soon tired – she knew her sister to be thoughtfully moody, and when such affliction (as Catherine saw it) came upon her, it was pointless to attempt further conversation. She left to seek out Michael. Perhaps he needed further advisement concerning his budding besottedness with Jane, though what he saw in a mere kitchen maid was not clear to her at all.

Absently, Anne picked up a nearby pumice stone and began gently rubbing the edge of her work. Catherine's departure did nothing to quell her speculation.

"Why indeed does the highest minister in the land come to Coudenoure?" she mumbled to herself. "And why the queen?"

Her childhood at Coudenoure had been played out against a vast, rhythmic and seemingly eternal backdrop. The fields and meadows, the high hills and ridges, the darkly wooded forests – the very essence of eternity. The slow awakening of each day as the estate came to life – the workers in the fields, the miller with his oxen, papa with his endless fascinations, mother holding it all together somehow in a steady weave across the loom – this was her world, punctuated only by the quiet progression of the seasons as they rolled gently past. It was an isolated, idyllic childhood, one in which only books and the occasional visitor gave a glimpse of the world beyond. There was nothing of note about the estate save its calm and steady presence in the world. And yet Elizabeth visited. The queen of all the realm visited this particular backwater estate. Why?

She could not remember a time when Queen Elizabeth did not make regular appearances. Indeed, these visits stood out against the estate's fabric all the more for the simple reason that hardly anyone else of note from the outside world ever

bothered to come to Coudenoure. Certainly Papa
had his fellow madmen, men who dreamed of other
worlds and of changing this one, too, but they
seldom engaged with the family, choosing instead
to disappear into Papa's workshop for days on end.
It was only as Anne had come of age that she began
to realize the distinctive nature of Elizabeth's visits.
It had begun when she was old enough to notice the
deference paid the queen by those who attended
upon her. When she arrived by barge, accompanied
usually by a not-so-small flotilla of guardsmen,
Anne began to notice the bowing, scraping, and the
immediate response paid to the Elizabeth's slightest
whim or order.

On occasion, Elizabeth appeared at Coudenoure
with a handful of courtiers – most prominent among
them one Robert Dudley. Even though he was
clearly her favorite, and even though they clearly
enjoyed a deep and meaningful friendship,
nevertheless, he too danced to her wishes. When
she was serious, he offered statesman-like advice
and counsel; when she was sad, he entertained her
with gossip and laughter; when tired, consolation
and simple companionship.

But while Anne could surely map the strangeness
of it all, she could not see a reason for it.
Occasionally, she was almost certain that she caught
furtive glances pass between her parents when
Elizabeth's name came up in a conversation. But try
as she might, she could not ascertain their reason –
the looks seemed tethered neither to any particular

topic nor to any one visit. They seemed random to her, and it was this randomness that she had patiently stored away with the other mounting evidence that there was some unknown tie between Coudenoure and the queen. But what? As she stood rubbing the marble before her, a sudden reflection from the past caught in the folds of her conscious mind and she stopped and raised her head, staring at nothing and everything. There it was.

Without bidding, an ancient memory of Prudence rose in her mind. She, Anne, was sitting in the old woman's lap in the kitchen. She knew it to be Prudence, for the woolen dress she always wore – a pale blue with a gray apron – never seemed to have quite made it through the fulling process. The result was a blend of aromas and streaks which Anne always and only associated with Prudence. That smell was part of what she was now recalling. And Bess. Yes, her mother was nearby – was she sitting across the table from them? Or reaching down to stroke her hair as she spoke? As far back as her memories went, Bess' hands were rough and slightly gnarled, the result of the endless hard work she performed in her studio. Anne unconsciously touched her face as the memory came upon her. Yes, it was her mother's hand. But all of that was backdrop to the few words which had come forward with the memory.

"Bess, child, you must tell her one day."

Her mother's hand, gentle and kind on her face.

"Why? It will all pass into history and should she know it, it would only bring trouble."

Prudence shook her head.

"Look at her, Bess. Look at your child. And what you cannot see I will see for you. I knew them all. She is Anne. She is Elizabeth. The queen sees it as well."

"It will pass," Bess insisted, as though determined to protect her child.

"No, it will not," came Prudence's forceful reply, "For it was clear at birth as it is now. And the ring? Have you not seen the ring?"

The door opened and Jane appeared in the studio shattering the moment.

"Lady Bess says you must prepare for the dance, M'lady."

Anne nodded in an acquiescing manner – she wanted nothing but to be left alone again. But as Jane closed the door, Anne realized the memory was gone.

"What ring?" she wondered, and began pounding at her marble once more.

*****

Coudenoure was not grand, but its ancient architecture made it seem so. The high arched ceilings of the quondam monastery, medieval in form and vast in perspective, gave a quality of timeless grace to its interior spaces. The expansive carpets which lay upon its cold stone floors and the ancient tapestries which covered its equally cold stone walls muted the noise of the day-to-day world of the estate, lending a serene hush to all activity within. The family's activities revolved around the library, the kitchen, and the workshops of Bess and Quinn. The great rooms were seldom opened, for even with the children they were simply not needed save for special occasions. The stone construction meant the rooms were always cool and the great hearths of the monastery were always lit if only for a slow burn. While Quinn had seen fit to refit his own workshop, as Bess had done her studio, neither of them felt the main features and rooms of Coudenoure should be touched. They remained as they had been for centuries. Should those who came before suddenly stumble through time and find themselves back at Coudenoure, they would have recognized it in an instant. Bess found the continuity and antiquity comforting, as did her husband.

Bess was deeply satisfied with the self-sufficiency of the estate. The monies from the state treasury were still allocated by Elizabeth on an annual basis, and Bess accepted them happily. She tucked them away carefully, not even mentioning to Quinn the growing horde of hard coinage. Cecil occasionally stopped by the estate, and as its prosperity became more and more evident, his suspicion grew commensurately. His inquiries became so routine as to be almost scripted, for while his accountancy skills were legendary, so too was his almost complete lack of subtlety.

"Madame," so the conversation always began, "I notice Coudenoure does well this year."

"Indeed," would come the pat response from Bess. She knew his next statement by heart, but she had come to enjoy the formality and routine of the exchange.

"Our good and dear Majesty has many estates, you know."

A nod was called for and given by Bess. At this juncture, the script called for a deep sigh from Cecil. Occasionally, he removed his black woolen hat for emphasis.

"Many of them, Bess, suffer, for they do not have the sure and brilliant guidance you and Quinn so ably provide for Coudenoure."

Early on in these exchanges, Bess had bristled, for Quinn was oblivious to the running of the estate. In fact, she had often thought of staging her own investigation along the lines of one of her husband's experiments. How long would it take him to realize no one had called him for dinner or supper? She suspected that days rather than hours would be the outcome of the trial. But time had rendered her indifferent to Cecil's male-oriented view of God's division of brains amongst his creatures and she now ignored the innuendo. In fact, she mostly ignored all innuendo and found she was happier in doing so. As always, Cecil coughed at this point to pull her back from what he viewed as the feminine inability to focus. Indeed.

"Lord Burghley, you are too kind in your praise," Bess would give a shallow curtsey at this point, "As our good queen is too kind in her support of our small and inconsequential estate. Why, sir, were it not for her support I do not know what would happen!"

What would happen is that she would be forced to spend her ever-accruing coinage, something she had no intention of doing. This was not part of the ritualized conversation, only of her ritualized thoughts in this regard.

Another deep sigh from Cecil.

"Madame, at any point I would be happy to inspect your expenditure lists, your books, to see if I might be able to assist you. Who knows? Perhaps there are pockets of expenses which might save you

money, and think of that! Think upon what you
could do with such surplus!"

"Ah," would come the closing remark from Bess,
"I surely appreciate your offer, but I believe Quinn
prefers to keep his own accounts." It was only a
small lie. God would forgive it she was certain.
"And should we ever be fortunate enough to run a
surplus, why, Lord Burghley, we would never
dream of retaining it but would swiftly return it to
your safe-keeping!" A bigger lie. No certainty as to
God's thoughts on this one.

Part of those necessary if thought by some to be
extravagant expenses were bees' wax candles rather
than the usual ones fashioned from animal fat.
Quinn in his later years had developed a cough and
Bess found that the bees' wax light lessened his
discomfort. Quinn himself had only noticed he
coughed less.

Prior to the evening's festivities, Margaret and
Jane had marshalled the servants for a thorough
cleaning of the manor house. It was at this point
that Jane's second extraordinary skill came to light:
she was a task master. As shy as she was even yet
around the family, in equal measure did she dole
out orders to her fellow servants. For two days, her
barking commands could be heard throughout the
house. By the third day, exhaustion and a high-
regard for her organizational skills were written in
equal measure across everyone's faces. Out of
concern that fear might be the next emotion to play

across those same countenances, Bess and Quinn declared the cleaning venture a wild success and ordered ale for all who had participated. At this refreshment, Jane was not so much extolled as avoided. Except by Michael. A woman who could command, clean, cook and love him – what else was there to be sought from life? In his imagination, he launched himself upon endless fantasies of adventures by sea – and adventures at home with his wife…Jane. The detail was fuzzy but the intent and determination grew almost daily. Catherine chided him endlessly, but Anne was his true confidante.

"You must needs win over our parents," she told him as they sat together one evening in the kitchen. They had both slipped off their shoes and were warming their feet before the dying fire of the main hearth. "They may have their own ideas as to your future wife."

Michael scoffed.

"Sister, those two!"

Anne giggled, her usual acknowledgement of the eccentric natures of Bess and Quinn. Michael proceeded to tell her of his plan.

"I shall apprentice soon with one of father's friends," he began.

"...I hear someone – Drake? – a great sea captain, will be at our gathering," Anne interrupted.

Michael nodded excitedly.

"Yes – I am very hopeful. In any event, sister, after my apprenticeship I shall come home in glory and propose to my beloved Jane!"

Anne smiled, happy to see him so pleased.

"That sounds like an excellent plan – and with you going off to sea…"

Now it was Michael's turn to interrupt.

"Exactly! With my departure on a long adventure at sea, well, they will have to give in to my will. And, sister, do not forget: At that point I shall be a man."

Anne nodded.

"You may have to wait until the completion of your first voyage – an apprenticeship is not the same as a becoming a seasoned professional."

Michael waved his hand as though doing so would make all problems with his vision evaporate.

"Be that as it may be. 'Tis fine! The end result will be a pleasant life with my Jane."

They munched happily on the pastry crisps which had been left out for them by said Jane. Life was fine.

*****

Before the guests arrived Quinn knocked tentatively on his own bedroom door. Michael stood close behind him. They had been warned that under no circumstances should they enter until specifically ordered thus. A mild scurrying, a little giggle and then a voice floated through the door.

"*Entre*, Papa!"

He did as he was told, surveyed those within and immediately began to cry. After a moment, he collected himself and spoke.

"What have I done to deserve such a family as this? Such beautiful daughters and my wife! My wife! Bess, you look like their sister, not their mother."

He came further into the room and sat before the fire. Michael sat opposite him. The fire glowed and candles lit the far walls.

"Now, each of you must do a turn before me and Michael so that we may appreciate your beauty and grace."

First was Catherine. A gown of fine silk, the palest of blues, had been fitted for her. The corset dropped to a sharp V at the waist, accentuating her lithe, slim figure. As she twirled a great swishing arose and she batted her eyes happily at her father. Michael clapped and Anne stepped forward next. Her gown, also a refit from those provided by Elizabeth, was the hue of a deep burgundy wine. Each girl had carefully chosen the shade that would most flatter her natural color. The blue of Catherine's gown made her eyes impossibly cerulean and deep, while Anne's dress fitted her dark, smoldering looks. Each wore a simple necklace of gold with a golden cross. In the fashion of the day, their hair was pinned, held in place by a jeweled caul consisting of gold netting with fine, small pearls woven into the mesh of the fabric.

Michael clapped once again and as they stepped back and Bess came forward. Quinn's eyes glowed with the love he felt for her – this woman, this marvel of creation who had given him three fine children, who ordered his life and respected his work. God in heaven, he thought, what did I ever do to deserve all of this happiness? Impulsively, he stood, bowed and held out his hand to his loving wife. Bess wore a simple white gown, but around her neck was the familiar ruby cross. Together, they danced slowly across the floor as they gazed into one another's eyes. They needed no music for their hearts sang their own song. They always had. Catherine, Anne and even Michael grew hushed and still as they watched – would they be as lucky?

After a moment, Bess bowed deeply to her partner, kissed him quickly on the lips, and turned to her children.

"Remember, speak when spoken to and girls, no flirting – you must be seen as chaste."

Anne nodded excitedly at her mother; Michael concurred quietly with Bess' directions; Catherine ignored her. Together, they went downstairs.

*****

All were present by the time Elizabeth arrived. Bess was immediately concerned. Cecil had not exaggerated. Elizabeth looked proud, but worn. Deep circles had appeared under her eyes since Bess had seen her last, and for the first time, she was so thin as to appear frail. She greeted her bowing subjects and passed on into the library. Quiet conversation was getting underway when a sudden loud gong sounded.

"What in heaven's good name?" Bess said in puzzlement. Again, a loud gong.

"Quinn?" Quinn was her go-to suspect when something untoward or unusual happened. He shrugged his shoulders and together they stepped into the hall. Jane caught sight of them and smiled happily.

"Jane?" came the query.

"Madame, we found this in the attic. 'Twas used by the monks to call their brothers in from the fields for their evening meal."

"Jane, the monks have not been here for many centuries, and we are not coming in from the fields."

Quinn saw the hurt look on the girl's face and stepped in to mitigate what was clearly viewed as a reprimand.

"'Tis lovely, Jane! And a fine idea as well! And what a festive call to supper!"

Jane brightened and straightened her cap.

"Now, go tell cook we are ready."

Jane left and Bess cut her eyes at Quinn while shaking her head.

"How do you ever bear to kill the insects which you so assiduously pin to every free surface in your workshop? Um? Your heart bleeds too easily, my love."

"I do feel for them, 'tis true. Why, just last week dear…"

"The gong?" Elizabeth interrupted them as they returned to the library.

Bess gave the slightest shake of her head to indicate it was a closed subject even as Quinn raised his voice and continued to discuss his insects. Dee listened to him excitedly. Catherine meanwhile was batting her eyes at a youth whose name Bess could not recall, while Anne was intently focused on the young man Cecil had introduced as a playwright. Hovering near the kitchen door was Michael, who seemed as though he might become apoplectic if he did not soon get another glimpse of his love. The musicians Elizabeth had supplied stopped playing, started up again, and then stopped once more, confused as to their role in the current situation. Elizabeth raised an eyebrow to Bess, who smiled and gave her a half-curtsey, half-nod. Coudenoure and its enduring chaos was home. She began to relax.

As Bess now beckoned their guests to supper, she suddenly realized that Michael was not shuffling about in anticipation of seeing Jane again, but rather was serving as her lookout. A moment of fear took hold of her.

"God in heaven," she whispered to Quinn, "What has that child wrought this time?"

"Whatever it is," came Quinn's reply, "'Tis sure to be covered in pastry."

On that point he was mistaken.

Michael disappeared into the kitchen before joining them minutes later, a bright smile on his face.

While the great room at Coudenoure was large, it was not large enough for a top table for the queen and their higher ranking guests. Instead, a fine chair had been placed for the sovereign at the head of the single, large table. On one side of the queen sat Bess while Cecil with a rather determined look on his face occupied the other. Clearly, business was on his mind. Quinn chose to sit with Dee and Drake at the farthest end of the table, oblivious to protocol and hierarchy. In fact, Dee, Drake and he were already hunched over some sort of scrabble Drake had produced from his pocket. Seeds from some unknown land? Minerals from afar? Special dirt perhaps? Bess almost snorted but instead just shook her head. All conversation ceased, however, as the door to the kitchen opened and Margaret, dressed in her finest linen frock, appeared. A collective gasp went round as the first subtlety was placed on the table. Jane leaned shyly against a far wall, watching the reception of her latest creation.

Bess had never seen such a delicate culinary creation as that which now graced her table. Jane had used marzipan and spun sugar to produce a glittering, icy recreation of Coudenoure in a snow-covered landscape. So real and accurate was her representation that Cecil put his finger out to touch the confectioner's sugar snow which draped the wintry fields and house. As Margaret bowed deeply to Elizabeth, she spoke.

"Margaret, is it not?"

Another deep bow.

"And who makes this subtlety? For even my kitchen cannot produce such fine artistry."

Margaret pulled her daughter close. Jane bowed repeatedly.

"'Tis lovely, child. Ethereal, fleeting and magnificent."

A huge grin broke out across Michael's face as though he himself were responsible for the queen's pleasure. Cecil, in the mood for business, could not hold his tongue.

"Why, Bess," he exclaimed, "'Tis a fine example of why the queen must support Coudenoure! Think how much together we might save her Majesty if we but cut back on such delicacies!"

"Cecil, you are an infernal wart upon cultured society." Elizabeth could be blunt when she chose. Cecil almost took the hint. But as the kitchen servants brought out meat after meat, pastry after pastry, pie after pie, he could not but attempt one last observation.

"Sumptuary laws..." he whispered sternly across the table at Bess, hoping the queen would not hear.

Elizabeth placed her fist on the table laughingly.

"Sumptuary laws allow me to have as many dishes as I choose."

"A sumptuary law? What is that?" The question came from Anne in wide-eyed innocence and once again Cecil looked sternly at Bess. His only answer from her was a deliberate spooning of meat and sauce onto her plate with a shrug in his direction. When the final subtlety appeared with the hippocras he almost fainted. Jane had made a splendid marzipan throne, replete with carving, newels, cushions and jewels, all covered in fantastically colored spun sugar.

The repast was a great success. Elizabeth allowed no one to touch the throne and ordered that it should be sent to Greenwich as an example to her own chefs. Jane beamed from ear to ear.

"I am done, and I wish to speak to the lady of the house alone." Elizabeth announced her intention and stood. "Bess, you will accompany me to the upstairs of your manor where we may speak in private. For you..." she paused and nodded at the remaining guests and family, "…the musicians will play for dancing in the library."

*****

Bess closed the bedroom door behind them. Elizabeth, sure they were alone, sat before the fire before speaking.

"Well, he left me."

"Auntie, the entire kingdom knows that."

Elizabeth smiled.

"You have not called me that in many a year," she observed.

"Yes, well, you have let that cumberground and his nefarious marriage wear you down."

Elizabeth stared into the fire.

"Bess, I have no tears left, no sorrow. Only exhaustion. Truly that man is the devil's own."

Bess remained silent.

"What? No words of advice? Everyone has advice for me these days! Marry a great prince and teach Dudley a bad lesson indeed! Send him to the new world with Drake. Send his *wife* to the new world with Drake; or my favorite one – send them both to Cathay and have their ship burned upon arrival. Umm, yes, now that would be satisfying."

"For how long?"

Elizabeth leaned back and closed her eyes.

"Ah, I see you understand my problem. Dudley's marriage is profane enough…"

"Profane? I was thinking it was more the act of a shallow, witless, offspring of a…"

Elizabeth interrupted.

"'Tis not his marriage that is at the heart of my problem these days. Initially, if I am honest, I must admit it was. But now, 'tis the loss of the man's companionship and friendship which prolongs my grief. Did you know, Bess, only Dudley understood my excessive need for gowns and jewels. We grew up together, and he saw the hardships placed upon me by always being the one without, always being the child "almost good enough" for court. Almost good enough, but never quite. And it mattered not how much I learned or what I did."

Bess again was silent. Elizabeth shot her a look that demanded an answer.

"I suppose 'tis true," Bess finally replied, "But then, so are a great many other things. You rule a vast and splendid kingdom, you have courtiers and princes lining up for your favors and hand in marriage. What is Dudley, after all? Hmm?"

She stood and turned the fire with a nearby poker.

"If you miss Dudley, bring him back to court. If you are too angry to do so, do not. But you cannot change what he did. 'Tis simple."

Elizabeth changed the subject.

"And then there is my cousin, that shrew of a woman, Mary."

"And where is she secreted away these days?"

"Chartley Castle. But I promise you by all that is holy, that woman still plots! Each day I hear rumors upon rumors of Spain this, of France that, all of them wanting me to burn in hell."

"Oh, Auntie, I do not think they want you in hell." Bess paused. "Well, perhaps."

They both giggled.

"Forget your heartache over Dudley – it will pass one way or another. But Mary, now that is a true quandary. And a dangerous one."

"Indeed."

"Do you have a plan?"

"No, but for my advisors, all roads lead to execution."

"And France? Spain?"

"Exactly! Drake and his sort are building a navy, but they must have time. For as surely as I move against Mary they will move against me. Even now Spain amasses an ever-growing fleet. Oh, I know they say 'tis for the new world, but 'tis also to remind me of their power, their will to see me gone. 'Tis only a matter of time. All comes back to time."

Now it was Bess' turn to change the conversation, for she sensed a melancholy settling over Elizabeth.

"You must see Anne's work in my studio."

Elizabeth brightened.

"Ah, she is talented, is she?"

"Oh, Majesty, what she has accomplished will amaze even you. I know that all of us here at Coudenoure have been stunned."

"Let us go dance, and tomorrow, or anon, you will begin chatting with us again here at your home."

Arm in arm they walked down the hall.

"Tell me, does that music seem uncommonly loud? For it plainly stirs me even up here."

"Yes, and what is that noise? Singing?"

Bess' brow furrowed.

"Surely Quinn did not leave our guests alone."

Elizabeth gave a wicked grin full of anticipation.

"Our guests? You mean your children and the other young people? Let us find out!" There was no need to open the library doors, or the door to the great room, nor to Quinn's workshop at the end of the hall. All stood wide and from all poured din.

By the window in the library three young men sat singing a ditty of unknown tune. Loudly. Beside them, so they would not have to bother carrying their cups, was a bowl of wassail. Catherine and the young officer (what *was* his name?) stood alone where the furniture had been pushed back to make way for dancing. Her hands, small and white, rested gently on his shoulders while his arms encircled her waist. The musicians were performing a lively tune suitable for dancing but the two of them had long since stopped moving as they stared, entranced, into one another's eyes.

In a far corner by the vast shelves sat Anne with Marlowe. A table had been pulled close and the two of *them* sat side by side. In fact, Marlowe, ostensibly to get close enough so that they might both inspect the manuscript laid out before them on the table, had carefully placed his arm along the back of Anne's chair. Close, indeed.

Elizabeth was now enjoying herself.

"But where is the other one?" she whispered. "Perhaps with his tart?" She cackled with laughter at her own pun. "Bess, his *tart*?"

"She is a talented scullery maid."

They entered the kitchen and yes, there was Michael, paying rapt attention as Jane demonstrated the making of pressed biscuits. The two of them never even noticed Bess and Elizabeth. Nor did they even seem to hear the sudden rumbling coming down the hall from the direction of Quinn's workshop. Out of a cloud billowing smoke scampered Cecil with the other men skipping quickly behind. Quinn closed the door, dusted his clothing, straightened his collar and began walking back to the party as though nothing had occurred.

Elizabeth nearly collapsed in tears and laughter on the stairway.

"Oh, God in heaven, Bess, wherever will it all end?"

Bess sat beside her but refused to be jollied. After a moment, Elizabeth rose, made a patent imitation of Quinn dusting his clothing, and still chuckling announced her departure.

"'Twas a fine evening, but we shall all now take our leave, for I am certain the lady of the house has need to speak with her family."

And that was that. For the first time in her life, Bess considered exploring the wondrous effects of too much ale.

Chapter Nineteen

Christmas 1579

The gray North Sea waters were chopped and
frothy. With each rise and fall of the massive prow
of the ship, an icy surge showered the decks with a
chilling spray. A strong headwind blew off the
coast of France, and as the tiny fleet beat northward,
every sailor and officer alternating their gaze
continuously between England's distant coast on the
leeward side and the waters ahead in which they
sailed. The coastline would tell the seasoned hands
what they needed to know of shoals, coves and
rocky graveyards – dead reckoning was in their
blood, a skill learned and passed through
generations. But as a heavy mist began to descend
upon them, obliterating even their fellow ships, only
the color of the icy waters through which they
ploughed whispered what they each yearned to
hear: home must be near, for the water muddied.

They were closing in on the Thames estuary and their homeport of Woolwich.

Michael Janyns' face was turned northward. His hair, dark and wild, framed his chiseled features perfectly while his deep, brooding eyes betrayed a rare intelligence. Since the turning of the sails to catch the homeward wind, his heart had beaten a consistent rhythm: almost home, almost home, God on high almost home. The refrain grew stronger even as the light from the low December sun began to cool and sink beneath the frigid horizon. The fog was upon them, but as the final ray of wintry light bid them farewell a shout arose from the lookout.

"Land ho!" he called. "Tack two aft and be quick!"

A cheer arose from every lip as the riggers began a short haul shanty. Suddenly, the ship crawled with activity. Great billowing sails slammed to the deck while another was raised, causing a wild veer in the ship's direction towards the shore. The sister ships sailing behind immediately followed suit. Every breath of every living creature on board now strained and sweated to the sweet music Michael had heard all day: almost home, almost home. The mousers stopped cleaning themselves on the upper deck and turned their heads, ears cocked slightly forward in wariness; Jacko the monkey – picked up by old Rastol in the jungles of New Spain – looked about expectantly. Almost home. With a final wrenching turn, the craft veered once more and the

sailors found themselves in the mouth of the estuary
with the lights of Woolwich now visible through the
haze, glowing in the distance.

There was no leisure as they dropped anchor,
however, for the captain intended to put back out
on the morrow – if he were quick enough, he might
yet catch the cargo offered to him in Calais. The
linen and spices would fetch a sum in London and
had he not already been loaded below the plim line
he would have spared this present landfall. No one
balked at unloading in the faded daylight – the
tavern keepers knew of their arrival and would wait
for them. Imagine! English ale on English soil!
And more pay if you were willing to put back out
with the captain for Calais – a short voyage indeed.
When the last bale was hoisted down the narrow,
swinging gangplank and the names of those sailing
at dawn noted, the captain was left alone on his
great beast of a ship rocking gently on the ebbing
tide.

Michael was carried along by the throng.
Woolwich taverns occupied a specific stretch of the
cobbled street nearest the river, just after the end of
the high road. Their doors were open and pitchers
of ale awaited the men. There was an odd, almost
mechanized feel to their movement, one well-
practiced: as they reached the first tavern, those in
the lead piled in until it was full. At that point, the
mass of sailors moved on to the next one and
repeated the operation until finally all had found a
seat and a glass. Michael settled comfortably into

the second such tavern and threw back the first pint like water. He looked around, grinning at his companions.

"Home!" he exclaimed simply. The fair-haired man next to him raised his glass and a great cheer went up.

"To England! To the queen!"

Pitcher after pitcher went down quickly until finally the ale could be felt, and a comfortable, warm feeling begin to envelope them. A few women, some old, some young, begin to circulate amongst the tables. The men eyed them appreciatively. Michael, with his dark good looks soon caught the eye of a young girl, no more than fifteen. His table mate called her over.

"Lassie," he began, "What is your name?"

"Helen." She answered his question while smiling at Michael.

"Well, Helen, let me tell you something about my friend here, Michael."

Michael grinned again, took a deep drink, and ignored him.

"You see, Helen, my friend is a strange, disturbed man."

"He does not look disturbed to me," she ventured, still smiling at Michael.

"He is, lassie, trust me."

"Perhaps I could help him." Her smile became slightly provocative.

"Helen, many a woman has said the same thing. Why, each time we make port women make for him like ducks to puddles, but you are wasting your time, for he has a sweetheart."

"Is she here?"

The men roared with laughter. Finally, Michael rose, bowed to the girl and spoke.

"What my nit of a friend is saying is that I remain true to my woman." He shrugged as a great cry of disgust arose round the table. "I surely appreciate your charms and wit, but I must decline."

Her smile disappeared and she looked at him like one looks upon a god. Again, the fair-haired man spoke.

"I have no such issue, lass" ventured his companion, "For my woman is most understanding, and if you were to sit here…" he patted his lap, "…she would not mind a bit."

Helen shot him a look, smiled at his brazen approach, and disappeared into the crowd. It was Michael's turn to laugh.

"Bring us some cards," he shouted, "For there is money to be made at this table tonight!"

Cards and two more pitchers of ale appeared, and the men settled into the night.

*****

His gray woolen cloak was thrown with careless élan over his powerful shoulders. He kept to the shallows, preferring to alternate between rowing and poling as he made his way up river. The Thames ran cold this time of year, its mist laying still and quiet upon the landscape. Woolwich still deep in early morning sleep showed no signs of life save for the smoke curling from its chimneys and he soon left it behind. So too the proper houses of the town's lesser streets disappeared in a silent slow march as he passed them by. Further on up river, the landscape became more rural, dotted with smaller houses with their livestock tucked away in the barns which joined their living quarters. Now silently he passed the small thatched houses of the peasants who worked the fields nearby. As the sun rose higher, he made Greenwich Wood, the great hunting ground of England's kings and queens. Almost home.

Up ahead, round a sharp yet gentle curve in the river, he saw a familiar site – the rickety dock of Coudenoure. How often had he played there with Anne and Catherine? How many tiny ships had he launched, sending them downstream with messages attached, with sails made of his sisters' old clothes, with tiny wooden men to rig them? He smiled.

And the dock itself. Had it shrunk? Had someone rebuilt it in his long absence? Michael had travelled the world in the past three years, had seen sights and lands and peoples that hardly anyone would ever see. He had known fear as they raided Spanish galleons, had seen gallantry which would break even the meanest person's heart, had felt the loneliness which came with being a stranger in a far away and unfamiliar land. He had even known Cathay with its mysterious and ancient culture. And yet none of these wonders had ever moved him like the sight of the tiny dock set slightly askew in the mighty Thames. He tied his tiny craft to the landing and laughed aloud – no one had rebuilt the dock for there, on the third plank from the end, were the initials he and Anne had carved long ago as children. There too was the tiny flag bearing the Tudor colors he and his sisters flew so that Elizabeth might know where to dock, tattered now, but still beckoning their sovereign come.

He tied the rope expertly, grabbed the bundle which lay securely tucked beneath the plank seat of the craft, and stepped onto the dock. He smiled with excitement at the thought of reunion – no one knew of his return, and he anticipated a mighty and wonderful surprise.

*****

Catherine was up early. She absently-mindedly nibbled on the breakfast of cheese, bread and tea her maid had supplied. Her hair had never darkened with age and a riot of pure blonde curls escaped from the long braid which extended down her back. Her cornflower blue eyes were wide-set, and when combined with a smile from her equally wide, full lips there were few men who could resist her charm. And while she was well aware of her effect on men, she did not much care. She had not cared for five years, since Coudenoure's first Yuletide feast and celebration. The tradition was being played out again that evening, and she knew Joshua Hill was coming. She looked out her bedroom window onto the rooftops of the servants' quarters nestled behind the manor house. Smoke was beginning to rise from several of them, and she watched dreamily as the stable doors were pushed wide and the plough horses led out for the day. There was no work this time of year but old Norman believed in exercise regardless, and so a stable boy would take them to pasture in the nearby fields. And there, trundling out the kitchen door with her round tea bowl held carefully between her hands went her mother to her studio. Catherine smiled – she had long since stopped pretending to an interest in the arts, but her love for her mother and her mother's talent was fierce. She had come to understand the relentless will it took to accomplish almost anything worthwhile, and Bess' devotion to her marble, year-in and year-out, endured only because Bess willed it thus. As she sat on the cold, stone sill of the window, she reflected on Bess' role at Coudenoure. Her mother was the iron rod, staked deep and secure, around which the estate whirled. Like a spinning top it sometimes veered now this way now that, threatening on occasion to spin completely out of control. But Bess always managed to right it, to orient it towards family and love, towards kindness and learning, towards all that she, Catherine, had been taught was good and right. It was amazing to her that one woman could accomplish so much. Would she be as successful with her own home?

She thought of Joshua and smiled. Since that first meeting five years earlier they had become inseparable. They had both known within seconds of meeting one another that they were destined to do so. Over time, they had overcome family expectations and concerns and weathered many separations. They viewed this evening as their fifth anniversary, and Catherine was certain that finally, Joshua would propose – it was time.

He had longed for a career as an explorer and finally, after a long apprenticeship, he had achieved his heart's desire. Sir Walter Raleigh was financing a voyage to the new world to establish a colony there, and Joshua had been chosen to sail with it. He would work under Arthur Barlowe aboard the Dorothy, the second and smaller of the two ships designated for the expedition.

Catherine had never even thought to question Joshua's choice of careers and the long separations it forced upon them. Since the evening they first met five years earlier, neither had ever doubted their love for one another. She had always been warned that courtship was fraught with heartache, and that a young maid must dance and court many before she might be fortunate enough to find a suitable mate. But that was not her fate. After the first Yuletide feast, she had known and was as certain as she was of the sun rising the next morning.

Bess had smiled and been maddeningly sweet when Catherine had proclaimed that Joshua would be her husband – she perceived it as a first crush and did not bother to hide her disbelief. By Joshua's appearance at their third Yuletide event, her mother finally realized the depth of feeling, at least on Catherine's part. Even Elizabeth had picked up on the steady and constant communion between the two and after much deliberation, the two women had agreed that while Joshua could continue to attend as one of Drake's officers-in-training, there must needs be a cautionary note placed upon the affair for Catherine's sake.

But in the end, nothing had dissuaded the two, and tonight, Catherine was certain that Joshua would propose. He would leave in March for the new world, and if they were to start a family of their own, they needed to begin now. A knock on the door interrupted her happy reverie.

Anne appeared with gowns in her arms and the two sisters immediately began discussing their options for that evening's attire.

"Will the queen be here?" asked Catherine as she admired herself in the looking glass they had years earlier purloined from their mother's room.

"Oh, aye," said Anne, using an expression she had picked up from her father, "And I am hoping that she may advance my Christopher's cause."

"Oh, yes – he needs her patronage, does he not?"

"Eh?"

Anne had searched high and low that morning until she finally had found the gown she was looking for – the one she had worn the first time she and Christopher Marlowe had met five years ago. The burgundy velvet, slashed with a fine burgundy brocade still suited her and she flashed her skirt now this way, now that, in the mirror. She hoped Christopher would remember.

"I believe Marlowe will advance marriage this evening."

"Anne, I am certain that Joshua is to do so – would not that be grand indeed? What would mother and papa think then?"

Anne laughed as she spoke.

"They would think, '…um, I must order new marble on the morrow or um…, I wonder what might happen if I convince a bumble bee to mate with a wasp…'"

Catherine snorted.

"Yes, but when we finally got their attention, they would be thrilled! We could have a double ceremony!"

While Catherine prattled on and they continued to try on gown after gown, Anne's thoughts stayed with Christopher Marlowe. He wrote regularly, and had attended every Yuletide feast since the first, but seemed somehow distant. He had the strange and irresistible habit of combining intimacy with aloofness. It nearly drove her mad with desire. His letters to her were deep, witty and full of learned observations about the very manuscripts they studied together each Yuletide. Yet in person, he seemed somehow absent, not quite in the moment with her. She believed that if she could only help him unlock his own reserve, he might be able to express what she was certain he felt for her. Oh, joy when such a time should arrive! Each Christmas, as they danced, played cards and combed the library together, she became more and more convinced that her feelings were being reciprocated on his part. His plays were becoming legendary, and his love of Coudenoure and its library had not gone unnoticed by Anne. They were, she had long ago decided, the perfect couple. He just needed to see it.

As the years had passed, Anne had come to realize that she was her father's daughter. Both loved adventure but both chose to seek it out only within the loving embrace of Coudenoure. But while Quinn's great adventures took place in his workshop, Anne's were centered within the books and manuscripts of the library. Both had a love of the order which cataloguing could bring to the study of a subject. Accordingly, Quinn spent a considerable amount of his time writing careful exegetical notes to accompany his many experiments. Anne, on the other hand, had stumbled across an early attempt at cataloguing and organizing the contents of the library. Both she and her parents were thrilled to find a careful list of manuscripts which might help round out their collection. She took it, studied it, and began to improve upon it. At that point, she had turned to Elizabeth for help and guidance.

Michael had apprenticed early, and what his relationship with Elizabeth might or might not become upon his return remained to be seen. But Elizabeth was protective of Catherine who viewed the queen as the font of all that was courtly, majestic, learned and pure. She also viewed her as the font of all gossip courtly and otherwise, gowns, hats, carriages and the other accoutrement of fine living. Both the queen and her mother had insisted that she was better off at Coudenoure than at court, and that belief had been an integral part of her childhood, so much so that it had now become an essential element of who she was. That Elizabeth provided such largesse as a means of buying off her great-niece's desire to mingle at court never crossed her mind. She was not a shallow person, only innocent and naïve.

But Anne's relationship with the realm's sovereign had taken a different turn. When Elizabeth visited Coudenoure, she spent as much time with Anne as Bess. They could be seen on sunny days strolling the wide perimeter walk which mirrored Coudenoure's outer wall. Together they practiced their languages, discussed art, politics and any other topic which might come to them. An ease of communication had developed and over time revealed the similar natures of the two women. Anne was too intelligent not to have noticed the phenomenon of their alikeness, but as when she was younger, she could not ascertain its origins. Perhaps it was mere coincidence.

Elizabeth of course knew otherwise. As Anne had grown older, each visit to Coudenoure grew ever more precious for the queen. The resemblance between her own mother and Anne had become so acute as to be startling: her sharp chin, almond-shaped ebony eyes and slight build all contributed to conjure up for Elizabeth an image of the woman who until now only lived in faint and whispery memories. The combination of similar interests and physical resemblance to her mother had given her a powerful, maternal interest in the girl. Unlike Catherine, whose proclivities were simple and in line with those of other young women her age, Anne's were complex and riveting. She never ceased to amaze her parents and Elizabeth with her requests not for gowns and ribbons but for books and tutors. Like Quinn and Elizabeth herself, she had begun to write and her work revealed a sensitivity and kindness unusual in their scope and development. She was mature beyond her years, and seemed to have the ability of long-term, strategic thinking even at her tender age. Elizabeth loved her as a daughter.

*****

Michael stood at the gates of Coudenoure, drinking it in. He had missed his home every day, but until this very second he had not known how much. His heart almost ached with the love he felt for place and family. The mist had finally risen, revealing the soft winter landscape of a December day at Coudenoure. The meadow was bedecked with snow and ice and as the sun began to beat down, a certain ethereal quality settled in upon it. The manor house remained unchanged as did the chapel ruins, orchards and cemetery on its western side. To the east, the old caretaker's cottage still stood, desolate and almost abandoned. On sudden impulse, Michael decided to further surprise his family. And Jane.

He ran quickly with a stealthy gait to the east side of the manor, hugged its wall as he circumnavigated to the back of the estate, and then paused. Would she remember him? Perhaps she had married or now loved another. He grinned at the foolishness of his own thoughts, for he and Jane were as one, now and forever. Quietly, he opened the back door to the main kitchen and grinned – some things never change.

"You there! That is right, you, you clod! Why is that fire not tended?" It was Margaret, yelling and throwing whatever was at hand at all whom she perceived to be morning slackers. They were never in short supply in her august opinion and the routine had not varied in twenty years. A ladle caught the offender on the head and he gave a short, frightened, "oof!" before skiddling over to the fire with apprehension in his eyes.

"You should move quickly, lad," Michael shouted, "...for I myself happen to know that if the mistress should find you slow, the ladle will be followed by a by a dough bowl! I speak with great authority on this matter."

Margaret turned and gasped. Jane fainted dead away into a scullery maid's arms. The lad blew the fire furiously.

"So I have achieved my goal and surprised all of you!" He said cheerfully. Margaret threw a dough bowl in his direction and flicked water in Jane's face as she came round.

"And a fine entrance, indeed! Did it never occur to you, Lord Michael, that such a surprise might be too much? Eh? Why, a knock on the front door with you on the other side would have been quite enough!"

"Oh, 'tis Michael, my lady, never mind with the titles." Even as he spoke, he knelt gently by Jane. Without thinking, he stroked her hair. She closed her eyes and smiled.

"Ah, yes," he said more to himself than anyone else, "I am home. Indeed."

*****

A short while later Michael entered his father's workshop.

"Papa?" he called loudly and tentatively. "Papa?"

"Shhh," came a whispered, furtive reply, but from where Michael could not ascertain.

"Papa? I am home, Papa!"

He felt a hand on his lower leg. Quinn was on all fours, motioning to his son to do the same. Michael did as he was bidden.

"Hello, son! I have surely missed you!" Came Quinn's whispered yet heartfelt welcome.

"Why are we whispering and why are we on the..."

Michael stopped mid-sentence. A sudden clabbering sound could be heard in the far corner of the workshop.

"Down, boy, stay down!"

"Papa, what is it?"

"I do not know yet. Drake brought it to me after his last voyage."

"What do you mean you do not know what it is? How can that be?"

Quinn looked at him and grinned.

"Oh that Drake, he is clever. He had it delivered to me! Otherwise I would have known his game. It was brought it to me in a box with only tiny air holes and Drake's man left before I could examine the creature within."

"But why?"

Quinn looked at him with exasperation.

"Why? Because, dear lad, the year previously I gave him a similar package."

"What was in that one?" came Michael's breathless question.

"Oh, 'twas a gift to me from a Spanish sailor."

"How did you come to know a Spanish sailor, Papa?"

Quinn waved his hand to indicate that Michael should not ask bothersome questions. Another clabbering. Then he continued.

"Anyway, dear son, I received it in good humor, but after the creature ate the Sunday supper that cook had laid out, and after it began eyeing the mouser in her studio, Bess made me pass it along. A real pity, that."

"But what was it?"

"I do not know, but I understand from Dee that Drake was much vexed for it is still growing and cannot be left alone with the farm animals. 'Tis some type of hooven creature but 'twas but a babe when I gave it to him. How was I to know?"

"A babe that ate an entire dinner?"

Quinn waved his hand at nothing. Another great clabbering, but this time, the sound was accompanied by something, what was that...ah yes.

"Tell me, Papa, is that the sound of claws scrabbling along wood?"

Quinn raised his head and listened carefully before he began crawling rapidly towards the door.

"Large claws?" Michael sounded alarmed as he half-crawled, half-walked behind his father.

"Come along, Michael. We must let your mother know you are here." A giggle. "You gave her no warning of your coming – she may throw her mallet."

"The women hereabouts seem fond of throwing things." Michael grinned as he crawled along.

They were behind a long table now, only feet from the door. Quinn looked his son in the eye.

"On my count. You must get out quickly lest we lose it."

"But we do not know what 'it' is."

"Exactly! If only I was certain it did not crave meat…"

The retreat successful, they closed the door behind them and went in search of Bess.

*****

In years to come, if asked about Coudenoure, Bess always chose to summon the memory of that night. Her children were mature, confident adults, her husband had not yet managed to blow himself up, and Elizabeth had finally come to terms with Dudley and her own spinsterhood. Her own sculpting had entered a new phase, one of quiet accomplishment, and she found peace easy to come by. These years had been golden ones. Her life had unfolded as a single piece of exquisite warp and woof, each color bright yet blended into the pattern, properly stitched and knotted as if with golden thread.

On that magical night, forever more in her memory, the candles seemed to glow more brightly. Their flames flickered and waved in a happy, shadowy dance upon the walls and ceilings of Coudenoure. There were Catherine and Anne, beautiful in their gowns, graceful and charming. And Michael, home at last. Quinn and she had spent the afternoon chuckling over their son's continued devotion to Jane, and hers to him. Before he had left so many years earlier, the queen had extracted a severe promise from him: she would have no baron of her land marrying a kitchen maid. Michael had insisted that he must, for they had been matched in heaven even before they were born. Impressed with the romantic sensibilities of her great-nephew, she had struck a deal whereby he would wait to marry until his 25th birthday. That was the age she had become queen, and she knew his temperament would be set by then and likely his mind changed as well. There were, after all, many women in the wide world he was about to explore – and he was an English baron. Michael had agreed, but had insisted that his wait should be rewarded not only with a bride, but also with the neighboring estate, Tyche, with the manor house Quinn had built. The deal was struck. Each Yuletide since then, Elizabeth had striven to move beyond her normal insistence that social hierarchy be observed, for after all, this *was* Coudenoure. As for Bess, she secretly breathed a sigh of relief. Her son would be fine, for any boy who could bargain with a queen would do well regardless of the circumstances of his life.

That magical night, the women's dresses seemed more elegant, their jewels more bedazzling; the men more courteous, life more charmed. And everything was still possible.

****

Later that evening, Bess noticed Anne and Elizabeth standing apart from the others. Anne was whispering shyly in the queen's ear. She moved to join them.

"And what is this? 'Tis a conspiracy?" She asked laughingly.

"Shh," Elizabeth demanded. "Anne has just told me of the listening post in the library wall just yonder. We believe we shall hear what the men have to say." She was clearly enchanted, as always, with her niece and her ideas, and if Anne wanted to listen, well, then, she would as well. Why not?

In a huddle, the three women moved cautiously to the wall. Bess shocked them by removing the mortar herself.

"'Tis an old trick, Anne. Old indeed."

Together, they leaned in close. John Dee's voice could clearly be heard.

"Old Janyns, my friend," he was saying, "Why are we not in your workshop this evening? Have you stumbled upon the secret of fire and wish not to share it with us?" He referred to one of Quinn's more recent interests.

"Um, no, no, I have not yet discovered the nature of flame, but 'twill come shortly, I am sure."

"Then why are we not in the workshop?" Dee raised an eyebrow and when Michael coughed politely the aged alchemist realized he was on to something.

"So, I see young Janyns is in on your secret. If you will not tell, surely we must investigate."

And just like that, all made a run for the door. Just as quickly, Bess, Elizabeth and Anne stepped back from the wall, all the while pretending to deep conversation. A mad and chaotic ruckus began at the end of the hall.

"Open the door, Quinn!"

"Oh, no. No, perhaps not this evening."

"Open it," came a voice from the herd which had thundered past the women.

In desperation, Quinn acquiesced.

"I warn you, gentlemen…'tis green with a tail as long as my arm."

They stepped in and closed the door behind them. Elizabeth heard a scraping sound as candles were lit. Silence. More silence. Then a great chaotic shouting.

*****

Finally cornered, captured, scrutinized and duly appreciated, the great, green lizard was retired to an appropriate cage, and the older men returned to the party amid hearty self-congratulations for their courage and exploits amid admiring astonishment at Drake's strange gift.

The women soon returned once more to their listening. Now alone in the library with Joshua, Marlowe, Anne's love, was speaking.

"Aye, my plays do well thanks to the Queen's patronage," he spoke happily. "She is my defender and I trust that will continue."

Elizabeth looked at her companions and smiled happily at the acknowledgment.

A deep laugh came from Joshua.

"Well, you must marry Anne, Sir Christopher, for she is your avenue to the queen's heart. And, as I hear, the young maid has already quite captured yours. I will tell you that this evening…," Joshua leaned forward confidentially, "This very evening I have been accepted by her sister. I must speak to Sir Quinn, but I tell you man, 'tis a fine feeling! You must act tonight – yes! How splendid would that be?"

Anne blushed and smiled as Christopher rejoined.

"She is pretty, aye, but she is not for me."

"What mean you?" Joshua sat up, for Catherine, with her belief that a secret was something one told one person at a time, had kept no detail from him of her sister's passion for Marlowe.

Marlowe gave a low, ugly chuckle, and a chill went down Anne's spine. Instinctively, Bess and Elizabeth attempted to move Anne from within hearing distance. She threw her arms out and her hands up to ward them off. Marlowe's next words fell like a mighty stone upon her slender frame, crushing it in an instant.

"I know she is the queen's favorite, you nit! Why else do you think I come to such a God-forsaken place as this each Yuletide and listen to the girl babble on about her splendid library? Eh? Why indeed? I have need of patronage, and Anne is my entrée, but nothing more. She is pretty, but not pretty enough. When I am done, I shall move on. 'Tis Fate which threw her my way so that my plays might be heard."

Tears filled Bess' eyes as Anne backed away from the library wall. Elizabeth put her arm around the girl's waist while Bess replaced the mortar piece. There was nothing to be said and the three stood in the middle of the grand hall, stung through with the harshness of Sir Christopher's words. Suddenly, the library door was thrown open and Joshua approached them. Marlowe was close on his heels.

"Majesty," Joshua offered a deep bow as did Christopher, "The musicians have finished their prelude and are eager to show off their full talents – come, let us dance!"

Through the open door came the sounds of lutes and horns. Catherine and a throng of young people joined them from the dining hall and all traipsed merrily into the library. All, save Christopher Marlowe.

"Majesty, come!" he gave another gallant bow and swept his hand towards the open door. His light brown hair fell forward across his dark eyes and pale skin. He smiled winningly at the queen, with no hint of what he himself had just pronounced only moments earlier.

"And Anne, you sly girl, you have neglected to tell me of the new incunabula the queen has gifted to Coudenoure! I must take you to task, for you know our common ground includes a love of this place and its marvelous library!"

Anne stared at him as though transfixed by some ancient and evil spell, unable to look away and unable to bear what she now saw. She almost fainted as fate snatched away love's veil and revealed the truth behind it. As pale as moonlight on a misty night, she jerked herself forward towards him. Bess and Elizabeth waited behind her, silently alert. In the dress she had hoped he would notice, she curtsied unsteadily.

"Sir Christopher, you must excuse me this evening. An ache has come upon me and my head, well, 'tis spinning. I am sure there are other young women who will gladly fill your arms this evening and ensure your good pleasure whilst you tarry here at Coudenoure. Unfortunately, I must retire. I bid you a good evening, sir."

Marlowe cocked his head and unconsciously narrowed his eyes. He sensed a change but could not ascertain its origins.

"What is this?" he asked, but with less bravado than before. "The fairest of them all will desert me? I shall die a thousand deaths should you not dance at least once with me this evening."

Anne stared a moment longer, unaware that she was now rubbing the soft, supple fabric of her special gown. As though in a dream, she brushed off her mother's attempts to aid her. With a heavy hand upon the marble railing, she seemed to pull herself up stair by stair, never turning back to look at the shattered remains of her own dream. She disappeared into the darkness of the upstairs hall. A short moment later, her door could be heard closing, slowly and gently, as though pushed by the void which now encircled her.

"And what ill spirit has come upon that girl, I wonder?"

Marlowe knew, instinctively, that something had gone terribly awry. Anne had looked at him as though beholding a monster with horror written across her soft, innocent features. That look, however, was far preferable to the ones he now faced.

"I must go," Bess whispered to Elizabeth. As Elizabeth nodded, Bess strode across the short distance separating her from Marlowe. Her face blazed with anger and disgust. She opened her mouth to speak but found herself unable. A hiss escaped her lips before she turned and hurried up the stairs.

Marlowe turned to the queen.

"Majesty, I know not…" his face was now a mask of innocence and confusion.

Elizabeth's face and neck were red with wrath. Marlowe backed away as she spoke to him in a voice barely human.

"So you would use a young girl and her innocence to receive my trust and patronage, would you?"

They must have heard. How, he did not know, but quick as he was, Marlowe had no time to curse his own stupidity and indiscretion. Elizabeth breathed fire upon him.

"Sir, you will leave *now*, and ne'er come back to this place."

Marlowe stood, vainly attempting to find words, words that would ease the queen's wrath. Elizabeth watched him for a moment.

"Ah, yes, the wordsmith seeks his tool, does he not? How best to move beyond the moment? How best to fill my ears with folderol?" She paused as though filling her lungs to their maximum capacity.

"Get out!" she bellowed. Within seconds, the great hall was filled with liveried guardsmen there to do her bidding.

"Take this, this, *rogue* from here, do you here me? He dares to stand before me after I have told him to quit this place."

Hands were placed upon Marlowe, lifting him from the floor and hauling him towards the heavy entry door.

"Take him," she breathed heavily. As Marlowe was put upon his steed, she walked uncertainly into the grand dining hall, falling rather than sitting on a chair.

"Majesty, are you ill? May we be of assistance?" The captain of her guard had seen her staggered walk.

Elizabeth shook her head and closed her eyes. Around her neck was a string of heavy, lustrous pearls, passed down to her from John of Gaunt's second wife, the love of his life, Katherine Swynford. She fingered them now, absently, thinking of Dudley and his massive deception, of her own father and mother, of broken hearts and half-lived lives and the heartache that love inevitably imparted upon those foolish enough to open the door when it knocked.

"Fetch my carriage and see that Lady Bess is told of my return on the morrow. That is all."

*****

Late into the night Anne lay on her bed alone, continually stroking the fine velvet of her ball gown.

"How ridiculous am I!" she exclaimed softly to herself. "And I thought he loved me. And the dress, what foolish sprite commanded such folly. And now all know, even Catherine and her beau, for he will not keep such mockery from her."

She stood up and began unlacing her gown. It was difficult, reaching first behind her waist, now over her shoulders, but finally, with a wiggle of her hips, she slipped it to the floor, stepped out of it and bundled it in her hands as she walked towards the fire. It had burned low and only embers remained. With a forceful toss she threw the garment onto the grate and for good measure took two small kindling logs from the copper log bin nearby. She threw them on the dress, picked up a poker and blew until the flame caught. Once satisfied, she sat in her favorite chair and watched the fire.

"And so it ends," she said quietly. "I have no art, no husband, nothing at all."

Sometime later, as Eos crept across the eastern sky and she finally crawled beneath the covers, Anne realized she had not shed a single tear. She smiled wearily. Tears are for wee cuts on one's

finger, she thought, for a bumble bee's sting, for
being bested in a game. There were no tears for this,
nor was there anyone to hold her close until it
passed. And never, for eternity and beyond, would
there be anyone to ever, *ever* make it better.

Chapter Twenty

It was officially published. Lady Catherine
Elizabeth Janyns was to marry Sir Joshua Edward
Hill. The match was deemed fitting and good by all.
Sir Joshua was a northerner, a highlander of noble
birth but a second son – no wealth or title had come
his way upon the sudden death of his parents years
earlier. He barely knew his elder brother, his
father's son from his first wife. He knew only that
the man lived across the border which separated
England from Scotland proper (for he had married a
Scottish heiress), and that he cared not for the
English, having adapted to Scottish ways
completely. As Joshua grew to manhood the
evident thinness of his circumstances became ever
more apparent, and he perceived only two choices
as possibilities for a way forward: he might enter
the priesthood or alternatively, he could put to sea –
the new world had opened many opportunities for
those second born. Since neither poverty nor Latin
appealed to him, he sailed with Drake.

As the weeks passed and the banns were read, a slow but steady change began to envelope Coudenoure. The idyllic isolation of the past was melting away, revealing the bedrock and sand which lay beneath. The mere presence of Joshua and Michael seemed to breathe new life into the old estate and the old ways. Immediately after the announcement of the approaching nuptials, Quinn, Michael and Joshua had determined that Agnes' old cottage, just to the east of the main manor house, would be the perfect place for Catherine and Joshua to begin their life together. But Fernwood Cottage, as it was known, had been severely neglected for years. Its thatched roof had fallen in or blown away in many places and its gardens had disappeared altogether. It now rose from a grassy meadow which extended all the way to its oak-planked front entry. Beneath the neglect, however, was a solid and small structure which was oddly elegant despite its disrepair. It had always reminded Bess of a fine-boned and attractive woman who perhaps had forgotten to comb her hair. For months Quinn was energized by the sudden prospect of turning his wandering mind back to its first love and without waiting for as much as a single approval from Catherine or Bess he began calling in glazers, masons, and all manner of other craftsmen. Quinn could be seen most days standing in the cold in the frozen grassland in front of Fernwood, rubbing his hands together delightedly or stretching his arms forward and using his thumbs and forefingers to form a square through which he avidly gazed. Almost unconsciously, he had adopted the clothing worn by his architect father before, dressing in monochromatic ensembles enlivened by colorful gay scarves draped casually across his shoulders and wrapped rakishly round his neck. Though he would have found it difficult to articulate, the new project had given him a sense of homecoming, of completion, as though a circle was being closed. His workshop lay forgotten for the moment and for that at least Bess was grateful. One more explosion and she was going to have to find a way to hide away the gunpowder and chemicals he and Dee found so appallingly irresistible.

The green monster had taken up residence in cook's glass house, having first been tentatively identified as a new world creature known in Spanish as *la iguana*. The small children of the estate dubbed it Terrence in honor of a bunny which had disappeared the summer before in the same glasshouse under what they all deemed to be mysterious circumstances. The fact that Margaret had served hare upon the very evening of the first Terrence's disappearance did not help matters. For months afterwards, she was subjected to their suspicious glances as she served them all at the children's table. Terrence the second was unlikely to suffer the same fate. He, or she, routinely ignored Margaret's name-calling and bruising remarks mainly because they were always delivered from a distance. He happily ate her lettuces and greens and sunned himself on the fire hearth which rose from the one brick wall of the glass house. His satisfaction was evident and he began to put on weight.

Quinn's conservatory was given over to new world plants supplied him by friends and colleagues. The only distraction from his new architectural duties came from the seeds his son had brought home to him as a gift from the exotic lands he had visited. As Michael described the circumstances of their acquisition – clime, humidity, season – Quinn carefully wrote his words down in one of the very many notebooks which filled an entire bookcase in his workshop. Endless, happy discussions between father, son, and the occasional visiting alchemist or plant enthusiast ensued and the resulting plan was not just satisfactory to all, but highly exciting – the planting would begin in the spring.

Bess, too, seemed to find a new beginning with the marriage of her youngest child. She realized that her recent frustrations with her sculpting were due not to the work itself but an underlying ennui which had crept into her life. Despite her multiple blessings, she caught herself drifting on occasion upon a sea of discontent. She could not identify the cause. Age, perhaps? Or maybe simple boredom? Whatever the reason, a change of pace was in order, at least temporarily. Catherine was completely caught up in her wedding plans, and wanted nothing more from her mother than reassurances and resources – the legion of servants and hires she had enlisted in her cause could do the rest. But

Anne. Anne's heart had been badly broken. Bess determined that as her mother, she should help the woman child heal. Accordingly, she turned all of the attention previously given to her work upon Anne. Yes, she, Bess, through assiduous attention would help Anne find her way; so much assiduous attention, in fact, that Anne commented to the queen about it on one of their perambulations round Coudenoure's wall.

"If you do not distract her I shall have to kill her. 'Tis that simple."

Elizabeth laughed aloud as they walked along. It was a fine wintry day with a bright sun.

"So Bess has decided to mother you after all these years."

"God on high, I shall not survive her ministrations. Can we not get the woman a puppy?"

"She worries about you, Anne," Elizabeth was still laughing, "You have lost weight and your complexion has suffered on account of that oaf Marlowe. You must forgive your mother for feeling the need to help you somehow."

Anne looked steadily down the path in front of them. It was not that her heart had turned cold, but simply that it had turned to other things, other pursuits. She was not one to put her hand upon a hot object twice. The constant attention to her emotional state had indeed helped her heal and move on, but not because of the empathetic hugs and reassuring words which seemed to flow from the household like water in a brook. Rather, in order to be rid of such heartfelt yet annoying sympathy, she had forced herself into a happier mode on the outside which was slowly giving her peace psychologically. The only person with whom she felt free to speak her mind about the recent events was Elizabeth, for she, too, understood viscerally the impact of Marlowe's betrayal.

"There is nothing left to get through, Majesty," Anne shrugged, " If that cold-heartedly playwright could not love me and my books then I am certain there is no hope for me in that connection. I have decided to live happily here at Coudenoure with my books and manuscripts and bid adieu to such destruction as love may bring. I am done with that manner of waste and ruin."

"The heart is a strange, resilient organ, Anne, and you may yet find someone to be yours. Do not imagine that life without a mate would be as simple as turning deeper into your books. You may find yourself wanting warmth one day, and they shall not provide it."

Now it was Anne's turn to laugh.

"I may not be as strong and as wise as you, Majesty, but I know that I shall spend my days striving to be as you are now – single and happy and blessed."

Single and happy and blessed, thought Elizabeth sadly. Strange how the perception of those around one, even those who loved you completely, could be so at odds with reality.

"Will you be at the wedding?" Anne asked.

"No, for my presence would distract from the bride and her merry day."

"Um."

"I shall send lavish gifts instead – I know my Catherine well, do you not agree?"

"Indeed," laughed Anne, "But how can anyone not love such a pure expression of life and joy? I am happy for her, for it is her path I am certain. And the gifts, yes, she will be pleased. Her Joshua seems a nice young man and Drake vouches for him a thousand fold."

"He seems somewhat vacuous, however, does he not?"

Anne smiled broadly while Elizabeth continued.

"*Tell me of your plans, Joshua.* I have asked this of him directly on several occasions. And Anne, I promise, he stands and stares at me like a cow at pasture."

"Did not you tell me that my father was so awed upon initially meeting you that he forgot to remove his own cap before bowing? So 'tis with Joshua, perhaps."

Elizabeth gave her a sideways glance.

"Perhaps. Perhaps not. I believe he loves the sea and he loves Catherine, in that order. They are well-suited for neither is deep."

She waved off Anne's objections.

"Anne, I love Catherine dearly and if Joshua is the young man of her heart then I consent readily to the marriage. Being shallow is not a sin, merely a trait. And if one loves such a person, one must accept that, for as you know, no one can change another soul."

The conversation turned, as always, to books and languages, the world in which they were most comfortable.

*****

Elizabeth was true to her word. On the eve of Catherine's nuptials, many large and ponderous wains arrived, driven by Elizabeth's own guard. The young bride-to-be was showered with great and somewhat gaudy gifts of furniture, clothing and jewels. Her world was now complete.

On the third Sunday after the reading of the banns, Catherine Elizabeth Janyns and Joshua Edward Hill were married in the small parish church of St. Michael. Bess and Quinn had told the couple of their own nuptials in Coudenoure's chapel ruins, suggesting the beginning of a tradition might be possible. In this they were ignored.

Renovations to Fernwood were coming along and the first floor had been readied for the young couple. There was no solemnity to the fete which followed their vows, only boisterous joy. The evening progressed, but Joshua and Catherine had long since begun to ignore the rowdy celebration. They danced to their own music in a quiet corner. Suddenly, Joshua was seen to whisper in his new bride's ear. A faint blush could be observed upon Catherine's cheeks as she returned a whispered answer. Joshua took her hand and together they threaded their way across the library, through the great hall and into the kitchen. As someone called to Joshua he turned, looked down at Catherine and grinned. She matched his with her own and with her free hand clutched the front of her dress, raising it slightly. His hand clasped hers more tightly, and they began laughing as they skipped lightly away without answering. Jane and Margaret turned a blind eye as the giggling newlyweds ran hand in hand through the kitchen to the outer door. Catherine, with her blonde rippling curls flowing nearly to her waist put her finger to her lips and gave them an angelic smile as Joshua tugged her forward and past them. Such happiness brought joy to the hearts of all who were fortunate enough to witness it.

Bess and Quinn had also tired of the dancing and revelry and stood outside the heavy front doors of their estate in comfortable marital bliss. While they stood arm in arm their reverie was interrupted by Catherine's peals of laughter as she and Joshua ran from behind the manor house and across the meadow to their new home. Fernwood was gaily lit with a thousand candles so that their way might be clear both to their front door and throughout their lives. Quinn smiled as the laughter floated across the still air. Through the candlelight they watched as Joshua threw Catherine over his shoulder, smacked her bottom as she squealed and giggled with delight – and disappeared through their new front door. It closed behind them, and Quinn and Bess were once more alone in the night.

"My love, I believe they will be happy." He tightened his arm around Bess' waist.

"As happy as we are, dear? Could anyone ever be?"

Quinn turned her towards him and kissed her. Together, as always, they went back inside.

Some weeks later, Joshua and Michael sailed for the new world aboard the Dorothy, one of Raleigh's new world fleet. They stood once more on the tiny dock of Coudenoure and bade family farewell. Catherine, sad at her young husband's departure, was buoyed by her new station in life.

*****

On September 7th, the queen's own birthday, a child was born unto Catherine Elizabeth Janyns and Joshua Edward Hill. She lay swaddled in her mother's arms surrounded by family, a thatch of brilliant red hair peeking above the blanket. Catherine's labor had been difficult, and her hands shook as she held her newborn in the crook of her arm. She caught Anne's eye as she gently wiped her face. She kissed her child one last time and indicated to Bess that she should take the infant. A faint whisper came. Anne leaned forward but missed its meaning.

"Sister, dearest, rest, you must rest. Do not worry about anything now, for you need to rest."

Catherine shook her head gently. Anne began to cry, fearing what was yet to come.

"Look after her. Promise me," Catherine whispered.

Anne ignored the implication. Bess was caught up with Jane, busy wrapping the newborn in warm blankets.

"What shall we call your beautiful daughter?"

Catherine's small faded voice replied, "Henrietta. She shall be Henrietta Elizabeth."

She reached feebly for Anne's hand.

"Please hold my hand, sister dearest, for I am so afraid and very tired."

"Please do not leave, Catherine. Please do not." Anne gripped her sister's hand. She held it long after Catherine's lay limp in her palm, like a melted snowflake.

*****

On a far away shore, a great battle was pitched. The Dorothy lay at anchor and help was on the way – their comrades could be seen scrambling into the lifeboats and rowing furiously to aid them. The landing party had been blindsided and nearly all were on the beach when a sudden roar burst forth from just beyond the tree line. Joshua grabbed his revolver and made to step out of the boat. But even as he did so, an arrow pierced his chest. He fell back. Michael abandoned his oar and reached for his friend.

"Steady, Joshua. 'Tis only a bruise you have received." Did God forgive lies told in the service of a friend?

Joshua passed his hand over the wound and smiled weakly at his comrade while closing his eyes.

"You are either dumb beyond measure or a pitiful liar, I am not certain which."

Michael pressed his kerchief to staunch the endless flow of blood.

"Perhaps I am both, eh? We must consider all possibilities."

Joshua opened his eyes. His face was losing color now, and Michael fought back the nausea he felt.

"Michael, you must attend my wife and child. Tell Catherine of my love for her." He smiled faintly. "Of all the women I have known, 'tis only Catherine I think of when I am alone. Only Catherine."

"My sister is a fortunate woman. And to think I believed you had married her for her looks…"

"Michael, ssshhh! Do you hear?"

"Hear what, old friend. Stop talking."

"What? No, no, dear, I see you. Michael, what is Catherine doing here? I do not understand! Yes, yes love, I am coming. Do not fear, for I will be with you."

He died that day on the beach. In the evening, as prayers were said and sorrows put away, Michael thought of Coudenoure. It would be years before Catherine would know of Joshua's death. Years, indeed, before he himself would see his beloved home and family.

As days became months and seasons repeated endlessly, Michael came to have enough of the sea. He had no desire to die in a far away land amongst strangers, his body given over to the sea. He wanted home, hearth and family, just as he had known as a child. Perhaps he and his father could launch a venture of some sort together. If not, just helping the old man with his endless puttering about would be joy enough. Unconsciously, he became more cautious in his work aboard the Dorothy. In his cramped cabin, barely more than a cot and small desk, he began to keep a calendar, and he crossed off each day without fail. He was already home in spirit, but for now must bide his time.

Chapter Twenty-One

January 1586

The wooden step created especially for him and for Augustus, his mule, creaked wearily as Cecil put his weight upon it. For his part, Augustus waited patiently while the stable boy helped Elizabeth's minister of state adjust himself in the saddle. The tow-headed lad took pride in being the only one the old man trusted when getting on and off the most faithful and oldest animal in the entire stable. In fact, he was uncertain which was older, man or beast, for both had been bowed and gray even when he had begun his apprenticeship some years earlier. But age was not the stable boy's primary concern, for aged or not, both rider and mule were capable of inflicting serious damage upon him.

Cecil's assaults were the easier to manage in the short run – the old codger was given to tongue lashings on all manner of subjects, most of which pertained to a perceived lack of various and sundry virtues in his staff. Early on, these vituperative, rambling homilies had produced tears and agony in the boy. Eventually, however, he noticed that all servants were subject to the master's stern warnings, but only he, the stable boy, seemed to take them to heart. He quickly adjusted his attitude and had been the happier for it ever since.

But the other old codger, Augustus, was an entirely different matter. He could be equally vicious but was also moody, making his rebukes – in the form of kicks and bites – wildly unpredictable. The sun could be shining, the old mule could be enjoying the pleasures of a summer pasture, have a full stomach and a clean stall to which to retire and yet, if the spirit moved, might well bite the very hand that had helped him attain such a paradise. Screaming and name calling would get you nowhere, for Augustus was regal not just in name but also in temperament. He could have cared less what those around him thought of him. Except, of course, for one: Cecil. Like a sovereign who bows in wary and fearful acknowledgement before his one true god, Augustus treated Cecil with differential and distinct respect. He clearly knew the one person who could take away his happiness in this life and he patterned his behavior accordingly. All others need take care.

Cecil and Augustus had ridden together so long that the calluses on Augustus' swayed back exactly matched the warp of the saddle, which was also of an ancient heritage. As always, Cecil declined to change into appropriate riding gear, preferring to remain in his ecclesiastically-oriented cassock with the deep burgundy sash at the waist and a round, pillbox of a cap to finish the look. A worn cloak, obviously a favorite for some years, was pulled securely across his shoulders. As the older man grunted and strained to sit comfortably, the stable boy struggled to keep his face blank and focused. He had once thought it polite to make a small joke about his master's efforts in this area, but after Cecil had explained things to him in scathing tones, he kept such jokes to himself. The cassock's skirt rode up Cecil's legs, revealing patched stockings and shoes from another era. As he pulled his cape forward to cover his exposure, he caught the servant boy's stare and chortled.

"You would do well, young sir, not to waste your money on such niceties as those that no one will see. 'Tis extravagant, and if you do so despite my warning, you will never inspect your own palace such as this."

He looked over the grounds before him and clicked his tongue at Augustus as he loosed the reins slightly. The old mule lurched off in grudging compliance. For days it had threatened rain or even snow but today was clear and Cecil had decided to ride up country and inspect his new estate. The trip had been uneventful, and the message he had sent ahead ensured that Augustus was saddled and waiting. He rode slowly up the makeshift drive, noting with satisfaction the ruts and holes which now graced its gravel surface – so the work *was* continuing apace. Augustus was slower than usual this morning and in a fit of mercy, Cecil leaned forward and patted his neck.

"We are all moving a bit slower these days, are we not, old friend? Um? 'Tis particularly difficult in the cold, do you not agree?" Augustus snorted as though appreciating the sentiment and ambled on towards the main construction area.

It had been twenty-six long years since the death of Mary and the accession of Elizabeth. Cecil sighed as he considered the toll those years had taken on him, on them all really – himself, Walsingham, Dudley – England had survived and peace had prevailed across the land, but at what cost? So many plots against the queen had been uncovered during that time that he had been forced to hire someone to deal with them and manage them en toto, one Francis Walsingham. A better spy master could not be had, and Cecil frequently congratulated himself on what had proven to be a brilliant move on his part. He knew how much they owed the twisted man who kept his own secrets even while exposing those of others, particularly of those who might do Elizabeth harm. Yes, a fine hire for an ugly, sometimes desperate job. Why, just last year the man had prevented one of the more carefully planned attacks upon England and the queen that had been seen in recent years, the wicked plot devised by the Throckmorton brothers. Cecil shuddered as he briefly contemplated what the outcome would have been had it not been for the faithful Walsingham. He pulled his cloak tighter against a rising breeze while his thoughts continued to wander about in the past. After a moment, they settled upon Robert Dudley.

Robert Dudley, the famous Earl of Leicester. Never far from the queen's side, nor her thoughts. Cecil turned back to the early years, when his greatest fear had been the queen's apparent and passionate love for that peacock of a man. He chuckled, causing Augustus to slow and turn an inquiring eye in his direction. A click of the spurs and he plodded on. How could he know that the knave would marry in secret? How could anyone have guessed that the man was an idiot in the first degree? It was true that Elizabeth had worn it hard for some time, but once he was sure she would recover emotionally, he had not thought of it again. And he had not cared when Dudley had reappeared at court, for there was no question now that Elizabeth was out of danger. But inevitably when he thought of Dudley, he had to admit to a grudging admiration for the courtier.

Over the years, the preening nit had proven himself far more loyal than any of Elizabeth's other subjects. Again and again, he proved his steady and deep love for her through various acts and mechanisms. Over time, he had become the confidant that he, Cecil, could never be, for Cecil was first and foremost the queen's servant, while Dudley was first and foremost her closest friend.

Both he and Walsingham had come to trust the man despite a hearty dislike for his temperament. He served the realm and its sovereign in his own way, as did they – what more could be asked?

Augustus rounded a corner in the rutted road and there before them lay Burghley House. A long, satisfied sigh escaped Cecil's lips and he pulled the mule to a halt in order to enjoy what lay before him.

In 1571, Elizabeth had rewarded his efforts on her behalf and those of the kingdom with a barony. Despite continuing on in the administration of her rule, he was henceforth the first Baron of Burghley. It had taken years for his methodical mind to determine how best to outwardly express his growing wealth and display his very own title. In the end, he had chosen this place to do so. The estate which was slowly rising was built on the ruins of a medieval settlement. Each time he visited profound thoughts on the continuity of the English peoples washed over him in deep, almost primordial waves of pride. His kind were ancient, and his home would be built upon a base established by them in the distant ages of long ago. Heraldry was Cecil's abiding passion and great care went into the design of his own crest – a blue and white shield beneath the Tudor crown.

True to his desire, the architect had laid out his estate in the shape of an E, for all he was he owed to Elizabeth. He was fond of the privy quarters at Richmond palace and his own home would bear more than a passing resemblance to their structure and layout. The sun came out from behind a cloud as he sat upon Augustus and admired the rounded turrets and ongoing work along the northernmost wing. Altogether, the house exuded an almost ethereal lightness and cheer, a sense enhanced by the pale limestone he had chosen for its outer walls. There would go his great gardens, he thought lovingly, while there, in that small wing, would be his very own library, fit for a man such as he. Of course, that library at that small manor house the queen insisted upon loving, that place known as Coudenoure, had quite a head start on him, but he would soon catch them. Perhaps, if he were lucky, his own collection might one day surpass that of Quinn and his brood.

As his eyes scanned the landscape, he was surprised to see a fine steed tied to a low-hanging branch near the house. He was even more surprised to see its owner step from the shadows. He urged Augustus forward.

"Forgive me if I do not dismount," he spoke lightly, "...for I have no stool upon which to stand as my usual aid."

The other man quickly mounted his horse.

"Then we shall walk our beasts as we speak."

"Fine. And a good day to you, Walsingham. What brings you to the beginnings of my humble estate?"

Francis Walsingham snorted. He was a tall, lean man with deep-set, hooded eyes which took in everything. Today, he was dressed as a simple traveler upon a long journey might be, belying his powerful status and role in the kingdom.

"Lord Cecil," he began, "Your house is neither humble, nor is it in the early stages, or, if it is, then it will not be finished until it reaches London. And 'tis a fine place, by the by."

"Indeed," came the reply, "And I will be moving my family in shortly."

"Ah, and how many little ones now? Ten? Fifteen?"

Cecil shot him a look – for reasons which eluded him, Walsingham was fond of pretending that Cecil had unbridled passions in the bedroom. He suspected its origins were in his somewhat short stature. He ignored the remark and continued on.

"You did not ride to this place to involve yourself in my domestic affairs, nor to admire my new estate. What brings you to Burghley House, my lord?"

"The woman."

"Ah."

They rode in silence.

"News?" Cecil asked after a bit.

"You know, of course, that the bastard Jesuit John Ballard has several times been abroad in our land this past year. He seems to be gathering a network about him, a network centered on Mary."

Cecil grunted in disgust and cried out in frustration.

"Always Queen of the Scots. Why will Elizabeth do nothing? Why?"

Walsingham ignored the outburst. His work was to leave emotion out of the equation.

"The plan is to assassinate our royal highness Elizabeth and put Mary upon the throne."

"'Tis always the plan, Walsingham. You rode this far to tell me what I have known for years?"

"No, I did not. I rode to tell you that young Anthony Babington is at the heart of it on the English side."

Again, thoughtful silence. Finally, Cecil continued the conversation.

"What is your plan?"

"I have a young genius working for me now who decodes the messages which are being sent between Mary and her believers. His name is Phelippes and he is quite valuable."

"How are they smuggling messages to her? How? I believed our plans to keep Mary isolated were impenetrable."

Walsingham laughed.

"Nothing is impenetrable, my friend – that is why you hired me. We have a man up north, an agent whom they believe faithful to themselves and their cause. He smuggles the coded messages in and out in the wine caskets which come and go from the kitchens. In turn, they are deciphered by Phelippes before being sent on."

"Clever. And the goal? Can you get something from that witch in writing? For Elizabeth will do nothing unless Mary implicates herself in her own hand."

"It may take some time, but yes, that is my goal. In the meantime, however, security must be tightened around our sovereign, for should they see a chance, they may forsake their own plans and seize the moment."

"Still, why did you ride here to tell me? Could it not have waited?"

"Just as we watch them, Cecil, they have set a watch upon us. They must not hear whispers in the wind, for if they do they may well cease their activity, and I swear upon all that is holy, if we can keep them in the dark about our knowledge, we shall have her head this time."

Cecil nodded in understanding.

"Was a palace ever built that had not a thousand listening posts?"

"Not in England," came Walsingham's jaundiced reply. "I will go now, and what words we have will be in unexpected places."

He left Cecil as he found him, plodding along, deep in thought, on the old mule Augustus.

*****

"God's wounds," Elizabeth said to no one in particular, "Where has the time gone? How can I be fifty-three? I am still the same person I was at twenty, yet my unkind looking glass tells me a different story."

She stood before the mirror in her bedchamber, arms outstretched so that the sleeves of her dress might be fastened. It was a new gown, and she thought back again to her youth.

"Perhaps not *quite* the same person – at twenty, I would have been elated to wear such a bejeweled creation! And the colors! How do you suppose they saturate them to such a deep hue, um? These burgundies – never have I seen velvet of such abiding beauty. And these teals! Magnificent! And yet my heart does not sing as it did when I was twenty!"

Her ladies ignored the remark and continued dressing the sovereign. Her mood had improved considerably since the return of Dudley from the Netherlands' campaign, but even he could not turn back the clock for the queen. Her figure, once slim and lithe, had slowly become frail and thin. Her strength was still with her, but not the vibrancy of youth. She knew this, and her ladies knew that she knew. It was a subject best left alone, however, for the moment one of them spoke of it in an effort to bring cheer to the queen's heart, the queen would turn on her as if she spoke a curse in the devil's own tongue. No. 'Twas infinitely best to let Elizabeth have the conversation alone with her looking glass.

"I shall have tea now," she said as a rope of heavy, tear-shaped pearls was draped about her neck. "Tell them to bring me some honey as well – I have come to esteem the combination."

As they bowed and picked up the gowns not chosen for the day's attire, Elizabeth snapped her fingers.

"And, are you listening? Tell them to fetch John Dee. I wish to speak to the man."

"Majesty, I do not know if he…"

"He is here," Elizabeth said firmly, "For I saw him skitter across the drive yesterday, chasing some hapless winged creature. Tell him the queen has need of his services. I shall see him in my privy hall."

The tea was duly delivered and she sat by the window, thinking of the past. She smiled as she remembered Bess describing the pell-mell exit of courtiers during her bout with smallpox. Bess, too, was getting older. On sudden impulse, she collected writing materials and commenced drafting a note to her niece.

> *"My dearest Bess,*
>
> *I sit now in the window of my bedchamber at Hampton Court, remembering your time here. How jolly and irreverent you were! I wish you were here now, and that time were not our enemy. What a silly wish, when my kingdom seems to be in daily peril. Better I should wish for success against the legions who now seem to come against me, and yet, in my heart, I wish for simpler times, times when you and I were still ignorant about the vicissitudes of the future.*

Listen to such dreadful sadness! When I was young, I believed that the throne was the solution to all my problems, that all difficulties would melt away if I could only have my heart's desire and be crowned. What a silliness!

Dudley has arrived from the Netherlands. He says he needed to see England, that his time away from her precious shores was too difficult to bear. I suspect otherwise, that Cecil and Walsingham had need of his council, for they creep around in the shadows these days, seeing assassins and usurpers behind every pillar. Perhaps they are right and I should take care. We agree that if there be plots, they derive from my northern cousin, that witch of a woman. Oh Bess, what shall happen? If I do as they wish, I shall have an eternal stain upon my hands and if I do not, I shall spend the rest of my days in grave danger. And England, what would become of her?

I miss the quiet certitude of time at Coudenoure: I am sure Quinn's clothes are on fire or some new alchemy has taken hold of his thoughts; I am sure that Anne is busy in the library, cataloguing and buying, for she asks for a steady stream of coins for the purchase of ever more rare books and manuscripts – what a library you have! I tell you, 'tis the envy of all bibliophiles at my court! I believe they are tempted to take it for themselves should no one be looking!

And Henrietta. How is my little darling? She sends lessons and work for me weekly, along with corrected versions of my responses! 'Tis too sweet for words. In her tiny script, she writes stern messages as to how I should complete each assignment. Occasionally, I achieve a laudatory note in the margin, but the child is a born general. With this letter I send along my latest work for her consideration – this week, she has chosen to help me with my Greek and French.

Cecil and Walsingham fear that should I visit Coudenoure, the assassins would seize the opportunity to do my person harm – they say Coudenoure is remote and unguarded and indeed, they are correct. For me, I believe I would be putting you and our kin in unnecessary and grave danger, for no other reason than I long to see you all. And so for now, I must content myself with memories and epistles.

Elizabeth R.

She passed the sealed letter to her maid with delivery instructions, and went in search of Dee.

*****

"I want to know the future."

"As do I, Majesty."

John Dee was not one to mince words. He tended to deliver sharp, pithy comments while gently twirling strands of his long white beard and staring mystically off into space. He did so now.

"Dee, I am surrounded …"

He raised his hand to stop her, the only person on earth allowed to do so. After a moment he spoke.

"I do not need to be a seer of secret things yet to pass, or a practitioner of magic to understand you, Majesty. You are surrounded by men fearful of coming events, but while 'tis true that they fear the unknown, 'tis more true that they fear the known."

"Holy Mary, say what you mean, just once."

Dee turned his deep, serene eyes upon her.

"Is Mary plotting your demise? Majesty, yes! Of course she is. She has been imprisoned by your hand some many years now. She is jealous of you upon the English throne, jealous of your power and jealous of all who are free to walk abroad in this land."

"Go on."

"The question you wish answered is not a vague prediction of future events, but the outcome of one event in particular."

Elizabeth nodded and spoke.

"Will she be successful, Dee, in my assassination?"

"No, she will not. You have taken care to hire able ministers who shall see to your safety and the safety of your kingdom. But Majesty, you must prepare for her execution, for if you do not, you will not live to old age."

Elizabeth laughed.

"Well, you are wrong there, sir, for my knees already ache when I rise from prayers and my face has more lines than…"

Again he cut her off.

"Mary is not your biggest problem. The continent is."

"What do you mean?"

"Spain has amassed great wealth from its new world ventures, and even now is amassing a vast armada to come against you whether Mary is successful or not."

"I know this. Drake and Raleigh are building a fleet for England as fast as timbers may be hammered and sealed."

"They must move faster."

"Dee, they cannot!"

"They must, for Spain plans to sail against you in two summers' time."

"How do you know this?"

Dee smiled and rose.

"I am a seer, Majesty, the last of the Merlins. Now, I bid you good day." He bowed and left Elizabeth sitting alone, wondering how to face so many threats from so many quarters. She began to pace as she considered the few options open to her. After a bit, she strode from the hall in search of her friend.

*****

"My queen, why do you always call me to walk with you on such cold and dreary days? Is it not enough for us to sip some of that tea you love beside a warm fire? Hampton Court is full of such luxuries we need hardly to ever step outside. Let us admire its tapestries and paintings and walk its warm halls."

"Mary is causing trouble and must be dealt with."

Dudley laughed. Elizabeth had sought him out in his quarters and found him deep in conversation with Cecil. They had looked up with guilty faces as they rose and bowed. But Cecil was not invited on the queen's walk.

"Mary, your cousin, is causing trouble? Why, Majesty! What a surprise!"

"Stop it, Robert, or I shall scream. I am fearful of what I must do for England to be rid of the threat of her."

"But if you had it in that witch's own hand that she intended extreme treason against you, you would have no choice, would you?"

"No, I would not, but the woman is of my blood – she is clever and she will not indict herself by doing something so stupid. How many plots has Walsingham uncovered only to find that while they all lead back to her, no trace may be found of her direct involvement. Ooohhhh, that woman is clever indeed, and she will have my throne and England will be no more if she is successful."

"She will not be successful."

"Are you Dee, now? A seer of future things?"

"That old twaddle is about as prescient as Terrence, the lizard that eats cook's lettuces at Coudenoure."

Elizabeth laughed in spite of her concerns.

"Dear Quinn paid a king's fortune for two more of the creatures, did you not know? And now there are little Terrences and little Elizabeths running amok in the glass house."

"Elizabeths?"

"Henrietta did me the great honor. She adores me and I adore her. When last I was there she had dressed them for a wedding. Jane sewed the gowns – the hats were particularly jaunty. I understand Cook was apoplectic, for they served her best lettuce at the wedding feast."

Dudley smiled and changed the subject.

"Walsingham is onto something, my queen. He has uncovered a great sin and conspiracy but has cleverly concealed his knowledge of the treasonous plans. This time, she shall spin her web upon herself and be caught."

They walked on, and spoke as old friends do, of nothing in particular. Feeling better, she dismissed him and continued in the bright cold sun alone.

Chapter Twenty-Two

February 7, 1587

Elizabeth awoke in a cold sweat. As she had almost every night for the past month, she dreamt of her mother. The dreams were nonsensical, with no clear end or beginning. Sometimes Elizabeth was running through a forest, panicked that she was late for some event she could not remember; other times, she was at Hatfield, frightened by a heavy, demanding knocking on the door; in still other dreams her mother was whispering in her ear, but try as she might she could not make out the words. Yet she knew they were frantic, urgent and terrified. The disturbed sleep patterns and the dreams themselves left her weary and desperately afraid. In her rational self-deliberations she assured herself that her conscience was clear and that suppressed guilt had nothing to do with these dreams. In her heart, however, she knew better. And differently.

All through the previous summer, she had refused to believe the mounting evidence against her cousin, Mary. She dismissed Babington as an isolated idiot until even she could no longer believe her own words. And the letters. God in heaven! She had lashed out at Walsingham, at Cecil, at anyone she could, for she felt the net closing in around her.

But Walsingham, damn his soul, had anticipated her every move. You do not believe your cousin would write such treasonous words, that she would not write of your own overthrow? Here, Majesty, here is the letter. And look, Majesty, she encoded her own writing, lest someone find her out. Babington is too great an idiot to plot such devilry? Here, oh Queen, here is his confession and those who counseled with him in the dark and evil alleyways of sin. You must act, Majesty, you must act.

Over and over again: you must act, you must act. She felt her whole court whispered the words and watched her as she went about her days and evenings. She had nowhere to turn, no time to think. All through the fall as Mary's trial progressed, she found herself unable to focus on anything, unable to bring herself to the conclusion that everyone around her had reached months earlier: Mary was guilty of high treason. On the day the verdict was read aloud, only she seemed to feel any sadness, any remorse. Only she still struggled with what she knew must come.

*****

February 8, 1587

The sky was overcast, bleeding gray despair onto the earth below. When news reached her of the execution, she raged for hours, claiming her ministers had deceived her, that her understanding was that the death warrant would not be sent forward until her final word. But in her heart, she knew better. And differently. As she had now for months and months. Bouts of nausea assailed her even so, and she took to her bed, eating nothing, seeing no one until finally, she was forced to confront directly the tightly coiled knowledge with which she would have to live the rest of her life and answer for upon judgment day. She turned the ring on her finger endlessly, opening and closing it almost mindlessly as the words echoed through her head.

As her father had done to her mother, so she had done to Mary. Amen and amen, and may Christ have mercy on our souls.

It was done and there was no undoing it.

Chapter Twenty-Three

June 1587

Quinn Janyns' meadow at Coudenoure was at its finest in the spring. He was a strange man, but strange men often had beautiful sight and Quinn's vision of what this meadow should be had come to full fruition over the years. Whether it was his early training as an architect or simply a gift, his ability to translate complex mental images into ethereal objects of great physical beauty was astounding. As the winter snows melted away, his meadow sprang to life. Almost instantly, it was transformed by thousands upon thousands of purple crocuses into a soft low carpet of color. Even as they began to recede, yellow daffodils pushed upward and bloomed seemingly overnight, spreading their exquisite spring fragrance on the wind. As they finished their tour new flowers sprang forward to take their place, making an ever-changing and beautiful kaleidoscope of shape, color, smell and texture.

Elizabeth had ridden out early from Greenwich Palace, ducking her usual escort of courtiers and guards. The rampant conspiracy theories which always circulated at her court had lessened somewhat since Mary's execution, allowing all concerned with her well-being to take a deep breath and relax to some extent. On this particular morning, only Cecil knew her whereabouts. She nodded in silent affirmation to her guards at each gate she cleared until finally, the high road to London was all that stood between her and Greenwich Wood beyond. She waved away the guards shrill attempts to halt traffic for her crossing, preferring instead to disappear into the woods without fanfare, in anonymity. The musty smell of the forest floor rose to meet her – complex, strong, heavy. Only the high call of an occasional hawk on the wing and the soft hoof-beat of her mount interrupted the heavenly silence. No one called her name; no one threw themselves prostrate before her as she walked along, wanting things she could not give; no one tugged at her sleeve or begged alms. Peace. She gave rein to her horse and as so many times in years gone by, it began picking its way along the ancient trail used by her father on his own visits.

Coudenoure. Elizabeth had not visited the small manor and its eccentric inhabitants for some time. As she cleared the wood the high ridge of the place came into sight and she urged her mount forward. Once past the meadow the horse made for the banks of the Thames. The old road which abutted its muddy shore and lead to the front gate had not improved with time. It snaked and wound its way around obstacles which no longer existed, or had never existed in the first place. Perhaps it had followed some ancient border between neighboring plots or farms. Perhaps the Roman soldiers who settled the land had travelled its treaded ruts as she did now. The tiny dock of Coudenoure came into view and a sharp turn brought her to the perimeter gate of Bess and Quinn's estate. She rode in silence up the long drive. Suddenly, a small figure popped up in the meadow. Dressed in a bright linen frock with a knitted overlay the child came bouncing towards her, crying out in delight. Long auburn hair flew behind her and despite the obvious efforts to tame it with braids and ribbons it lent a wild and unkempt yet strangely charming aura to the little girl.

"Lizzie! My Lizzie!"

Elizabeth fairly jumped from her mount and ran to meet Henrietta. Of all the personalities she had ever encountered, none came close to Henrietta. The child was a marvel of nature. Physically tall for her age, she was lithe and well-proportioned. Her Tudor lineage was unmistakable – it was there in her auburn hair, in her gray-blue eyes, in her square jaw. But unlike Henry or even Elizabeth, Henrietta's face was not just intelligent and interesting, but undeniably beautiful. Her high cheekbones, prominent even now, gave great promise. But all of that was naught compared to the child's temperament and intellect.

Henrietta had begun walking early, talking early and reading early. Her facility for languages was remarkable. She had begun with the English alphabet, moved on to Greek, and from there had even conquered the strange orthography of the Moormen. Her vocabulary had soon outstripped that of others in the household and she reveled in learning new words, rolling them off her tongue with evident enthusiasm. Elizabeth loved the child for all these reasons, but there was another, more profound one which caused her to smile whenever she saw the child: Henrietta loved Elizabeth unreservedly, without purpose or cause, without artifice. It was true that the child's aunt, Anne, also loved Elizabeth without reserve, but Henrietta had somehow managed to endear herself to Elizabeth in a way that pulled the sovereign out of herself. Each time the child engaged with her Elizabeth felt the veil which had always separated her from those around her rise, as though it were a curtain on a stage. Smells became more acute, sights more interesting, life grander and finer. The child showed the woman things long forgotten or buried by time and age. They were alike, Henrietta and the queen. But Henrietta exuded a personal magnetism and charm that overwhelmed those around her for seemingly no reason. She did not use this gift to gain favors, but accepted the attention which rained down upon her without question. Her confidence was magical.

Spring was in the air and Elizabeth laughed as Henrietta closed the gap between them and threw herself into her arms. Round and round they swirled, Elizabeth free, both of them joyous.

"Where have you been? I have waited for you almost every day!"

"Almost?" cried Elizabeth in mock dismay.

"Well, sometimes the old people must be cared for, but almost every day!"

"And who are these old people?"

"I tell you this in the strictest confidence."

Elizabeth nodded.

"I am the only person under one hundred years old that lives at Coudenoure. Grandpapa, Grandmother and Anne are all paper thin and ancient."

"My word!" declared Elizabeth, "Are you certain?"

Henrietta nodded grimly.

"I am, and so, like Terrence and his Elizabeths, they are my responsibility." She sighed dramatically. "They are my burden, and I must carry on."

"'Tis too sad for such a young maid as yourself."

"Oh, I agree," said Henrietta enthusiastically. "But 'tis my lot in life." Her self-satisfaction with her own altruism made Elizabeth laugh.

"Yes, what a little soldier you are."

"Indeed," came the reply accompanied by another happy sigh.

They walked on up the drive and were met by Bess and Anne.

"You have come back to us!" Bess cried.

"But I understand Henrietta is now forced to look after everyone on the estate."

Bess looked lovingly at her granddaughter.

"Cook has just taken jam biscuits from the hearth."

Henrietta was gone in a flash.

"The child is a born caregiver," said Anne. "She mothers everything and everyone on the entire estate."

They went inside.

*****

Henrietta, thought Elizabeth grimly, was only a few degrees from wrong. When Catherine, Michael and Anne were small, the house seemed to shake with their activity. Quinn was ever in his workshop and ever in danger because of it. Bess was constantly at her stone. Somehow, in the time since she had last visited, the estate had lost a measure of its vibrancy. But where? Elizabeth tried to ascertain the difference between then and now.

The ploughmen were still in the fields, the miller still grinding with his oxen. Stable hands could be seen walking the horses and maids could still be heard calling gaily to one another through the open doors of the dairy barn. Gardeners with their barrows trotted to and fro on the grounds, busily putting into action Quinn's latest landscape scheme. On the surface, all seemed the same. But beneath the façade a creeping lethargy had set in. All were about their business, but all moved slower, as though the years were catching up to them. Elizabeth shook off the sense of maudlin emotions such thoughts produced and turned herself to her loved ones.

Quinn and Bess were now showing signs of deep middle-age. Both heads were streaked through with gray, and both had a comfortable girth around their middle. But their physical changes were not what echoed through the queen's mind. The twosome had always finished one another's sentences, sensing the other's thoughts almost before they were formed. Now, they seemed to have taken their private world a step further. They did not speak much to one another and yet their communication was complete and complex. Elizabeth wondered what such a grace might feel like.

Anne, on the other hand, still had the dark hair and charm of youth but had aged psychologically well beyond her years. Her love for Christopher Marlowe had not been a girlish crush as first believed. She had never recovered from the blow struck her so long ago by his cruel and thoughtless words and in an effort to protect herself she had turned inwards. The wound's impact was deepened by Catherine's death shortly afterwards. Together, the two events had provided definitive proof for her that love was not a kind and gentle force, but a raging fire that consumed all who were foolish enough to answer its call. She could be seen each year on the anniversary of Catherine's death at the young girl's grave in Coudenoure's cemetery, placing flowers on the headstone, gently patting the earth beneath which her sister lay. As for any remembrance of Marlowe, she never again spoke his name. Only the quiet and still lack of emotion, year after year, told the tale of her lost youth. She loved Bess and Quinn and adored Henrietta, but even these familial ties were now laced with a caution and a distance that was usually seen only among the truly aged, those who had lost everything and everyone through the sheer and steady force of time.

As the foursome sat together that fine spring morning, Bess told Elizabeth of the estate while Anne spoke with pride of the many additions to Coudenoure's burgeoning library. Soon, she declared, the shelves must be expanded, and an assessment of conditions of care be considered for the older treasures.

"Papyri, you see, begin to crumble if the atmospheric conditions they require are not met. They do best with a mild humidity which inhibits mold, but yet with just enough so that the fibers of the plant do not separate and become brittle." On and on she went.

Even Elizabeth and Bess, her two biggest supporters in her library expansion efforts, could only absorb so much. They simply nodded and smiled as on she tripped, displaying an encyclopedic knowledge of all things paper, parchment, papyrus and vellum.

Suddenly, the sound of a galloping horse coming up the drive caught their attention and en masse they moved to the window.

"'Tis a young man, that is for sure," declared Quinn, "For no one but a youth would ride at such a pace-"

He stopped mid-sentence. Bess gasped and together they ran from the room and threw open the manor doors.

"Michael! Michael!" Bess screamed with joy, pulling her son from the saddle and weeping in his arms. Quinn too cried unashamedly, hugging them both again and again. Their boy was home.

A muted scream came from the great entry way and all turned to see Jane fly out as though catapulted by some unseen force. In an instant, Michael tore himself free from his parents and ran to her, collecting her in his arms as she sobbed and clutched him frantically, as though he might disappear again should she let go.

"Do not cry, my Jane, for I am home now," he whispered soothingly in her ear. "And I will not leave you again."

Despite her initial worries about class and status, Elizabeth had come round and recognized that somehow Michael and Jane had found one another despite the great divides of wealth and background which separated them. She turned slightly away so that no one would see the tears she shed upon seeing their happy reunion. Were they tears of happiness for the young couple, she wondered, or tears of sorrow for herself? For even a queen cannot summon such bliss at will.

Chapter Twenty-Four

June 1588

The two mules struggled against the leather harness which yoked them to one another. The ridge was steep, and Michael stood at the top, waiting impatiently as the wain moved inch by inch up what was now a rutted track. The stableman at the reins shouted and whipped them onwards until finally they crested the top and slowed to a stop. Far behind them yet another wagon turned and began the ascent onto Coudenoure's high ridge. At the top, young men lined up to lift the heavy stones that were the cargo of the creaking wagon. Some distance away at the apex of the top of the ridge, older men shouted and motioned to the young ones to hurry along. As each barrow of stone was dumped, it was picked up and prepared for placement by the masons and their apprentices. A small group of foremen and masons watched, concern written across their faces. Michael was among them, as was Quinn.

"Can we do it in time?" asked a small boy whose father was deep into discussion with the masons. Fear was in his voice and instinctively he reached out and clutched Michael's hand, looking up in wide-eyed terror for reassurance. Michael smiled down at him and patted his head. After a moment, he squatted and looked at the child frankly.

"Aye, of course we can, but we must all pull together." He paused. "Have you ever been on a ship at sea?"

The child's pale green eyes grew bigger as he shook his head.

"Have you?"

"Oh yes," Michael replied. "And I have often been in battles both on sea and on land."

The boy stared at him in wonder.

"The trick to success, you see, is that every man must understand his duty to his fellows, to his country, and to himself. It matters not if you are outnumbered or out-maneuvered. What matters is what is in here." He thumped his chest. "Have you a brave heart, young boy?"

"I do." The child pulled himself up straighter.

"Then go see how you might help those masons, for we must build quickly."

The boy saluted before running off. Michael smiled and as he stood the sound of hooves from the far side of the ridge could be heard. He turned to see Henrietta and Jane dismounting with large baskets of food. They were followed by others and in short order all work ceased as everyone settled in for dinner. Quinn, Henrietta, Michael and Jane sat comfortably to one side, noshing on bread and cheese. Michael sighed and Henrietta looked at him sharply.

"Have they been sighted?"

Michael shook his head in consternation.

Since the previous Christmas, England had been warned that the great fleet of ships being assembled by King Phillip of Spain was almost ready. Early rumors had caused panic in the streets of London – thousands of ships with unlimited supplies of gunpowder and men. Walsingham's spies soon debunked this huge number, but their intelligence was not much more encouraging than the unfounded rumors. The armada, put together with new world money and a crusade taxation plan (blessed by the Pope and supported by the Spanish populace), numbered well over one hundred ships. The Pope chose not to leave the matter there, however. Indulgences were issued for all who sailed with the mighty fleet and assurances given that those who killed a Protestant were bound for heaven regardless of past sins. The Queen of England was the worst of heretics, for she enslaved her kingdom and forced them to worship outside the true Catholic faith. The battle Spain was enjoining was therefore holy in God's eyes, a crusade against the evil Elizabeth. God would surely bless all of their efforts and England would be freed at last.

Elizabeth, meanwhile, had mounted her own campaign of words and ships. Drake, Frobisher and sailors great and small had responded to the threat and made themselves available. Every shipyard in the realm had risen to her call to protect England's sacred shores from the Spanish infidel, and Elizabeth now possessed more ships than the armada. But not more gunpowder. Even as plans were being drawn, the severe shortage was recognized and Drake was assigned to steal Spanish powder from the armada itself once it drew close. Without his piracy, England would fail despite its advantage in number of vessels and all knew the consequences if the English fleet should fail. Elizabeth had no standing army to speak of, while Walsingham reported with conviction that at least eighteen thousand foot soldiers sailed aboard the Spanish ships, ready to invade the moment the armada made landfall. There would be no second chances for England or for the queen in such an event.

Michael Janyns had been called early for Elizabeth knew of his skill and experience firsthand. He had been home barely a fortnight when Drake contacted him, drafting him into England's service. His time was split between war councils in London and Coudenoure, for the high ridge there had been determined to have superb sightlines for a signal station. Beginning in Cornwall, these stone huts were built upon the highest ridges and hills of the towns and countryside between England's southern coast and London. Each of them had openings in their roofs to support tall, sturdy iron rods, upon which hung enormous iron fire baskets filled with kindling and wood. Should the sharp-eyed men assigned to any one post spy the dreaded armada approaching England's shores, they were directed to light their fires and hang them high, alerting the next station in line. In turn, like pearls dropping onto a golden chain, the message would be forwarded onward by each station along the chain, each lighting its baskets until minutes later the fiery warning reached London. The enemy had arrived and battle was to be joined.

As he sat upon Coudenoure's ridge that June day, Michael pulled his thoughts back to the moment at hand.

"Have they been sighted? No, but they are coming."

Henrietta looked defiantly southward. The sky was clear and ten miles hence, the station in line before Coudenoure could be seen. She turned northward, and by straining could just make out the one to Coudenoure's north, the one that would wait to relay the baton of fire from Coudenoure and send it yet further along.

"We must be ready." Her declaration was simple yet determined. "Jane, you will see to provisioning Coudenoure. Do not leave the supplies where they can be easily taken from us but hide them so we will not starve should the bastards get this far."

"Henrietta!" Quinn chuckled even as he tried to sound stern, "...you must not use such language."

"Then they must not try to take what is ours." Again, simple yet determined. Her confidence and childish determination made them all believe.

"Margaret and I shall provide for Coudenoure. You need not worry."

Michael smiled at the soft-spoken words of his love. Jane had evolved into a woman of substance, one who continued to amaze him and win his heart over again each time she revealed a new facet of her complex nature. Early on, when he had realized that their passion for one another ran deep and eternal, he had worried about the difference in their social rank. He was a baron, she a kitchen maid. But together they had shut out the naysayers and focused on building commonalities for their future life together. Just as she had learned to read, had studied politics and learned to manage an estate, so he had learned to respect others for what they contributed to the world, whether it be great or small, whether it came with a title or not. His time aboard ship had only reinforced his lack of concern and interest with rank and title, his deep appreciation of skill regardless of background. He knew that the world he and Jane would build together at Tyche would be one of peace and harmony for all fortunate enough to inhabit it.

Lunch was over and Michael helped Quinn to his feet. The old man had lost something physically but not his keen curiosity about the world around him. Michael had brought him trinkets, seeds and even a strange tree from the new world. It now lived with Terrence and his harem in the glass house and produced six-inch long green fruit which grew in clusters, the fruit's peel changing to a yellowish hue as it ripened. Terrence loved it, Cook avoided it, Quinn studied it and Bess ignored it. Not everything at Coudenoure had changed over time.

*****

July 19 1588

What was that – was it a sail? Finally? He ran up the earthen mound and quickly climbed the ladder which leaned against the round, stone signal house. Gaining his balance, he turned south, peering anxiously into the swirling gray fog. He had seen this evil watery veil coming, watching it in alarmed silence as it grew and spread out over the high seas. A wind kicked up mid-morning and blew mist landward as it fed ravenously off the warm waters below. Like the devil's own brew, it dissipated, then reformed, swirled and roiled as it sank ever lower until finally, it rested upon the land and the sea, hiding both good and evil in its gray, cold embrace. He cursed it and continued staring – he thought he had caught a glint of red appear and then disappear on the far horizon. Without warning, an eerie stillness settled uneasily upon the land. The wind came to a sudden stop, as though pausing to consider the grave options which lay before it: should it blow the infernal veil of fog and mist away and reveal all, or should it move on and leave England to a deathly fate? The watchman turned all round as though expecting to see some reason for the sudden cessation. But the decision had been made, and as suddenly as it had stopped the wind began again. It blew with determination down from the hills, across the valleys and out to sea, parting the clouds and fog, creating a rift through which the gray-blue ocean appeared. Yes, he had been right. It was them, but what he now saw in the widening gulf of clouds caused a knot in his stomach.

"Dear God," he said aloud. He tried to count but realized it was futile. For a hundred years or more, his family had kept this signal above England's southern coast, but never had it been imagined that such danger would come to their realm's coast or that upon their actions would ride the fate of the nation. He watched in horror as the great war-galleons continued to appear, the horizon now obliterated by their billowing sails, each painted with the red cross of Spain.

Even as he watched, a score of men came running and riding up the hill.

"Light the fire! Quickly, man, for we must get word to the Queen!"

The torch was put to the baskets. Five minutes later, ten miles away, they saw the next signal house light their own baskets, sending the word inland. From Dover to London, the fires were lit in a steady stream. It had begun.

*****

August 8, 1588

Jane had not been happy with the news.

"But you said you would not leave again. Michael, you are twenty-five in one month! We are then free to marry by the Queen's own resolution!"

"I know, but England has great need now of naval men, Jane, for the Spanish are throwing everything they have against us. They will stop at nothing to overthrow our sovereign and impose their false religion upon us all. They have a fleet of one hundred-thirty warships! Jane! Hear me! I must do my part."

Tears welled in her eyes.

"I do not feel good about your going."

"Of course you do not, my love, but I promise by all that is holy that the moment Phillip's armada is defeated, I will come home to you and Coudenoure. We will marry and have a family, as we want. Just one more short separation, my love. This will be the last."

Bess was of a similar mind. Only old Quinn and young Henrietta seemed to understand his need to answer the call. Anne understood it too but was so consumed with worry about Coudenoure she took almost no part in the arguments and conversations which swirled about his leaving.

"When you are back you will marry Jane."

"Yes, Henrietta, but you must look after her. I fear her state of mind at my going more than I do all the guns of the armada."

Henrietta did not smile.

"We will plan your wedding. Choosing a day, a dress, all of those things. The pastries alone will take weeks of planning."

"Not so," replied Michael laughing, "For we have already had serious and momentous discussions about our wedding feast's menu. That issue is, to put it mildly, already in hand."

And so he had left. The entire estate turned out to see Michael go, knowing that their fate rode upon his back and the backs of other men like him. Many of the aged among them crossed themselves, still oblivious to the change in religion which had caused the hostilities in the beginning. They cared not for quibbling about the will of God, hoping only that he heard their own prayers, their own private supplications for grace, for sustenance, and for forgiveness. If he saw to their needs and those of their clan, well then, it mattered not what the great powers of the world wanted. This much they knew with certainty.

*****

As the three-masted ship sailed into battle in the early morn of that bright August day, Michael loaded his weapon and with his shipmates sallied forth to meet the enemy. Salvo after salvo fell around them and yet they pushed forward, forcing the Spanish vessels out of formation and into chaos. He felt no fear, only exhilaration that the moment was upon them and that the great danger would finally be brought to an end. Hour after hour of choking smoke and cannon fire at last allowed them to pull within musket shot range of the armada.

"Load and fire!" came the order.

Michael said a quick and fervent prayer as he stepped forward and quickly steadied his gun on the rampart. Across the blue and smoke-filled waters, a young Spaniard, just turned fifteen, was ordered forward aboard a Spanish galleon and told to fire as well. Terror filled his heart and his hands shook as he lifted his musket. What was he doing here? His dark eyes filled with frightened tears and he struggled to control their flow. He wanted to go home, to see his mother and father again. Battle was not for him and he had known it all along. Only the draft, sent forth from the King himself, had forced him into such brutal service. He closed his eyes and uttered a prayer heavenward that his bullet might not find a home but might instead sail onward into harmless oblivion. He did not aim, but closed his eyes tight and pulled the trigger. The kick from the butt forced him backward and he fell on the deck with a scream.

Michael squinted and focused on the cohort now at the Spanish galleon's rampart. Smoke began to rise from the line as each man fired. He saw a soldier standing somewhat apart from the others and carefully put his finger on the trigger while taking aim at him. A slight hesitation: was the soldier crying? Another second of hesitation and keener focus: why, he was not a soldier but a child! And yes, he was shaking and crying. He could not…

Perhaps God did not hear their prayers above the din of battle that afternoon in early August. Michael fell back too, but silently. His gun dropped from his hand and his eyes closed in eternal death.

*****

In her studio, Bess sat listlessly alone. John Dee's words describing Coudenoure, spoken years earlier, echoed through her mind. He had said it was a place "…without sadness." And she had believed him. What a fool she had been to think that such a thing was possible. She felt impossibly sad, and worried that perhaps she was experiencing the beginning of the same sadness that had spelled the death of Constance her mother. And where was Elizabeth? It had been a month since the news of Michael's death. Surely the queen owed her some small pittance of acknowledgement for the sacrifice of her only son. But it seemed that now no one remembered Coudenoure. All about the kingdom celebration raged, and the queen's name was spoken in reverence and joy. Holidays were declared, feasts celebrated and hallelujahs to God were never ending it seemed. Only Coudenoure grieved for Michael; only Coudenoure remained isolated and alone in its sorrow. Try as she might, Bess could not deny the well of anger which rose within her each time she thought of Elizabeth. Where was she now that Bess needed a friend so desperately?

*****

Late August 1588

"What have you heard?" Dudley walked slowly into Cecil's chambers at Whitehall.

Walsingham glanced up. He was not dressed for court, but for business. Like Cecil, he preferred a longer cassock than was popular at court amongst the queen's courtiers. He also preferred darker colors and had more than once referred to those who chose more flamboyant attire as peacocks. Dudley was one who had been so labeled by Elizabeth's spy master. In response to Walsingham's wry critique, he had taken to wearing a peacock's feather in his hat. Always. He had one today which perfectly accentuated the teal of his doublet and his rose-colored, silken hose. His beard, trimmed yet full, was flecked with gray, lending him an air of statesmanship despite his choice of clothing. In other times, Walsingham would not have let such a moment pass – he would have chided and laughed at his fellow-minister. Today, however, as he turned and surveyed Dudley, he held his tongue.

It was true that the queen's favorite was bedecked and festooned like a royal barge but the clothing could no longer hide the man beneath. Dudley was not a well man. The beard could hide his sunken, hollow cheeks. His dark eyes still glowed with the intelligent mischief which was his hallmark but they were now circled by dark and deep shadows. His frame, once tall and muscular, was as thin as Walsingham had ever seen. His color was that of a haunt, a shade of the night with no business amongst the living. No, the man was not well. Best to address the issue at once.

"I have heard you are taking several cures," he said, and Burghley turned to inspect the newcomer. His friend was right – Dudley looked as though he might not make it to the chair Walsingham pushed out for him. He raised an eyebrow and waited. Dudley looked at them and gave a crooked grin.

"'Tis the cures, I am certain. They are worse than any pain I assure you."

Neither Walsingham nor Cecil said anything – they continued to stare at him waiting for a serious answer about what was obviously a serious issue. After a moment, Dudley acquiesced.

"Gentlemen, I fear my illness is more than I have admitted to. I cannot eat, nor do I care to, and I have grave pains and aches about my chest and stomach. I have taken many cures, in answer to your question, and am currently taking several new ones, but alas they seem to do no good. Perhaps they do me harm. I do not know, and some days, no – many days – I no longer care."

Cecil leaned back, assessing the man. Yes, he was mortally ill, there could be no doubt. He spoke kindly to Dudley.

"Have you taken the waters? At Buxton? I understand they are quite effective and soothing. Such is perhaps what you need. That, and to leave court so that you may rest your head unfettered by such worries as still beset the kingdom. All is well in hand now."

"Show me." Dudley leaned forward and Walsingham spoke, gesticulating at the map upon the table as he did so.

"After Gravelines, as you know, Drake continued to harass and scatter the armada. With Howard blocking the southern exit from the channel, they had no choice but to sail northward. They are even now being picked off, one by one, by locals and fiefdoms alike. We have no qualms with this – should some Scottish warlord see fit to enhance his own stature by attacking Phillip's precious ships, well then, we are obliged on all accounts."

"And danger?"

Now Cecil spoke.

"There is none to speak of." He leaned back, crossed his hands across his considerable girth and gave a satisfied sigh. "Mary the witch is gone and now Phillip's threat as well. England's two greatest foes vanquished within a year. Grace to God Almighty!"

Dudley leaned back as well, and both men noticed a catch in his breath, as though he were combating his pain only with the greatest difficulty. His next words confirmed their suspicions.

"Well then, gentlemen, you have no immediate need of me. I will ride to Rycote this evening and from there onward to the healing waters. I shall see you anon."

"You will notify the queen?" asked Cecil.

Dudley turned back at the door and looked at them through deep and sorrowful eyes.

"Indeed I shall," came his sad reply.

"Anon," Walsingham said as the door closed. "Anon my friend."

The next morning, as promised, Dudley sat down to write his beloved queen. Strange, he thought, how they had managed to remain friends through the years. Two headstrong individuals, neither willing to yield, but neither willing to forsake a relationship that had lasted their entire lives. Not just lasted as though it had never been tested but one which had endured against all travails and all likelihoods. It had defined them both, for good or for ill. Strange too, he had never thought this would be his end. He had always believed he would die in battle, or perhaps through accident. Something swift so that his thoughts might not linger upon the great beyond and his utter lack of communication with God over the years. But that was not to be his lot. Nor, he realized with a jolt, had he thought he would die before Elizabeth. Since childhood, her life had been lived in a state of constant danger from within the kingdom and without. It had been a given, he now realized, that no one could survive such threats into old age. And yet she had. He grinned to himself – the old girl was her father's daughter indeed.

How would she take his death? What should he write to her? Should he tell her himself? He chose not to break the pattern of their world, their mold. He would put her first, as always, for she was his queen. Let others tell her of his death – she had no need to hear it from him. He picked up his quill.

"*Majesty,*

I most humbly beseech your Majesty to pardon your poor old servant to be thus bold in sending to know how my gracious Lady doth and what ease of her late pain she finds, being the chiefest thing in this world I do pray for, for her to have good health and long life.

For my own poor case, I continue still your medicine and find it amend much better than with any other thing that hath been given me. Thus hoping to find perfect cure at the bath with the continuance of my wonted prayer for your Majesty's most happy preservation I humbly kiss your foot, from your old lodging at Rycote this Thursday morning, ready to take on my journey, by your Majesty's most faithful and obedient servant,

R. Leycester"

He closed his eyes for a moment, and lovingly bade Elizabeth farewell. After a time he looked up and rose, forcing his thoughts onward towards the greatest adventure of all.

*****

Elizabeth could not bear the pain. Her kingdom spared, her love taken; Her people jubilant, her heart broken.

She slipped away, that day they finally broke the news to her. In a daze, she locked the bedchamber door behind her, closing out the world and all its foibles. There was no grace to be found as she sat for hours before the fire with her eyes closed, remembering Dudley. Dudley with his ridiculous charm and manner, with his dress more stylish than her own, with his heart more true than she had ever deserved. He was her own, and she now cared not about their many raging fights through the years. Nor did she care about his marriage, for what was the man to do?

Where did they go wrong? There, yes, that was it: the circumstances surrounding the death of Amy Robsart. Elizabeth thought back to that time and place. But if Amy had not died an unnatural death, Dudley still would not have been free to marry her for years, perhaps never. They had been doomed from the beginning, only they had not seen it until much later. And when they did, neither could accept it, and so on they had gone. Until now.

Two days later, Cecil had the door to the bedchamber forced open. Elizabeth lay in wretched grief upon the bed, clutching the letter Dudley had written her only hours before his death. Doctors were called and ladies maids gently attended to the devastated queen. Quietly, Cecil excused himself and went quickly to his chambers. He never hesitated as he put pen to paper and as he sealed the note he rang for a courier. On the outside leaf, he wrote the name of the estate to which the note should be delivered with all haste – the one place where Elizabeth might find healing.

Three days hence, Henrietta stood at the front of manor house with the great wide doors open behind her. She glanced up toward the ridge and noted that smoke was billowing forth from the signal watch tower Michael had built. She had ordered a young servant boy to raise a fire basket when he saw the queen's retinue approaching. Even as she looked, a somber parade of black-clad guards appeared at the far end of the drive and slowly made their way to Henrietta, the only one there to meet the sad party. She bowed deeply as the queen stepped down from her carriage and as their eyes met, the queen's breath jerked in her chest.

"That will be all. Wait outside the wall, all of you." When they were halfway down the long drive, she began to sob and threw herself into Henrietta's arms. After a moment, she raised her head.

"But where is Bess? And Anne and Quinn?"

Young Henrietta was not an emotional woman. She was sensitive and kind, but her practical streak always ensured that she would act rather than allow emotions to freeze her. But today, with Elizabeth sobbing in her arms, even she could not escape the raw power of loss which had so recently swept through Coudenoure.

"Michael." Her voice said it all.

"Oh dear God," Elizabeth sobbed. "How?"

As Henrietta collected herself and told her sovereign what they knew, she turned and pointed towards the estate's cemetery.

"She refuses to leave his side. That is her yonder, sitting on the bench."

For an instant, Elizabeth remembered her first visit to Coudenoure, when old Agnes had been sitting thus. She forgot her own grief momentarily.

"I must go to her."

Henrietta's arm held her back.

"You should know, Elizabeth, that she is not herself."

"What do you mean?"

"She believes she is back in Rome."

Elizabeth pulled her arm free and began walking towards the place of sorrow in which Bess now resided. Not herself, she thought. Who could be? She has gone to happier times. That is all. Even I am not myself these days. What loss has come upon us!

She sat down gently next to Bess and patted her hand. Bess turned to her with a vacant stare and spoke to her in Italian.

"Shall we go see Papa today?"

Elizabeth wept anew.

From the door to the manor house, Henrietta watched the two old friends as they sat upon the bench in the distance. Perhaps Elizabeth could pull her through. She felt an arm slip round her waist.

"Oh, Anne, I did not hear you."

Anne laid her chin lovingly on Henrietta's head. Her tears were spent, but a deep sadness hung over her. When the soldier had arrived with the letter telling of Michael's death, she had watched in horror as those around her fell apart. She could not bear the destruction she was forced to witness, and all because of love. She had withdrawn to her room, taking several medieval Latin texts with her. As the days passed, she had remained there, isolated from the sorrow, occupying herself with translations of the various manuscripts. It was exacting mental work and when she felt sadness knocking upon the door of her soul, she redoubled her efforts and focus. It was never clear to her if the debacle with Marlowe at such a young age – devastating in its completeness – had forced the tendency to withdraw upon her, or whether it had always been part of her nature and only awakened by his callousness. With the deaths of Catherine and Michael, however, it had become more pronounced, and she knew in her heart that distance from such roiling emotions was her only hope of maintaining a steady peace within. Her ability to comfort others was there, but severely limited, not from a lack of caring but from an inability to cope herself.

She raised her head and looked at Henrietta, a young woman so different from herself that some days she could hardly believe they were related. As Anne was shy and reclusive, Henrietta even at her young age was outspoken and gregarious. Anne worked hard to learn her languages and mathematics; such things seemed to come to Henrietta with no effort whatsoever. It was as though a grand experiment had been set in motion by the fates when they were born – one child dark, serious and studious, the other fair, brilliant and gifted. How would their lives unfold? Who would go the farthest? Anne sighed, reminding herself that they had more in common than what was apparent to the eye. Each was intelligent, each was beautiful, and each had been raised at Coudenoure, an environment not conducive, but insistent, upon the expression of the individual. In the end, all that mattered was that they were blood.

Anne roused herself from her thoughts and spoke quietly.

"Mother will be fine, do not worry. She just must accept what has happened before she can come back to us."

Henrietta literally snorted.

"I am worn thin by sorrow and grief. We must shake it off, Anne, or we will all go mad."

"How do you propose to do that?" Anne smiled ruefully at her young niece.

"By not indulging in such tears and anguish. And you, aunt, could learn much if you left your manuscripts upon the shelf occasionally."

"People must be allowed to grieve, each in her own way, Henrietta."

"God's wounds, Anne, for how long? Michael is gone. Catherine, Joshua, that Dudley fellow – I never cared for him anyway."

"Henrietta! Do not speak ill of the dead!"

Her niece ignored her, instead looking up towards the heavens with a searching eye.

"It must be quite crowded up there now."

Anne laughed.

"You are sacrilegious, child."

Again, Henrietta ignored her.

"We need a distraction. Shall I set the house afire?"

Anne smiled as she continued.

"What happened to that gun powder of Papa's? Is there any left? It makes such a lovely, such a lovely..." she searched for a word..."*bang!* Do you not agree?"

"You would blow up Coudenoure?"

"Do not be absurd." Pause. "Only a small outbuilding."

Despite her natural reticence, Anne began to catch Henrietta's infectious mood.

"Jousting," she said suddenly, looking at Henrietta with a gleeful grin.

Henrietta clapped her hands and began laughing.

"We would make mother, Papa and the queen engage in it – we will call it old peoples' jousting."

They both roared.

"No steeds, for they are too fast."

"Um," agreed Henrietta. "A stately walk is needed. Mules. If Cecil would loan us Augustus…"

"Perfect!" Anne continued the charade. "I shall write to him today, though I fear Augustus would not participate even if Cecil should send him along. What about lances?"

"No, they are too heavy," said Henrietta. "Perhaps they could attempt to snatch their opponent's hat as they mosey past. Like this."

Henrietta playfully began slapping at Anne who promptly began slapping back. The raw silliness was grand, and each felt better as a result.

"Michael would like the sheer ridiculousness of it but he would likely do something much more dramatic. And something that would raise poor Jane's spirits," Anne said when they had both stopped laughing.

She thought for a moment and then snapped her fingers.

"I have it! Come with me!"

She ran around the corner of the manor towards the back of the estate, towards Jane's small cottage. Anne was fleeter and Henrietta struggled to keep pace.

"What are you doing, auntie? Can you not slow down? I cannot breathe!"

She stopped and bent over double, then cast her eyes heavenward.

"Oh Michael, wait for me, for this nit, your sister, is killing me with running!"

"Hush!" floated back over the wind to her and she continued on.

Without waiting for an answer to Anne's knock, they barged into Jane's small abode. Jane was in bed, weeping. They ignored her tears.

"We are in need of a feast." Anne explained.

Henrietta began dancing around the room.

"Indeed! And musicians! Our loved ones must be sad and missing us as well. Let us send them love and cheer so that they will not forget us in their new home. Let us show them how much we love them even yet."

Anne nodded in agreement.

"Of course, the old people may not care for the idea." Jane struck a note of realism as she sat up and wiped away her tears.

"Nonsense," Henrietta assured her and reached for the bed covers.

She tore them back and ignored the appalled look on the pastry genius' face.

"You are our own kin, through marriage or not, and Michael must be shown that, his mind must be put at ease! Come. We have work to do!"

They pulled and pushed Jane, laughing as they dressed her and grabbed her hands.

"And shall we tell the old ones?"

Henrietta laughed.

"No, the look of horror on their faces will be thanks enough."

*****

When the threesome returned to the manor house proper, Elizabeth and Bess were in the library, speaking in low tones. They turned as the young women traipsed into the room.

"Bon Journo," said Bess, tentatively. Elizabeth held her hand.

"I do not speak Italian. If you wish to communicate, you must do so in English." Jane made a declarative statement and watched Bess matter-of-factly. Bess looked over at Elizabeth, then at her children, then at Jane. Suddenly, she shuddered as though throwing off a heavy load.

"Tea." She spoke in a loud, clear and somber voice. "The queen and I would like some tea."

The feast went as planned, though with no musicians. Quinn waxed poetic on the projects Michael had helped him with, Elizabeth told tales of her Dudley, and even Bess managed a laugh as Anne remembered Catherine and her love of all things bold and gold. Jane had prepared the favorite dishes of each of those who had passed, and as they sat in the grand dining hall, prayers both collective and individual went up to God for the well-being of those who had left them all too soon.

As Elizabeth departed that night, she and Bess hugged one another tightly, knowing that somehow their losses had strengthened their mutual bond.

The next day, Cecil sent a note of thanks to Coudenoure, and a mule.

Chapter Twenty-Five

It seemed that death had finally moved on, though the scars it left behind were sensitive ones. Some wounds were slow to heal, flaring up at odd moments when a gesture or word summoned a memory. Some were scarred over like a landscape scoured by glaciers in an earlier age. In a similar way, the spirits of those at Coudenoure had been flattened and changed by the terrible and relentless scourge which had passed over them.

Quinn was quieter in the years following the deaths of Michael and Catherine. Initially, it had been hard for him to grasp that Michael, his only son, would not be coming home again. He knew of other families whose sons had engaged with the Spanish during Gravelines. Their boys had come home – why had Michael not returned? Try as he might, he could not stop himself from straying into this line of thought over and over – why Michael? Eventually, he made his peace with his own grief, but never with the random nature of Michael's death.

He had spent his life studying nature, seeking
out the underlying unity which brought pattern and
form to all things. In mathematics he found the
eternal, divine proportion, with pi in all things from
roses to acorns. And that quest had taught him that
very few things are random: the bird's sweet tune
in the spring called out his desire for a mate; the
flower's scent was not for him, but for the Fibonacci
number and pi. Anne translated the work for him.
So with all that pattern and assurance why Michael?

Michael had been his best friend as well as his
son. He had understood the magic of numbers and
was likewise fascinated. His granddaughter
Henrietta understood them too, almost viscerally,
but was not so interested.

All things came easily to Henrietta but none
seemed to capture her. Even as a young child, she
had realized her own restlessness but could not
identify it as such. She only knew that once she had
learned something she had to move on, for it
seemed that no subject had the complexity or depth
to hold her firmly in its grasp. Now, as an adult, she
sometimes wondered if this refusal to be captivated
was due to a lack of complexity in the subjects she
studied or to a lack of willingness on her part to
slow down and see what lay beneath. The question
had a personal and very practical point as well.
Would she ever be able to find someone with
enough depth, enough hidden layers to be
discovered over the years, who might be able hold
onto her and her love? She felt that if such a man

existed, she could love him and follow him to the ends of the earth. Otherwise, as frequently happened, she despaired that like her auntie Anne she would remain unmarried for life. For Henrietta's other quality was an inability to compromise. She would have to love someone completely or not at all, for her there was no in-between. She had never known her mother, and Michael's death had not had the same numbing effect on her that it had on the other family members, not because she did not feel, but because she was better at letting go and getting on with the business of the living. It was not age which dictated this attitude but her nature.

Of all of them, Bess continued through the years to wear her loss the hardest. Now that Terrence and his kind had long since died out, done in by climate, children and possibly too many weddings, Bess had commandeered his old kingdom – formerly known as cook's glass house – and hired a botanical man to grow flowers for her, even in the deepest cold of winter. She could be seen most days gathering small bouquets from the glass house, taking them out to the burial grounds and placing them gently on the graves of Catherine and Michael. Quinn could often be seen standing by her side. Together, hand in hand, in grief as in joy.

The rest of Bess' day would be spent in her studio. There were two dozen projects she had started since the death of her children, each of them abandoned for reasons she knew not consciously but only suspected. She could not bring herself to finish anything. Each time she came close to an end, she thought of Michael and Catherine, their lives unfinished. And so she moved on to the next piece of stone. Then the next. And the next.

It was some years before she began to realize that, despite her best efforts, her children's faces were fading from her conscious mind – it was only in her dreams that they remained in sharp focus as they were in life. Bess determined to memorialize them in stone before they were gone forever. Like shades among the Greeks begging to be forgotten not, they haunted her now, and she found new purpose and healing as she worked most days to finish their busts, carved from the purest white marble she could find. Upon hearing of her project, Elizabeth had asked for one of Dudley as well.

The years passed on, and Elizabeth found herself more and more dependent on Coudenoure. And upon the young Earl of Essex, Robert Devereux, known to all as simply Essex.

He had come to court even before the death of Mary, making quite a splash with his charming good looks. He had a quick wit, and ambition which was quicker yet. It did not hurt that Robert Dudley was his stepfather. Dudley, older then and beyond the jealousy which might have marked a lesser man's acknowledgement of a younger man's favor, did not oppose him. He and Elizabeth had spent their lives together, and there was now simply no more room in their relationship for such petty and insecure emotions. They were as they had always been, and always would be. Dudley had quickly moved to a higher post, that of Lord Stewardship, so that Essex could fill his old post, that of Master of the Horse.

Elizabeth had first noticed young Essex years earlier and had remarked in passing upon his uncanny resemblance in manner and attitude to that of Dudley. Obviously, the older man had taught him well. And while Elizabeth knew that physical resemblances always struck a chord with her (she need look no further than Constance, Anne and even Henrietta with her remarkable Tudor looks to recognize this idiosyncratic quirk), she now found pleasure in the non-physical purely behavioral similarities between Essex and Dudley. Whether it was practiced artifice on the part of Essex, she did not know, but she enjoyed the common verbal means of expression they shared, using words in similarly odd ways unique to them. And then there was their manner of rolling their eyes at the most inopportune moments, causing her to break out in laughter when laughter was not appreciated, or standing with one leg forward, as though ready to move off on a mere second's notice. Such continuity between generations not only amused her, but gave Essex a place in her heart.

He was tall for his age, and uncommonly handsome, like his stepfather, and like his stepfather he was headstrong and willful, but he covered his obstinacy with a grace and charm that Elizabeth found delightful. Essex openly flirted with her, playing with remarkable consistency the eternal court-role of the lovesick swain. When reminded of their considerable age difference, some thirty-five years or so, he simply guffawed and remarked upon how much she might teach him should she be willing. It was all so overt and stimulating. Early on, his light banter and humor had taken her back to her youth with Dudley. How young they had been! She saw in him what Dudley had been for her and loved it all for that reason alone. As time went on, however, she had to acknowledge to herself at least that Essex was not half the man that Dudley was.

Dudley, too, had flirted with her, had plied her with charm and guile. But Dudley had also known his place. There was no question but that he owed his position, indeed his life, to his Queen Elizabeth. Behind his ambition and her vanity there had been a mutual respect, born of their deep knowledge of one another. They had sparred intellectually since childhood, knew each other's Achilles' heels, knew of the touch-points in the other that might evince either anger or fear. They had built upon this, and upon their deep natural love for one another, and their relationship had an easy but nevertheless hierarchical rigidity which neither violated.

Elizabeth's world for better or worse had been predictable. She knew her enemies, she knew her friends, and she knew which of her ministers she could trust. In moments of doubt or confusion,

Burghley was there, Walsingham guarded her back, Dudley was her comfort. But suddenly, the passing of so many years became apparent and it felt to her that they had passed not in a slow progression of time but somehow all at once. She now felt caught out in the storm with no shelter. Her generation had passed on and she was left alone among strangers in her own world. With the end of Mary and with Spain effectively hobbled by the destruction of its armada, she herself now felt lost.

After all, what happens, in the end, when you finally vanquish your mortal enemies? When you put them away with no mercy and no quarter given? Does peace flow out upon you like a mighty river when it finally reaches the eternal sea bathing you – in what? Forgiveness? And what if you have lived with those enemies your entire life? They were, after all, your demons, your life lived in their shadows, their darkness, your world revolving around them and their machinations, their schemes inhabiting even the darkest, most fearful corners of your own mind. What then? Do you rise up in glory and joy as you smite them? And what then? Does happiness fill their place in your universe? Does it pervade your world even as they did?

Elizabeth did not find it so.

And what happened if there were no one to understand? If you awoke in your glory to find yourself alone in this new world of strangers who called your name and spoke your language and yet knew you not. What then? Who to tell of your exploits, who to laugh with as you recalled those very enemies whom you had vanquished? Who would stand with you as a witness to your own life? To your own love? To whom would you confess your own sins? To whom? To the strangers among whom you now lived?

Elizabeth did not know. But she understood finally that old age consisted of this.

It seemed that all who had served her long and well had disappeared now. She no longer awoke to Cecil and his endless fretting about her morning routine. He no longer wheedled and whined to force her attentions upon this matter of state or that one. With the vanquishing of England's two mortal enemies he had called seen fit to retire, sensing that times were changing and that his work was done. But Elizabeth had no such luxury, for sovereigns must always remain for the final act, regardless of their personal will and desire. Strange, she thought. She could order the death of those around her and those far away, she could command ships and men and even the occasional battle, but she could not order her own retirement, nor could she order her own sought-after peace. William Cecil had finally departed and now lived at Burghley House, his fanciful home in the country where he devoted himself entirely to books and heraldry. He had at last been able to choose peace and quiet over life at Elizabeth's court. She did not blame him. His son had stepped forward and assumed his father's role.

And indeed, Robert Cecil was an excellent minister. But he did not know her and she was not interested in knowing him particularly. She felt she had seen it all and done it all – so what would be the point?

John Dee, her seer and friend, had also left her court far behind. He had immigrated to Poland and now chose a madman's schemes as his guiding principle. She smiled when she thought of him and his esoteric wisdom, always mixed with incredible folly but also with incredible intelligence. He, too, was gone now and she found herself living a half-life among people she barely knew. They did as they were told, but brought her heart no joy.

But then there was Essex. And there was Coudenoure. She put up with the Earl's growing ambitions, his unhooded hubris, his near insults, all for the sake of company. But unlike Dudley, Essex did not seem to entirely understand the bargain – she was the queen, he her suitor. Time and again he ignored the ritual which had to be observed in order for the relationship to work. Time and again he overstepped the boundary between royalty and courtier. Time and again – until finally Elizabeth could ignore it no longer.

Chapter Twenty-Six

Winter 1600

"He had a simple mission, Bess. As Lord Lieutenant of Ireland, all he had to do was destroy the Earl of Tyrone, that vicious little man who would see my rule over Ireland put to an end."

Elizabeth had appeared on the royal barge that morning at the Thames dock of Coudenoure. Her court was progressing to Whitehall, and on impulse she had ordered that her own barge stop while the others continued on. She had not visited her favorite estate in two months, an unusual state of affairs, for it was now once again the place where she routinely chose to go to refresh herself and to reflect. On occasion, she still preferred the old litter style of transport, and she used it now as she stepped from her barge onto Bess and Quinn's estate. Elizabeth batted away the footmen's attempts to assist her into the litter, and walked on a ways before allowing their help.

Coudenoure. The place seemed as unchanged as time itself. A new dock had been built at her own insistence, but the old one remained beside it untouched. She looked at it now, remembering the days when Bess' children were tiny and sent their model ships down river to defeat what dragons as may have been found. She was not in an unhappy mood, merely a reflective one, and the memories of those days made her smile. The path to the manor drive was kept clipped and tidy for the queen's visits, and she walked along in silence for a moment, well ahead of the small party which had stayed behind with her. The way become slippery with frost and dead undergrowth and she finally entered the litter as they approached the main drive of Quinn and Bess' home.

All was as it ever had been, and she enjoyed the unchanging, timelessness of the place. Her courtiers might come and go; Spain might threaten or recede; her own will might change or refine with age. All this was true, but Coudenoure, like a tiny isolated jewel, continued to shine with constancy. The children of the estate had long ago commandeered the signal station built during the time of the Spanish threat. Even these many years later it stood upon the ridge which separated the royal lands of Greenwich Palace from those of Coudenoure. Their games of pirate, of kidnapped maidens and daring swordsmen, played out upon the ridge and the

Thames below. Time and again, assaults were made upon the ridge to rescue whomever had been captured in that particular day's scenario. Frequently, the adults of the estate sat in the grand meadow which surrounded the gardens and main house proper and watched in amusement as first this ragged band with its homemade flag, now that, assaulted the hilltop where the unworthy villains de jour held this maid or that queen captive . England was always victorious, and usually around mealtime.

The children's lookout, ever alert for pirates abroad on England's great river, had seen the queen's retinue sailing past and had quickly incorporated them into their play. A contingent had been sent down to warn the household of an impending attack. So it was that the adults were waiting for Elizabeth on the steps of Coudenoure. As she stepped from her litter, all bowed, and she dismissed her servants and retainers, instructing them, as always, to wait at the end of the long drive they had just traversed. They were harried by bands of tiny warriors with wooden swords as they retreated down the way.

Elizabeth wanted to walk. Cloaks and mitts were provided for her and Bess and they meandered through the winter scene to the monastic church ruins and the graveyard beyond. Elizabeth repeated her previous statement but with evident exasperation.

"He had a simple mission, Bess. God's wounds, as Lord Lieutenant all he had to do…"

Bess interrupted.

"Yes, but Majesty, the question is why did he not do as ordered."

Elizabeth snorted.

"Because he is full of himself. That is why. He believes me to be so besotted by a mere subject of mine that he can fiddle and diddle with my commands as he pleases."

They walked on over the frosted ground.

"Tell me, how does the matter lie now?" Bess asked.

"Well, as if it were not enough that he squandered my money and resources and humiliated my kingdom, he has now come home against my explicit orders directing him otherwise."

"Explain, old friend, for I am not as conversant as you with matters of current statecraft."

Elizabeth sighed and repeated her earlier statement.

"As Lord Lieutenant of Ireland, all he had to do was destroy the Earl of Tyrone, that vicious little man who would see my rule in Ireland brought to an end. Instead, he ignored my orders, did as he pleased, squandered my resources and came home. What was he expecting?"

"My friend and queen, he sounds dangerous."

"Indeed. He would have my throne and I have known this for some time. He has the hubris and the ignorance of youth."

Bess asked the obvious question.

"What is to be done?"

Elizabeth paused before answering.

"Currently, he is banished from court. He writes nonsensical letters pleading with me to let him return but I have grown tired of his tantrums. He remains, for the most part, at his London home, Essex House."

"Much of his income, I believe, is derived from your favor, is it not?" Bess asked sensibly.

Elizabeth gave a satisfied nod.

"Yes," she said bluntly. "And I have grown tired of being used like a sow's teat. He had the lucrative sweet wine tariff and I have recently refused to renew it in his name. He is caged and he knows it."

Bess walked in silence for a moment before giving a quiet and wary response.

"Caged animals are very dangerous, Majesty."

"Indeed."

"You are taking away his income and his stature – be careful."

"Yes," was Elizabeth's only answer.

They walked on.

"Let us return to the manor house. I wish to see Henrietta – she is well?"

"Well, good, bored, and altogether a handful. The woman is a force of nature and I know not how to tame her."

Elizabeth laughed with delight.

"We should think of her marriage, my friend, for she is of that age."

Now it was Bess' turn to snort.

"And good luck, Majesty, in that quest. She refuses to marry before Anne, but I believe that is just a ruse – she intends to be ruled by no one."

"Ah, then we shall have to find a worthy suitor."

"Tell him to put on his armor when he arrives to court my daughter, Majesty, for he will need it against her intellect and independence."

They entered through the main doors and Bess ordered tea.

*****

No income, no access to Elizabeth upon which to trade. No standing. No money. But fury, and hubris enough for a thousand men.

There would be no turning back now. Essex rebelled.

*****

Deep Winter 1601

It began in the kitchen. Jane was about her late evening routine. Margaret was now too arthritic to run the kitchen or even provide much manual help, but she kept Jane company as she went about setting up for the next day's meals. A young child – a stable man's son – approached Margaret and warmed his small hands by the fire.

"I could tell you a story for a sweet." He continued warming his hands.

"Oh, aye, could you now?" Margaret smiled at the brazen attempt to get a biscuit.

The lad nodded and turned to her.

"But you must give me the scone first."

Jane had been listening and in amusement handed a scone to Margaret. The child's eyes grew bigger.

"You shall have the scone when you tell your tale." She spoke authoritatively and waved the bit of food under the youngster's nose. He capitulated.

"It is said that a great many men were seen just now passing upon the Thames. They had guns."

Margaret cocked her head and Jane stopped making her list.

"How were they seen? 'Tis dark!"

He shook his head vigorously.

"We keep a watch at the signal house on the ridge."

"Who does? And what are you looking for?" asked Jane.

The boy gave an exasperated sigh.

"We trade the watch, old woman." Margaret boxed his ears. He continued with the proper respect.

"We keep a watch for pirates, of course. What else? We shall slay them as they come up river!" He backed away and gave a demonstration of his prowess with an imaginary sword.

"You have not answered – how did you see these pirates?"

"They were in well-lit craft and we saw them coming. We ran to the river and told them we would either join them or defeat them."

Jane and Margaret laughed in spite of themselves.

"'Tis quite a range of options you presented to these pirates."

The boy nodded.

"And where were these ruffians going?"

"London."

"Why?"

"*To rid our kingdom of our nefarious queen.* So they said."

The women sat up, suddenly alert.

"Say again, boy, where were they going?"

He repeated himself. Margaret spoke quickly.

"And which direction were they going, young boy?"

The child pointed as he spoke.

"Towards London."

He realized he had the upper hand and reached for the scone. Margaret drew it back.

"You may have an entire tray of scones if you tell me everything you know."

The boy sat down upon the stool she kicked out for him from the table.

"They are going to London, for there is a great rebellion coming. But they would not take me, nor the others. They said we are too young."

Jane gave him a plate of food and told him to wait outside the door. Together, she and Margaret hurried into the library.

As always, Bess and Quinn were there eating a small repast before retiring. Near the window sat Anne, working away on a translation by the light of two stout candles. Henrietta was not present.

Attracted by the whispering of her parents and the others, Anne pushed back her chair and joined them.

"Yes? What is going on?" She demanded.

Henrietta entered the room, kissed her father and hugged her mother before helping herself to a blueberry-laced, sugary confection that Jane had invented and which lay untouched on her father's plate.

A deafening quiet was her only answer.

"'Tis trouble? It must be, for all of you look as guilty as if you had been caught in the treacle barrel."

Henrietta paused and looked around her. Slowly she put down her sweet.

She eyed them all purposely. Finally, Jane told the tale.

"But how can this be?" Quinn asked as Jane finished. "Who would do such a thing?"

Bess stood and stoked the fire before turning to the others.

"I know who."

She related what the queen had told her only weeks earlier. The fear in the room was palpable.

"Essex." The word hissed into the room from between Quinn's clenched teeth. "That evil upstart."

"But can we be sure? Perhaps it is someone else who foments such a rebellion."

"No, 'tis him," Bess said quietly. "I am certain."

Round and round the conversation went – who could it be, and why? An hour had passed by the time the young boy who had broken the news to Jane and Margaret appeared in the library door.

"Beg pardon, beg pardon." He bowed repeatedly. Suspecting something, Jane hurried to him.

"What is it, lad? Do not be shy."

"There was a name. I remember it now."

They waited holding their breaths.

"Essex. I heard the name Essex."

Jane directed him to the treats jar in the kitchen and he disappeared.

Panic and fear began to overtake those left in the room. Finally, Bess spoke authoritatively.

"We must warn her. And we must alert Robert Cecil."

"Tonight?" asked Anne incredulously.

Again, a heated conversation ensued. Over and over again they repeated the facts to one another until all felt exhausted. They were merely babbling in the face of disaster. As if to give credence to that fear, the clock struck the Matins hour. It would be dawn soon.

"We have squandered the time." Henrietta rose. "I shall ride to warn the queen." She turned to leave but not before Bess clutched her arm.

"I shall go, child, for there is likely danger."

"No, my love, 'tis my work to warn her." Quinn rose to leave.

"Stop!" Henrietta's voice rose to a pitch seldom heard at Coudenoure. "Only I know the quickest way to Whitehall, for I have been there many times with the queen."

She took a deep breath.

"I shall warn her, and you must find someone who can get word to Robert Cecil. He must rally the country now."

She paused before continuing.

"He is currently at Greenwich – I know this for one of the poachers from the village warned me to stay clear of the wood this fortnight."

Under other circumstances, Henrietta would have had to answer many questions about such knowledge and how it was gained, but not tonight.

"Then I shall ride to Greenwich, niece, and you to London." Anne spoke with confidence. "Papa, you and mother must stay here and fortify Coudenoure, for should the queen need shelter or men, she will rely on us."

As the women stepped out of the library, Henrietta hugged Anne.

"We must hurry, for they have a dreadful start upon us."

On impulse, Anne ran quickly up the stairway to her mother's room, returning in a flash. She carried an object in her hand. Henrietta raised an eyebrow as her sister put Bess' favorite necklace around her Henrietta's slender throat. The rubies on the cross were cold against her skin.

"Mother says this is not a necklace, but a talisman against harm and evil. Wear it, niece, and you will be safe."

Henrietta laughed.

"I have no need for such things. If you believe it has power, *you* should wear it." She made to take it off but Anne stopped her.

"I go to Greenwich, Henrietta, where there is no danger. You ride to London..." She left the sentence unfinished.

They ran side by side to the stable. Each knew the fastest mounts and they ordered them saddled and readied. It was done in a matter of minutes and as they steadied the horses and prepared to ride, a loving glance passed between them.

"'Tis some excitement for our evening, is it not?" laughed Henrietta.

Anne laughed, too.

"I think, dearest niece, that when this is over, you should truly consider the life of a pirate. I believe you have the makings of a fine one."

"Anne, ride safe." Henrietta turned and took the back path off the estate. Once upon the main London road, she turned and with a prayer in her heart, rode hard for Whitehall.

Anne too, turned, rounded the manor house and rode hard down the main drive. Her steed, Ajax, knew the way but was hesitant in the dark. It was difficult to force him to a gallop, and Anne wondered how she would get him to navigate the woods on the far side of the meadow beyond the ridge. She did not need to worry.

As she rounded the final bend of the Thames which coincided with the estate's ridgeline, she kicked the bay into a high gallop across the meadow. She had ridden that meadow a hundred times before, had played in it as a child, had picked flowers in it each spring. But she had never traversed it in such a panic in the dark. She forgot about the small rise which defined it near the queen's own wood on the far side. She forgot that on the backside of that rise was a gully which Ajax would never ever navigate no matter the speed or gait at which it was approached.

And he would not navigate it now. As Anne rode headlong and recklessly across the dark meadow, she forgot his dislike of the gully until it was too late. With a scream that no one heard, she was thrown from the now sweating beast onto the cold and frozen meadowland. Ajax snorted, and stood beside her as she lay motionless upon the wintry frozen ground.

*****

Dawn was breaking as the woods gave way first to simple houses and shops and then to more elaborate structures as she made her way into London proper. The streets were already busy, filled with merchants, wagons, beggars, servants –

all determined it seemed to get a jump on the day's activities. Vendors too poor to own shops set their wagons at right angles to the traffic of the road and displayed their wares from there. Some were organized – here was a market of fresh vegetables, there a market of textiles and raw wool, farther on the barrel fires of the smithies.

Henrietta slowed her horse to a stately trot and turned towards the Thames. She would attempt to enter Whitehall from the river side. If she were not allowed through the gates, she would call for courtiers she knew who would speak to her right to go forward into the queen's own palace. But the situation never developed.

As she turned onto one of the city's main, cobbled thoroughfares, her steed reared unexpectedly. Not twenty feet away a wall of angry men was advancing towards her. Their shouts were unmistakable.

"The queen must go! We are ruled by a mere woman – the queen must go!"

Their words became a menacing chant and Henrietta sat frozen, unsure of her next move. She had not anticipated meeting the rebels face to face and as her mount reared yet again, she lost her balance and fell from the saddle. A nearby urchin grabbed the reins and disappeared into the growing throng. As she stood and dusted herself off, she recognized the leader's face. Fury grew in her heart and she stepped forward to confront Essex.

"You! You malcontent! She has made you what you are and you repay her thus?"

His only answer was a sneer and a shout.

"The queen must go!" He looked directly at her, throwing the words in her face.

Henrietta raised her hand to slap him but a great noise from behind her brought a pause. Essex, too, heard the commotion and looked up. They were being confronted by a contingent of Elizabeth's guards and Essex knew that more would follow. He looked fleetingly at Henrietta and made to turn and flee but there was no time. More loyalists had appeared from a side alley. Essex, his men, and Henrietta were caught in a pincer movement as the queen's troops tightened round them.

"Henrietta!"

Someone was shouting her name. She turned and scanned the crowd.

"Henrietta! Quickly!" It was Quinn.

Henrietta had no time to wonder about his sudden appearance. Without hesitation, and with a strength she had never seen in him, he tossed aside rebels and guards alike, finally reaching out and grabbing her arm.

"Come, child, quickly!" He was trying to pull her to safety when the blow fell across his skull.

"Grandpapa! Grandpapa!!!" Henrietta's screams were drowned out by the rising tide of chaos which enveloped the scene. She tried to reach down and protect his prostrate, still figure against the rampaging crowds but once again someone grabbed her arm.

"So you would overthrow our sovereign, would you?" A guard with an ugly smear of a grin pinned her arms behind her roughly.

"No, you nit! I have come to warn her! Release me!"

The man laughed and passed her on to another who quickly tied her arms.

"This one says she is here to warn our Majesty."

"Oh aye," came the shout of a reply. "I shall let her cry her warning from the Tower."

She was thrown to the side with others who had been thus apprehended. Henrietta turned away in horror as the melee before her grew bloody. Without grace or warning, she was transferred to a heavily-armed barge. The oarsmen received an order and she knew, without being told, where they were taking her and the rebels, for there was only one place where traitors against the kingdom were lodged. Henrietta put her head down and tried not to panic, reminding herself again and again that she was here to warn Elizabeth of the very rebellion in which she had been caught up. She must convince the oarsmen that she was well-born, and should be released – clearly, she did not belong with riffraff that would presume to harm their sovereign queen. She lifted her head and looked at her fellow prisoners.

There were ten of them on the barge. She was the only woman. As she assessed them, her heart sank for she realized that they looked as she did – not poor. Their clothing was well-made, their mien one of confidence, although at this point, clearly overlaid with fear. Who were these men, she wondered? She pulled her mind back to her gambit for freedom and looked down the length of the shallow craft at the two oarsmen and guards who occupied the far end. They showed no signs of worry about their prisoners, for she and her fellow passengers all had their hands tied securely behind their backs. Should they choose to attempt escape, they would surely drown, and as a result the guards had a nonchalant attitude and remained somewhat aloof from their human cargo. She sucked up her courage and shouted down to them now.

"You! Release me at once, for I do not belong here!"

None of them gave her even the slightest glance. She called out again. This time, one of the guards turned and looked steadily at her. He was young and tall, with raven-dark hair which fell in gentle curls to his broad shoulders. His cheeks and nose were chiseled stone and from where Henrietta sat, she could see, and feel, the piercing intellect of his brilliant blue eyes. Their raw intelligence caught her off guard and before she could speak yet again, another of the guards looked her way and laughed.

"You do not belong here – oh aye, I am certain you do not. My bed would be a better place for you by far, young girl. Shall we tarry there before your visit to yon tower? Eh?" He made a move as though he would advance down the barge towards her. Only the uneasy rocking of the craft upon the river stopped his advance.

Henrietta should have been fearful. She was not.

"Mind your tongue, you idiot, for my father is a baron and our sovereign is a dear and steady friend of my family! Mind you keep away from me!" She snorted and looked out over the Thames.

Her outburst had inspired the others who rode with her that day, and a great cry went up from a number of them as the barge passed under London bridge.

"I am an earl! Release me!"

"And I an earl's son! I say as my comrade does – release me!"

A dozen cries went up, diluting the effect of Henrietta's claim to nobility. She looked out over the Thames, thinking desperate thoughts about her situation. They would be at the Tower soon, and she knew that the latticed, iron gate would be lifted on the watery entryway known as Traitor's Gate. The barge would slide past and it would close behind them. No one of her family knew of her fate that morning and should the gate close behind her would they ever know. Many years earlier, as she had sailed with Elizabeth upon the royal barge up the Thames, the queen had described her own entrance into the tower through the very passageway which now awaited Henrietta. She looked back down the barge at the guards, and was surprised to find the young one staring at her still. Their eyes locked in a silent moment. Had something passed? He casually turned and shifted his gaze, and she looked away.

Behind her, a great shout arose and a loud scraping noise engulfed them. They had arrived at the tower. The smell of algae and stale river water assailed her as the barge rocked perilously and passed through the slimy underside of the gate. She had felt rage before. Now she felt terror.

One by one they were pulled roughly from the barge and led through a narrow stone entryway. As her turn approached, the guard who had made the lewd suggestion to her called out.

"Oh, she deserves her own cell, gentleman. I shall take her to it myself. And fear not if I am not back shortly, for I may choose to tarry there."

Henrietta was appalled and as he approached her she spat in his face.

"I tell you I am the queen's own woman, and if you touch me you shall pay."

The guard wiped her spit from his face while staring at her with a malicious smile. Suddenly, his focus shifted to something behind her. After a moment, he bowed with a fearful look and without another glance at Henrietta moved away. She could not turn to see what had caused the man's sudden respect – someone grabbed her arm and led her to the door. Now, her terror became absolute – the steps inside the doorway led down, not up. She was shoved and forced with her fellow prisoners to descend the cold stone stairs. Round and round the narrow steps curved, sinking ever deeper into the earth. When she thought they would extend even unto hell itself, they stopped, and she found herself in a filthy, darkened pit of a hallway. Without ceremony, her arms were untied and she was thrown through an open door. She heard the lock being bolted behind her and turned to face her surroundings.

*****

A slit in the stones, high above the floor, told Henrietta that night had fallen. Her cell, barely six feet square, was bare and cold and she was suddenly possessed by an involuntary shivering. There was an iron, sliding panel at eye level in the door to the corridor beyond, and just before the last light faded it slid open. A small cup of water and a single slice of bread appeared. She grabbed them both, speaking rapidly to whoever might be on the other side.

"You must hear me – I must see the queen!"

A soft chuckle floated in the air.

"Child, you will not see the queen, but before tomorrow is out, fear not, for you will see God on high himself. Perhaps he will listen to your pleas."

Henrietta's stomach churned.

"What do you mean?" she asked in a whisper.

"You are all traitors, and will receive traitor's deaths on the morrow."

Henrietta thought fast.

"You there," she spoke in a confidential whisper, "I have something of great value. I shall give it to you if you open this door for a brief moment only."

Pause.

"What is it?" came the gruff and cautious reply.

"You must open the door to find out." The tease was in her voice.

After a long moment, the bolt was slid back and the door opened barely two inches. Henrietta knew she would not have another chance. She backed away from the door, crooking her finger and inviting her jailer into her cell. After a moment, a great hulk of a man shuffled in. Henrietta moved as lightning. A swift, unexpected knee to his groin caused him to double over in pain. With all the strength she had she half-hurled, half-shoved her warder across the floor and dashed through the open door. Down the corridor she flew, on and on until the steps she had descended earlier in the day came into view. She was almost there! She was panting and out of breath as she skipped the first step entirely and landed on the second. Round and round she ran until finally, at the top, she cleared the last course of stone and stepped out into the fading light. A strong arm went swiftly round her waist and spun her back against the wall. A guard with a torch came running, and as he held it up to identify the prisoner who was brazen enough to try and escape, he also lit up the face of the man who had caught her. It was the guard from the morning, and again, as she looked into his intelligent eyes, she thought she saw a slight flicker – was it pity? She reached beneath her dress and in a single hard jerk broke the chain with the ruby cross which hung there. Before anyone could touch her, she looked into his eyes, took his hand, and placed the cross and chain there. They began pulling her away.

"Give it to the queen, I beg you! She will recognize it. I promise! Sir – I *beg* you!"

She was dragged back down the stairs screaming and spitting.

"Please, kind sir, show it to the queen..." Her voice echoed from the dungeon. The young man pocketed the jeweled piece and turned as his commander appeared.

"What was that? Did that wench have some stolen property? Did she give you something? Eh?"

His jet-black curls shook as he nodded.

"No, she was just looking for another chance to escape, sir. That is all. Nothing new from those wretches below."

His commander agreed and stroked his beard.

"'Tis the end of your day, Roman. You may leave now and I will see you on the morrow."

The man with the piercing blue eyes nodded and walked away. Once outside, he patted the pocket in his vest where he had hidden the necklace away. It jangled, and he strode on into the night.

Henrietta had acted on her best hope. As the door slammed behind her and night cloaked the cell in darkness, she began to pray.

*****

[Continued by Royal Sagas 3: "King James' Aversion]"

Made in the USA
Coppell, TX
21 July 2020

31367728R00232